Cursed with prophetic visions and desperate to atone for a death she could have prevented, Gianna York swears she will never again ignore the chance to save a life. When she is hired by Landen Elmsworth to serve as companion to his sister, Gia repeatedly sees the image of her employer's lifeless corpse floating in Misty Lake. As subsequent visions reveal more details, Gia soon realizes her best chance to save this difficult man is by becoming his wife.

At first, Landen Elmsworth believes the fetching Miss York might be right for a meaningless dalliance, but he grossly underestimates her capacity for cunning and soon finds himself bound until death to a woman he may never be able to trust. Yet in the dark of their bedroom they discover an undeniable passion—and a capacity to forge their own destiny . . .

Books by Thomasine Rappold

The Sole Survivor Series
The Lady Who Lived Again
The Lady Who Saw Too Much

Published by Kensington Publishing Corporation

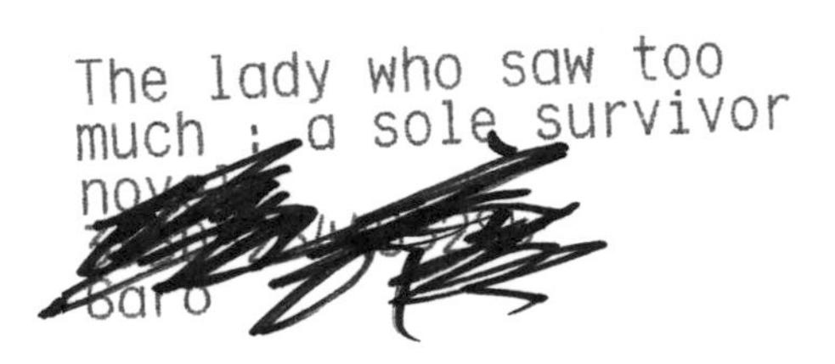

The Lady Who Saw Too Much

A Sole Survivor Novel

Thomasine Rappold

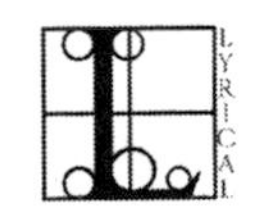

LYRICAL PRESS
Kensington Publishing Corp.
www.kensingtonbooks.com

Lyrical Press books are published by
Kensington Publishing Corp. 119 West 40th Street New York, NY 10018

All Kensington titles, imprints, and distributed lines are available at special quantity discounts for bulk purchases for sales promotion, premiums, fund-raising, and educational or institutional use.

Special book excerpts or customized printings can also be created to fit specific needs. For details, write or phone the office of the Kensington Special Sales Manager:
Kensington Publishing Corp.
119 West 40th Street
New York, NY 10018
Attn. Special Sales Department. Phone: 1-800-221-2647.

First Electronic Edition: June 2016
eISBN-13: 978-1-61650-993-4
eISBN-10 1-61650-993-7

First Print Edition: June 2016
ISBN-13: 978-1-61650-994-1
ISBN-10: 1-61650-994-5

Printed in the United States of America

For John. Who would have thought...

Acknowledgements

Special thanks to my agent, Stefanie Lieberman, my editor, Paige Christian, and the entire team at Lyrical/Kensington for their gentle guidance and patience with a newbie.

Thank you to my critique group, also known as the BFS, for saving me from the "fancy ferns in the forest" and so much more. You guys rock!
Thanks also to the Capital Region Romance Writers for all the knowledge, encouragement, and friendship through the years.
To my wonderful family, friends, and readers, for all your love and support, I thank you from the bottom of my heart.

Chapter 1

Troy, New York 1884

She was about to be tossed to the street. Gianna York folded her trembling hands on her lap, lifted her chin, and did her utmost to maintain her dignity.

Prolonging the torture, Mrs. Amery tidied one of the tall stacks of papers covering the surface of the large desk between them. "I'm sorry, Gia, but my decision is final." The woman's usually stern voice softened beneath her crushing words. "You've done a fine job these past months, but in light of your recent disclosure, I simply cannot keep you on any longer."

Gia slumped in her seat. She'd expected the worst when she'd been summoned to Mrs. Amery's office so early this morning, and that's precisely what she'd been handed. She stared down at her lap as she fought to contain her dismay.

"Our students are impressionable young women, as you well understand. The precarious situation in which you've placed yourself by fleeing your home as you did, leaves me with no other choice. And I'm afraid it leaves you with limited respectable options."

Bristling at the unnecessary reminder, Gia rued the moment of weakness during which she'd divulged this part of her past. Lesson learned. From here on out, she would lie. The thought made her angrier. Not at Mrs. Amery, who'd always treated her fairly, but at herself. It wasn't weakness but pride that had prompted Gia's confession. Her stubborn attempt to challenge society's perception of what she'd done had failed miserably. If a woman as forward-thinking as Mrs. Amery couldn't be swayed…"I understand," Gia uttered.

Mrs. Amery sighed. "It's a bitter pill to swallow, I know, but all is not lost. I may have a solution."

Gia glanced up, surprised.

"I've learned recently of a position that might interest you. Of course it's not as a teaching assistant, nor here at the school, but—"

"Where?" Gia leaned forward.

"Misty Lake."

"Misty Lake?"

"A small town in the country a mere half-day's ride from here. The position is for a companion to a young woman from an upstanding family who summers there. The poor girl suffers with a crippling shyness, and her family feels a companion might help alleviate her condition. Their trust in the Troy Female Seminary has brought them to me for a recommendation." Mrs. Amery tilted her head. "I've told them only of your quality work here, nothing more," she said sternly.

"I appreciate that."

"I know it's not ideal, but if you still refuse to consider returning to your family, I truly believe it's your only recourse."

Gia stiffened at the mention of her family. Returning to Boston meant abiding by their conditions, and Gia knew all too well the terms of those conditions. Blind obedience. Total conformity. Mind-numbing medications to "restore her health" and "quiet the spells" from which she'd been afflicted since the accident but rendered her senseless in the process.

No. She refused to go back to that life.

Gia had survived the icy water for a reason. And while she'd never understand why she'd lived while her brothers hadn't, she'd conceded, after much painful resistance, that all that ensued was a part of that reason. Gia had to accept this. Even if her parents couldn't.

Gia straightened in her chair. She could be a companion. She could be whatever was required of a companion, so long as it paid sufficiently.

"And it pays quite well," Mrs. Amery added as if reading Gia's thoughts. "The position must be filled immediately, so if you decide to accept, you must depart at once."

"I'll do it," Gia said.

"Very well, then." Mrs. Amery reached into the desk drawer. "The Elmsworths are expecting you tomorrow." She handed Gia an envelope. "All the information is there. Along with travel expenses."

Gia stood, feeling better. A quiet summer in the country would not be so bad. While she'd miss the girls here at the school, she was fortunate she'd have a roof over her head. Beggars couldn't be choosers. "I'd better start packing."

Mrs. Amery nodded. "I'm due at an appointment upstairs." She plucked up a file as she rounded the desk. With a sympathetic smile, she patted Gia's arm. "Good luck to you, my dear." She hurried from the room, deserting Gia to the fate contained inside the envelope in her hand.

Blowing out a long breath, Gia opened the envelope. Fingering through the contents, she bypassed several crisp bills before slipping out a gold-embossed card. The fine parchment bespoke wealth and status as did the bold print. With her thumb, Gia traced the raised letters of the ornate script. *Landen J. Elmsworth.*

A chill of foreboding crept up her spine. The print shifted, fading slowly from focus before her blurry eyes. Her heart pounded. With a fortifying breath, she braced herself against the inevitable—and all that came with it. Fear and dread gave way to total helplessness as the vision emerged like a slow wave of nausea.

Closing her eyes, she sank to the chair. She clutched the parchment in her palm, the buzz in her ears growing louder, drawing her in. Brisk air filled her lungs. Gooseflesh formed on her skin. The smell of pine loomed amid tall trees and shadows. Entranced by the sound of babbling water, she waited as a picture took shape in the darkness.

A man lay at the bottom of a rocky creek, face down in the shallow water. His long black coat clung to his lifeless body. The crimson scarf around his neck drifted like a thick stream of blood on the mild current.

And then as insidiously as it had appeared, the vision was gone. Gia opened her eyes. Panting, she unfurled her trembling fist, then stared down at the crumpled card. She hadn't experienced a vision so vivid in months. Nor one so ominous. Especially of someone she'd yet to meet.

She leaned back in the chair, still reeling. Visions of strangers came rarely but were no less disturbing. She shoved the card into the envelope and tried to stay calm. The thundering pulse at her temples refused to recede as each detail of the vision pelted her brain.

She remained seated for several long moments before attempting to stand. Rising on shaky legs, she composed herself. Exhaustion in the wake of the vision struck hard. She clutched the chair for support. She'd almost forgotten how draining it could be—it had been so long. Why this was happening now, after all this time, she didn't know. But of one thing she was certain.

Landen J. Elmsworth, whoever he was, was going to die.

* * * *

Gia stared at the gable-roofed house, urging her feet to move. She dreaded meeting the man she'd seen dead in her vision, dreaded meeting his family. A part of her longed to ignore the vision, run miles in the opposite direction and try to forget it. While she was unsure if she could prevent her visions from becoming reality, she was determined to try. She had to.

The memory of Prudence Alber's death pierced her chest like a dagger. Gia had stood idle, and a young girl had died. The heavy weight of her guilt kept her rooted in the gravel drive in front of the large house, too ensnared in the past to move. She took a deep breath, then stepped to the porch. She had to do something to make up for what she hadn't done for Pru.

Somehow—some way—she would save Mr. Elmsworth.

Gia rang the bell. After announcing herself, she was led by a tall housemaid through the foyer and into a finely decorated parlor. "My name is Florence, Miss York. Please make yourself comfortable while I get Miss Elmsworth."

Gia took a seat on the small settee, glancing around. The spacious room was styled to perfection with elegant furnishings and bright hues and only a hint of the musty smells so common in summer retreats. Outside the large windows, the lake sparkled amid mountains and trees, a scenic painting come to life.

There were several such lakes in the area. Were there as many creeks as well? Gia pushed from her mind the thought of her vision and the challenge ahead. She had to stay positive. A few moments later, Florence returned. A young woman followed demurely behind her.

"Miss York, this is Miss Alice Elmsworth." Florence urged the girl forward.

"I'm pleased to make your acquaintance, Alice," Gia said. "May I call you Alice?"

Alice nodded, staring down at her shoes.

"I will bring tea," Florence said.

Alice watched Florence exit the room. From her forlorn expression, Gia half expected the girl would follow. "She won't be but a few minutes," she uttered instead. She said nothing more as she took a seat across from Gia.

Beneath Alice's clenched hands, her knees bounced with nervous tension. The timid creature appeared as though she wanted to be anywhere but in the presence of this stranger who'd been hired to be her companion. Gia sighed, feeling increasingly uncomfortable for causing the girl's palpable distress.

Gia fidgeted in her seat, wondering how best to approach the situation. They waited for tea in excruciating silence until Gia could bear her own discomfort no longer. "May I ask how old you are, Alice?"

"I turned twenty in March," she replied without looking up.

"I turned twenty in March, as well."

Alice glanced up, and Gia smiled. "Six years ago."

Alice smiled too. A brief little smile that came and went so quickly Gia almost missed it. Alice shifted in her seat, relaxing a bit, but the strain in her voice remained. "You attended the Troy Female Seminary?"

"That's right. But I'm originally from Boston." Gia worked in her mind the tale she'd concocted to explain her relocating to Troy. "After the death of my parents, I took up residence at the seminary," Gia said, feeling guilty for the lie.

"My parents are deceased as well," Alice said. She lowered her gaze to her lap, but not before Gia glimpsed the pain in her eyes.

If possible, Gia felt guiltier. She was also perplexed. So, Landen Elmsworth was not Alice's father as Gia had presumed. Her uncle perhaps? Florence entered the room with a tea tray, and Gia was grateful for the distraction.

Alice and Gia drank their tea amid bits of conversation that consisted of little more than Gia's questions and Alice's yes or no answers. Although it was obvious the girl lacked the usual self-esteem that came naturally to most young women of her class, Gia sensed that a treasure trove of fine qualities lay buried beneath Alice's severe anxiety. When she wasn't avoiding eye contact by fidgeting with her hands or the folds of her skirts, her large blue eyes sparkled with wit and intelligence.

Unfortunately, the effort involved in exhuming these qualities would exhaust anyone attempting to draw them to the surface. Gia imagined the girl in a crowded ballroom. Alice would disappear into the wallpaper. Gia understood, now, why her family had resorted to hiring a companion. The security of having someone at her side might help build Alice's confidence.

"Alice!"

A male voice boomed through the foyer.

"Alice!"

Alice straightened in her seat. "We're in the parlor!"

Heavy footsteps sounded outside the room, and then he was there, posed in the doorway. Gia stared. The black coat, the dark hair. The wide shoulders. Was this him? The man in her vision?

He stepped into the room, addressing Alice as if Gia weren't there. Anger blazed in his blue eyes. "I just saw Mrs. Folsome in town," he said.

Alice set down her tea.

"She told me you declined the invitation to her dinner party next week."

Alice shot to her feet, hands on hips. Her entire demeanor changed as she challenged the man, face to face. The timid mouse was a tiger at heart. "I told you, Denny, I do not wish to attend."

Denny. Gia exhaled in relief. For some reason, she felt inexplicably grateful that this particular man was not the man in her vision. Not that she'd wish such a fate on anyone, but the thought of this young, virile, and stunningly handsome man's end seemed a terrible waste.

"And I told you, you must make an effort," he said to Alice. "You are twenty years old now. Much too old to spend your days holed up in the house."

Alice motioned with her eyes toward Gia. "We will discuss this later," she said through clenched teeth.

Ignoring the cue they had company, he said, "There is nothing to discuss. You will attend Mrs. Folsome's dinner and that is the end of it." He turned toward Gia, finally acknowledging her presence in the room. "You're the companion?"

His blunt question sounded more like an accusation. Gia nodded.

"Then please explain to this stubborn miss the importance of socializing."

Reluctant to engage in their familial dispute, Gia opened her mouth, but nothing came out.

"Denny!" Alice gaped. "You have yet to introduce yourself to Miss York, and you're already barking orders at her."

He frowned, lips pursed tight. For a moment, Gia thought he might protest. But with a sigh of resignation, he affirmed that Alice was right. "My apologies, Miss York," he said as he yanked off his hat. He tossed the hat to a chair and a stern look at Alice. "But my sister has a habit of distracting me from my manners."

He turned toward Gia, and she swallowed hard beneath his bold scrutiny. He moved closer. The tense slant of his brow slackened, as did the taut line of his mouth. His perfect lips parted, luring all lucid thought from her head. "How do you do?"

Even the smooth sound of his voice had turned pleasing. She licked her suddenly dry lips and managed a nod.

His gaze held hers as he extended his hand. Clasping her fingers, he gave her hand a slight squeeze, all the while appraising her with those placid blue eyes. The heat of his touch pulsed through her veins. He released her, but she remained gripped by a strange giddy sensation. The reaction was girlish and silly, and as overpowering as her visions.

She stared into his face, lost in a moment of mesmerizing desire. Like a cuff to the head, his next words jarred her back to her senses.

"I am Landen Elmsworth."

Chapter 2

Gia stared at the man, absorbing the confirmation that he was, indeed, the subject of her vision. *Oh, please, let me be wrong.* But her visions never were wrong. Gia had learned that the hard way. The curse of her prophetic ability had never felt so heavy. She glanced from Mr. Elmsworth to Alice and felt suffocated by the crushing weight of it.

Thoughts of his tragic fate raced through her mind with imagined scenarios. Whatever might lead to his landing at the bottom of a creek bed, his present confidence unnerved her. She longed to warn him, to stress his need for caution, but she couldn't. Not yet. She had to act carefully if she hoped to influence the outcome of his future. The details of her vision were vivid. There were tinges of color in the leaves on the trees and a brisk chill in the air. She had until late summer at least to figure out something—some way to save him. This prospect gave her the fortitude necessary to pull herself together.

"Alice, would you mind if I spoke with Miss York in private?" he asked, snapping Gia back to attention.

"Not at all." In her haste to escape, Alice set down her cup, sending tea sloshing over the rim. "I'll be out in the garden," she said as she dabbed at the mess.

"My sister spends much of her time in the garden," Elmsworth muttered.

Gia turned from Alice's affronted frown to the tall window and the garden beyond. Clusters of budding flowers and neatly pruned shrubs enclosed a stone patio, complete with a fountain. "I can understand why. It's lovely."

"Do you enjoy gardening?" Alice asked. The avid gleam in her eye made Gia smile.

"Unfortunately, I lack the green thumb required to nurture a garden. Perhaps you can teach me your secret."

"Alice wastes enough time in the company of plants," Elmsworth said. "Your job is to see to it she focuses her attention on people."

"In other words, Miss York, you've been hired to be my friend." Alice shot to her feet. "Wasted effort on my brother's part, since I neither want nor need your services."

Gia fidgeted in her seat. Alice's opposition would have Gia out of a job before she finished her tea.

As if sensing Gia's distress, Alice reclaimed her manners. "No offense to you, Miss York, but I prefer to keep to myself."

"That's precisely the problem," he said.

"My problem, Denny, not yours." Alice lifted her chin. "This entire idea is humiliating. How do you intend to introduce us? As your pathetic sister and the companion you hired to tolerate her company?" Her blue eyes welled with tears.

Elmsworth sighed but said nothing.

Trying not to sound as desperate as she felt, Gia said, "If that's your worry, Alice, I'm sure we can come up with a more discreet solution. I can be introduced as an old friend of the family who has come to spend the summer with you."

Alice considered this before glancing to Elmsworth.

"Problem solved," he said.

Gia breathed a sigh of relief. While she sympathized with Alice's dilemma, Gia needed this job to save the girl's brother.

"I suppose I have no choice," Alice said.

He shrugged. "You can always attend the season's affairs with Aunt Clara."

Alice cringed at this alternative before turning to Gia. "Welcome to Misty Lake, Miss York." With one final frown at her brother, she swished from the room.

* * * *

Landen turned to his sister's new companion, studying her reaction. Despite the awkwardness of Alice's little fit, the woman remained poised and collected as she sipped her tea. She was older than he'd expected. And a hell of a lot prettier. Long lashes fringed her brown eyes. Her dark hair was coiled and tucked into her hat, but its unique citrus scent could not be contained. And that mouth…

He cleared his throat—and his wandering mind—amid his pleasant surprise. Aunt Clara's former companion had been a spectacled, dowdy woman who'd claimed to speak fluent French and prattled incessantly in English.

Miss York's attractiveness might work in Alice's favor. Men would flock to this woman, and Alice would be at her side. Perhaps Miss York's grace and confidence would be contagious and Alice would contract some for herself.

"You're very hard on her," she said suddenly.

He blinked at her critical tone.

"Have you tried being patient?"

"I've tried everything," he said. "And I've indulged her solitary behavior for too long. Years spent hoping she'd grow out of it. It's time my sister came around."

"She's a lovely young woman."

"She may as well be a toad for all the good loveliness does her." He glanced out the window to where Alice knelt amid a thick patch of tall daisies. "She shrinks from the world as if she were the ugliest creature under the sun."

Craning her neck, she watched Alice with a faraway look in her eyes. "Has she always been so shy?"

He nodded. "Even as a child. She never joined with other children to play but instead would watch from the sidelines. Her mother feared there was something wrong with her, but our father wouldn't hear of it."

She turned from the window to face him. "Her mother?"

Landen leaned back in the chair, impressed she'd been listening so closely. He added "keen intellect" to her growing list of attributes. "I am a product of our father's first marriage," he said. "My siblings—Alice and Alex—were born during his second marriage to their mother."

"Alice mentioned her parents were deceased."

"Yes," he said. "Four years now."

"I'm sorry."

The stark sincerity in her voice took him aback. As did his reaction. He brushed off her condolences without meeting her eyes. "After they died, I sent Alice away to school, hoping a new environment might be the solution. She lasted barely one semester before she begged me to let her come home."

"How did she fare academically?"

"She's an excellent student. But each report I received contained the same assessment. Her lack of class participation and timidity concerned her instructors." He shook his head. "Her apprehension has gotten only worse."

"Why do you suppose that is?" Gia asked.

"She's of marrying age now. I imagine the pressure of that has added to her anxiety."

"Pressure?"

He bristled at the accusation in her eyes. "I pressure her to get out of the house. To meet people. If she can't manage to attend a simple dinner party, she'll never mange to find a husband."

"So you're hoping I can help you marry her off?"

Her erroneous assumption rankled him more than her audacity. He leaned forward. "I want a husband for Alice, yes, Miss York. But I'd prefer she land a husband who cares for her. I want people to see my sister for the woman she is. The bright, caring person inside the frightened shell she presents to the world. This will not happen if she remains crippled by her fear of participating in any and all social activities."

She lowered her eyes.

"I don't want my sister to end up an old maid."

Her brows rose in surprise. She met his gaze, her posture stiff.

Satisfied he'd hit his mark, he leaned back in the chair. "Mrs. Amery's recommendation for a companion was sterling but brief. Now that I've met you, I'm left wondering why an attractive woman of your age would take a position as a companion when you could be—"

"Married?"

"Yes."

"Not every woman deems marriage her ultimate accomplishment."

Her outspokenness was refreshing, but he didn't believe her for a minute. The debacle of his past had taught him the extent to which some women would resort to secure their futures. The bitter memory roused his ire. He'd never again be so foolish as to step into that trap.

"Some of us old maids remain happily unattached. Some of us enjoy traveling and meeting new people."

"A position with the right family would expose you to the right people."

She frowned, fluffing her skirts.

He took a long breath, exhaling his anger. He was being unfair. Something about her didn't add up, but she deserved the benefit of a doubt. Alice was a sinking ship, and he sensed this woman could help keep her afloat. Through the summer, anyway. "I'm a blunt man, Miss York. I did not intend to insult you."

"Yes, you did, Mr. Elmsworth." She lifted her chin. "But you did not succeed."

He couldn't help smiling. "Your impertinence may be just what Alice needs."

He motioned for her to refill her empty teacup, and her tense expression softened a bit as she poured. "You may address me as Landen, if you please."

She glanced up in surprise.

"Formality is more lax here," he said. "An aspect of the country most people seem to enjoy." He glanced to Alice outside. "The season is just beginning. It's important Alice attend as many social affairs as possible. Ensure that this happens."

"I imagine crowds make her anxious."

"That's an understatement. Upon entering a crowded room, Alice slinks to the deepest corner, claims a seat, then remains planted for the duration of the affair."

"Has she no friends?"

"None to speak of. Her timidity makes people uneasy."

"She seems to have no problem engaging with you." She smiled in reference to Alice's earlier exhibition.

He smiled too. "No, she doesn't. She's different with me and my brother. Once she's comfortable with someone, she's free to be herself. She's especially comfortable with Alex. He'll join us here in a few weeks."

She nodded. "So the challenge will be to help build Alice's confidence in public," she said.

"Yes. And a challenge it will be. The girl can be as stubborn as an ass."

"So I've seen," she agreed.

"You will accompany Alice to all social affairs here in Misty Lake." He eyed her dress. "Is your wardrobe sufficient?"

"I…"

"No matter," he said. "Alice will require several new gowns. I will set up an appointment with the dressmaker for you both. At my expense, of course," he added. "I also would like you to familiarize yourself with the town and the people here. You and Alice will join me for dinner at the Crooked Lake House when my schedule permits. Next week, perhaps. I will make the proper introductions so you'll know who's who."

"Instead of pushing Alice into a crowded roomful of diners, might you consider easing her into society more gradually?"

"How?"

"You could host a small reception here at the house. In the garden perhaps. That way she would feel more comfortable. A familiar environment and all that."

He considered this, wondering how he hadn't thought of it himself. "That might be a better idea."

She nodded.

"An afternoon reception?"

"Yes," she said. "Something intimate."

"You and Alice can see to the details. My Aunt Clara arrives late next week. She can assist with the preparations."

"All right. In the meanwhile Alice and I can get to know each other better."

"Florence will arrange for your things to be brought up to your room."

She stood, then started for the door. The subtle sway of her hips as she walked drew notice to her curvaceous figure. Whether coming or going, the woman was alluring. As was that scent.

"One more thing, Miss York."

She stopped, turning to face him.

"Please keep in mind that you are here to help Alice."

Her full lips thinned as she gave a firm nod. "Of course."

"You are new to Misty Lake, and as such, you'll surely receive plenty of attention this season. See to it that some of that attention trickles onto my sister."

Chapter 3

Gia awoke groggy from another restless night spent tossing and turning in the turmoil of her vision of Landen Elmsworth and thoughts of Alice, the dependent young woman who also would be affected should Gia's vision of his death become a reality. Not to mention his brother and his aunt and anyone else who might care for him.

Her head ached from the pressure of it all. Lack of sleep didn't help. For the briefest of moments, she longed for the opiates and the temporary diversion from the enormous responsibility her prophetic vision had dumped in her lap. *What have I gotten myself into?*

She flung aside the covers and proceeded to dress for breakfast. After almost two weeks here, Gia barely saw the man, but each moment in his presence was torture. And in more ways than she'd imagined. Despite the man's irritating arrogance, Gia felt drawn to him. The admission frightened her, and she did her best to shake free of her bizarre attraction to this total stranger.

She made her way downstairs, past a harried housemaid carrying a tall stack of linens. Rounding the corner, she walked down the wide hall toward the dining room. She nodded to two more housemaids who were busy polishing the woodwork and floors. Following the aroma of bacon, Gia entered the dining room to find Alice alone at the long table. She exhaled in relief that Landen was nowhere in sight.

"Good morning, Alice," she said, taking a seat at one of the awaiting place settings.

Alice straightened, shoulders stiff. "Good morning."

Gia poured a cup of coffee and helped herself to the large plate of bacon on the table. The unmistakable sound of Landen's voice carried from outside the room. Gia froze in the midst of spreading jam on a biscuit.

His voice grew louder, and another housemaid scurried past the arched doorway.

"Aunt Clara arrives tomorrow," Alice said to explain the commotion. "Denny is wasting his time. No matter how tidy the house or sparkling the crystal, she'll find fault in it, anyway."

"Your aunt?"

"She's a domineering old shrew," Alice said. "But Beatrice is worse."

"Beatrice?"

"Her long-suffering friend."

"Misery enjoys company, they say."

With a nod, Alice retreated to her eggs, taking refuge, once again, inside a shelter of silence. Gia frowned. Alice's timidity made Gia miss the spirited young girls at the female seminary. Luring this girl from her shell might prove as challenging a task for Gia as changing the outcome of her vision.

Turning her focus toward the direction in which she'd been hired, she said, "Your brother has finalized the guest list for the garden party."

"How many?" Alice asked in a tone that said she dreaded the answer.

"Including your aunt and her friend, we'll total twenty," Gia said. "Shall we write the invitations and send them for delivery before Mrs. March arrives to fit our new gowns?"

Alice shrugged.

"I'll take that as a yes." Gia wiped her mouth, then set down the napkin. "We can work outside on the patio."

After breakfast, Alice followed Gia outside. Bright sunshine warmed the quiet spot, and the smell of dewy plants and shrubs filled the breeze.

"If we relocate those potted ferns, we can set up tables there," Gia said, pointing.

Alice glanced up, then gave a quick nod. She stood, arms crossed, staring down at the ground. Her anxiety was unnerving. Irritating. After all the time they'd spent together, Gia's patience was running thin.

"For goodness' sake, Alice. It's just us two and the daisies. You needn't be so tense," she snapped.

Alice gaped. "Easy for you to say," she snapped back. "You have no idea what it's like."

Gia sighed. "What is it like?" she asked as she sat on the bench. She looked up at Alice's pretty face, which was now marred in pain. "Help me understand."

Alice lowered her gaze. "I hate parties. And people. They stare."

"Stare?"

Alice hugged her arms tighter. "I feel their eyes on me, watching me. I hate it."

"You're a pretty girl, Alice. Even so, I think you exaggerate their interest."

Alice shook her head.

"Unless the neckline of your gown is exposing your bosom or you're dancing with one of your potted plants on your head, people probably aren't focused on you any more than anyone else."

Alice glanced up.

"It's been my experience that people are too self-involved to squander time studying others so diligently. Especially when there's food to be had and music to be enjoyed. And even assuming that what you believe is true, and people are watching you, what do you imagine is the worst that can happen?"

"I could make a fool of myself."

"How exactly?"

"I could do something stupid. Say something stupid."

Gia nodded. "And the guests would then toss you, kicking and screaming, into the lake?"

Alice frowned. "Of course not."

"What, then, would ensue if you said something stupid?"

"I don't know, Miss York, and I don't intend to find out."

"Please call me Gia," she reminded the girl for twentieth time.

Alice huffed. "I don't intend to find out. *Gia*."

"And why don't you intend to find out?"

"Because," Alice fired back.

"Because anything you have to say is stupid?" Gia asked. "Or because you are stupid?"

Alice's eyes flashed wide. "I am not stupid!"

"I know that." Gia smiled. "And I'm glad to hear that you know it too."

Alice shook her head in defeat. "When I'm among people, my heart pounds and my palms sweat. Oftentimes I feel as though I might faint."

Gia sighed. "Have you? Fainted, I mean?"

"No."

"Well, that's something to keep in mind. You've survived crowds before. No matter how nervous you are, you must remember that soggy gloves will not cause you to faint."

Alice considered this. "It's still dreadful."

"Well, I promise to do my best to make it less dreadful for you." She smiled. "I've a feeling the two of us will have a fine time together."

Alice shook her head. "Please don't relay that prediction to my brother. A companion was his idea, and I simply couldn't bear it if he were right."

Gia laughed. "Very well then," she said. "Let's start on the invitations."

* * * *

After a productive day of party planning and dress fittings, Alice and Gia shared another quiet dinner that evening. According to Alice, Landen was having dinner in town with the Widow Filkins. Again. Gia was curious about his relationship with the widow, but refrained from inquiring about her. It wasn't Gia's business, and it definitely wasn't her place. Even so, Gia looked forward to the garden party and meeting the woman with whom Landen spent so much of his time. He'd listed Charlotte Filkins' name at the top of the guest list, which confirmed her significance.

After dinner, Alice retired to her room to read. Gia sat in her own room, attempting to do the same, but failing miserably.

Her thoughts kept returning to her vision. Possibilities of what might lead to Landen's death played through her mind, yet none of her imagined scenarios seemed plausible. From what little time she'd spent with him, she knew he was smart, physically fit, and seemed too in control to succumb to overindulgence or addictions to gambling, alcohol, or other dangerous behaviors that might land him at the bottom of a creek. Perhaps he'd be tossed from a horse or slip while out walking.

Whatever the cause, there had to be some way to stop the tragedy from happening. But how? Was it possible that another vision might help? She'd never before attempted to encourage a vision, but she'd never before attempted to stop a vision's forecast from happening.

If she could manage to touch some of his personal belongings… She stood, heart racing. She could sneak to his room, poke about, and see what transpired. It was a long shot, but it beat sitting here doing nothing.

Abandoning the book, she tightened the cinch of her robe and made her way to the door. With each faltering step, with every painful memory of her failure to save Pru, Gia's resolve grew stronger. All she had in this world were her visions and the promise she'd made to herself to follow them. She'd go wherever she had to, do whatever she must, to honor that vow—to lighten the burden of guilt she'd carry for the rest of her life.

Like a thief in the night, she crept down the hall to his room, her thoughts spinning. While she was rummaging around his room, she would search for the red scarf as well. Could the omission of just one minor detail change the course of the future? She didn't know, but she had to try. His aunt and her friend would arrive tomorrow, and there'd be no better opportunity.

She eased open the door, then slipped inside his room, moving quickly. Enough moonlight spilled through the windows to guide her along. She picked up his cigar box from the tall bureau, then closed her eyes. Nothing. She grabbed the whiskey bottle next to it. Again, nothing happened. Frustrated, she opened the top drawer of the bureau and searched for the scarf. She moved to the next drawer, then the next. The blasted thing was probably packed away with his winter garments somewhere. He didn't need a scarf in the summer after all.

The sound of heavy footsteps carried outside the room. Gia froze. *His* footsteps! The carpet absorbed the sound of most foot traffic, but not his. Her gaze darted wildly, searching for some place to hide. She dropped to the floor and slid under the bed, tugging her flowing robe with her.

The door opened, and she squeezed shut her eyes, as if that might help. Her nose twitched from the dust, and she plugged it to stifle a sneeze. Just her luck. She'd hidden in the one nook of the house the thorough team of housemaids had managed to overlook during their cleaning frenzy.

Alice had mentioned Landen was a private man. Even the help was not allowed in his study downstairs. Obviously, his desire for such privacy extended to this room as well. She was doomed.

She watched his large boots moving toward her. She shriveled amid the soft glow of the lamp he'd turned on. Coins clanked on the wood surface as he emptied the contents of his pockets onto the bureau.

She held her breath, her body stiff as a board. There'd be no explaining this caper, no reasonable excuse, and she wasn't clear-headed enough at the moment to concoct one. She had no choice but to hold out until he fell asleep, then sneak out. *Please, let him be a deep sleeper.*

He paced the room for what seemed like forever before he began undressing. He tugged off his boots, then kicked them aside. She held her breath, listening as he loosened his necktie. It dropped to the floor, followed by his shirt, undershirt, and trousers. A moment later she was eyelevel with his discarded drawers.

She stared at the garment, trying with all her might not to think about what he might look like naked. Craning her neck, she tried for a peek. The sound of movement drew her back into the dusty shadows. The mattress slumped against his weight as he plopped to the bed. He gave a few sharp fluffs to the pillows, then settled in for the night. The silence was deafening. Why didn't he turn off the lamp?

And then, just like that, he was up again. He strode to the table to pour himself a drink. Rolling her eyes, she screamed in her head, *go to sleep!*

As if hearing her desperate plea, he climbed back into bed, released a loud sigh, and finally turned off the lamp.

Closing her eyes, she exhaled in relief.

"Sweet dreams, Miss York."

She flashed open her eyes, so startled by his voice she smacked her head on the bed slats. Her heart pounded.

"Since you're obviously comfortable enough to remain under there, I'll bid you good night."

She cringed, her blood pumping through her veins.

"The next time you conceal yourself beneath a man's bed, you might consider forgoing the perfume."

She mouthed a vile curse. "Soap," she muttered instead.

"Pardon me?"

"It's soap. Not perfume."

"Come out from under there," he demanded.

"I can't."

"And why's that?"

"You're naked."

"You might have considered that before you invaded my room. Where I sleep. Naked."

She clenched her teeth at the unexpected humor in his voice.

"At least cover yourself up with a blanket," she said.

She heard a rustle of covers.

"Done."

She crawled out from beneath the bed. She brushed the dust balls from her hair, off her sleeves, anything to avoid looking at him. Her heart hammered. She forced herself to face him, then wished she hadn't. He sat on the edge of the bed, a thin sheet wrapped around his waist. He was magnificent. Moonlight cast him in shadows and light. Her breath caught in her throat. Firm shoulders, muscular arms. A silken layer of dark hair graced his broad chest, trailing in a fine line to his taut stomach and beyond.

"Well?"

She could barely breathe, let alone speak. "I can explain."

"I am listening."

"I was…looking for something."

He patted the space next to him on the bed and smiled. "You've found it."

She gaped, shaking her head. "You misunderstand."

Securing the sheet around his waist, he stood, moving toward her. "Enlighten me."

The scent of his skin filled her senses, heating her blood and her flesh and her bones.

"Are you a thief?"

She took a step back. "No."

He moved closer. His tousled hair pronounced a wildness about him, giving weight to the carnal look in his eyes. She couldn't help wondering how many women had seen him this way, but she knew, without a doubt, she would never forget that *she* had.

He stopped, reaching toward her. She couldn't move as his hand touched her hair. Twirling a lock around his finger, he grazed her temple, her ear. He leaned closer, and she closed her eyes, melting in the wisp of warm breath in her ear.

"A wanton?"

She shook her head slowly, her voice barely a whisper. "No."

"What, then, are you doing in my room?" His lips skimmed her neck with each word. "Why are you here?"

To save your life, she wanted to say. But when she opened her eyes and gazed into his face, she discovered she wanted something else more.

So she kissed him instead.

Chapter 4

Landen didn't know whether it was the effect of the whiskey he'd enjoyed earlier or some sudden, inexplicable bout of insanity that had him kissing the companion he'd hired for Alice. He knew only that it felt too damn good to stop.

He'd wanted to kiss her from the day she'd arrived. From the moment he'd looked into her dark eyes and been lured by something more potent than her beauty or intelligence. And here she was, in his arms.

Pulling her firmly against him, he kissed her harder, deeper. The sound of her soft moan rumbled through him, setting him ablaze. He pushed his tongue through her lips and into the warmth of her mouth. She tasted so sweet. The heady scent of her, the heat and the feel of her body pressed to his was consuming. In all his summers spent in this house, he'd never before had a woman in this room. He felt like a randy schoolboy, rock hard with want, mind void of all rational thought.

She drew her mouth abruptly from his, panting for air. Her lips were parted and dewy and so irresistible he had to have more. "Gia," he uttered.

Her eyes sparked with yearning at his use of her name. His chest swelled with the conquest, along with parts down below. He bent toward her but she stepped back, blinking hard.

"I..." She shook her head, struggling for words, a dazed expression on her face. Wrapping her arms across her breasts, she stared at him like a frightened child, so unlike the woman who'd kissed him with such passion only moments before.

She'd engaged him in a dangerous game but hadn't the nerve to continue. He, on the other hand, was ready to play through to the end. The chill of disappointment helped him reclaim his senses. Was soliciting danger her pastime? Whatever her game, he should have known better than to participate. The stakes were too high, and nothing was worth risking his freedom. But looking at her now, her hair all disheveled, her eyes shining in the moonlight, he could almost forget that. He took a long breath and gave a reluctant nod toward the door. "Go."

Gathering the robe around her, she hurried for the door. He watched, aching to stop her, as she halted briefly to compose herself. She turned the knob hard, then flung open the door. The sound of a loud gasp filled the room.

Landen cringed at the source of the gasp outside the door.

Aunt Clara stood in the hall, mouth agape, hand clutching her chest. Beatrice stood next to her, on the verge of a swoon as she took in the sight of their state of undress. Two wide-eyed housemaids rounded the corner. The trunk they carried between them hit the floor hard. The loud thud echoed through the hall with the sound of their giggles. This wouldn't be good.

He moved to shield Gia from the audience of stunned faces, but his half-naked stance did little to defend her or the shameful situation. Clutching the sheet at his waist, he took a step forward. "Aunt Clara." He clenched the sheet in his fists to combat a curse for this stroke of bad luck and Gia's obvious disgrace. "You're early."

His aunt stared at him, speechless. Her loss for words was a rarity, and despite the unfortunate circumstances, he couldn't help the momentary surge of satisfaction her stunned silence brought him. As if sensing this, she narrowed her eyes, her pale face turning three shades of red. "No, my boy," she said, shaking her head. "Unfortunately for you—and this girl—it appears I'm too late."

* * * *

Pandemonium erupted, echoing through the hall. In the midst of the chaos, Gia made her escape, leaving Landen alone to defend against the squawking women who flapped around him like a pair of frantic hens. Gia bolted down the hall. He watched, resisting the impulse to chase after her and console her, to make it all right. But things were far from all right.

"Get that trunk to my room," Aunt Clara snapped to the snickering maids. Shoving Landen back into his room, she followed after him. She slammed the door, leaving a sputtering Beatrice outside.

She strode to his discarded clothes on the floor. "At least have the decency to get dressed." She tossed him his trousers, then turned her back as he put on his clothes. He was still buttoning his shirt when she spun to face him. "Sit." She pointed to the bed.

Landen plopped to the mattress and prepared for her wrath. She paced slowly, ensuring ample time for him to stew in the juices of her latest disappointment.

"Had you taken my advice, you'd be married by now and well past such tawdry behavior," she said.

"I wouldn't dream of depriving you of this opportunity to crow."

Her face hardened. "Who is she?"

"Gianna York. The companion I hired for Alice."

"Convenient." She stared down at him in disgust. "You're sleeping with the help."

"No," he said. "I kissed her, nothing more."

She arched her brow skeptically. "Your restraint will be a great comfort to the Widow Filkins."

He frowned at her sarcastic jab. He hadn't slept with Charlotte Filkins in weeks, but that was none of his aunt's business.

"The damage may be controlled," she said. "We will send the girl away in the morning, and that will be that."

His disappointment trumped reason, and he averted his eyes.

"If you're questioning the necessity of this, let me remind you that the audience to your little encounter included two housemaids. The help loves to talk. The girl will be ruined by daybreak."

He nodded, unable to dispute this point. "I'll speak with her."

"No!" She shook her head. "You've done quite enough. It's obvious you can't be trusted to be alone with her."

Landen stiffened but held his tongue. No wonder Uncle Howard had died so young. Aunt Clara's incessant jabs had prodded the poor bastard into an early grave.

"I will take care of it." She straightened her spine, preparing for business. "Just as I always do," she muttered before she marched out the door.

* * * *

With a deep breath, Gia answered the loud knock on the door. The old woman barreled into the room. She'd recovered from the shock of discovering Gia and Landen together and currently seemed well in control. Her stern expression articulated the severity of the situation before speaking a word. "I am Clara Elmsworth, Miss York. Landen's aunt." Her formidable tone demanded respect—the respect Gia had denied her earlier by behaving so scandalously in her presence. "You're in very hot water."

Gia nodded.

"It will be best for all involved if you left town immediately. I have several connections and will find you gainful employment elsewhere." She narrowed her eyes. "I will also compensate you handsomely before your *quiet* departure."

Gia turned from the woman, wringing her hands. She couldn't leave. She had nothing. No one. Her desperate need to save Landen filled her with a swell of crazed panic. She had to stay. For him. For Alice. For Prudence and her brothers. Her visions came to her for a reason, and she'd been led here for that same reason. She was certain of it. She would not leave until she accomplished what she'd come here to do. No matter the cost.

But she needed this woman's permission to stay. After what had transpired tonight, and Clara's ensuing disdain, it would take drastic measures to get it.

"No."

The woman's shocked expression turned defiant. "Pardon me?"

"I can't leave. Not yet." Desperation prodded her onward. She forged through her fear and shame and guilt, well aware of the consequences. Fully knowing he would hate her. But at least he'd be alive. "I must stay for at least a month." She touched her stomach. "To be sure." She lowered her eyes, in part from the lie, in part for effect. "Once I'm certain all is well, I will go."

"What…?" The woman's face drained to white as she absorbed Gia's meaning. Although Clara had likely assumed the worst all along, Gia's open admission had undoubtedly stunned her.

"Are you telling me that you may be… That my nephew defiled you?"

Gia winced at hearing the words out loud, but said nothing to dispute them.

An earsplitting silence filled the room. Clara grasped Gia's hand with surprising strength for a woman her age. "Come with me."

* * * *

Landen paced in the parlor while he waited for his aunt's return. While he regretted not being able to speak with Gia before his aunt sent her away, after experiencing Gia's kiss, he didn't trust himself to be alone with her any more than Aunt Clara did. This was a delicate matter, and he wasn't a delicate man. It would be less embarrassing for Gia to have the situation handled by a female.

Even if that female happened to be Aunt Clara.

Gia certainly would be eager to go. Especially since she'd brought this mess on herself. She should have considered the consequences before sneaking into his room. Even so, his response to her kiss made him guilty for his part in the debacle. He would have done far more than kiss her, had she been willing. This admission struck him with the force of his mounting regret. What the hell had he been thinking?

The door opened and he rose to his feet. Aunt Clara charged into the room, dragging Gia with her.

"Sit," she told him. "You too." She all but shoved Gia toward a chair.

Gia straightened in her seat, looking more frightened than Alice did while in the midst of a crowd. His chest tightened at the stark panic on Gia's face, and all at once, he rued allowing his aunt to *handle* Gia as he had.

"There's been a change of plans," Aunt Clara announced.

"What do you mean?" he asked.

"After what she's disclosed to me, her leaving town is no longer an option."

Landen stared in confusion. He turned to Gia for help, but she averted her eyes. She stared down at her knees, her face unreadable.

"She's not leaving?"

Aunt Clara shook her head. "No, Denny, she's not leaving." Her smug tone sent a chill down his spine. "You and Miss York will be married instead."

* * * *

"She is lying!" Landen shot to his feet.

"Perhaps," Aunt Clara said matter-of-factly. "Unfortunately, you can't prove it. And given the witnesses…" She tossed up her hands. "Besides, it doesn't matter. Word will spread through town and everyone will believe the worst." She lifted her chin. "You have no choice."

The four words enclosed him, squeezing the air from his lungs. The one thing he swore he'd never do was fall victim to a woman's manipulations again. And here he was. The victim.

Apparently, he'd learned little from the mistakes of his past. And nothing of scheming women. "And if I refuse?" he asked for the hell of it.

Aunt Clara shook her head. "You won't. You're an honorable man, Denny. You'll do nothing to discredit yourself. Nothing that might cause your business dealings to suffer." She shrugged. "You know it. I know it." She tossed a nod toward Gia. "And I've a hunch that Miss York knows it too."

Gia stared at the floor. He strode toward her, glaring down in disgust. "You conniving little—"

"Enough!" Aunt Clara waggled a finger. "That's no way to speak to your future bride."

His anger rose at his aunt's obvious elation. Her desire for him to settle down and have children was no secret. She'd been hounding him for years. "You wished for this," he said. "The two of you may as well be in cahoots."

"Don't blame me for your self-inflicted plight," Clara said. "You're the one who was caught red-handed and half-naked with the companion you hired for your sister."

If possible, hearing this truth made him angrier.

Clara tilted her gray head, her tone softening beneath her underlying pity. Despite all her berating, he knew that she loved him. "Accept it, my boy. You've been outsmarted."

He turned to Gia, but she still refused to look up.

His heart thundered as he struggled like an animal caught in a trap. His thoughts spun in futile circles for some way out. Drained and sickened, he exhaled in surrender as the icy calm of defeat settled over him. "So it seems."

Gia glanced up, finally meeting his eyes.

"You're a clever girl, Miss York," he said, as evenly as he could manage. "And I intend to reward your cleverness by being the husband you deserve."

Chapter 5

Gia stepped from her room the next morning, dreading having to go downstairs. With every descending step, she felt the hellfire of Landen's fury waiting to incinerate her alive. Prompted by the remote possibility he might be absent at breakfast, she quickened her pace. Clara's friend, Beatrice, was still snoring loudly in the room across from Gia's. With any luck, Landen was a late sleeper as well.

Gia entered the dining room to find Alice seated at the long table with Clara. "Good morning." Gia took a seat across from Alice, exhaling in relief at Landen's absence, however temporary.

"I've been waiting for you."

Clara's cordiality seemed genuine, and Gia swallowed her shame. She'd lied to the woman, setting in motion a turn of events she hadn't expected. Gia had been so desperate to extend her stay, she hadn't fully considered that Clara might actually insist Landen marry Gia. Or perhaps, deep down, she had, and didn't want to admit to this possibility. Either way, Gia would now have to live with what she'd done.

"Landen has left for business in Troy," Clara said. "But not to worry. A few days in the city will give him some time to adjust to your sudden engagement."

And the distance to keep him from wringing my neck. Gia's heart plummeted at the memory of the scene in the parlor yesterday. His hatred of her was obvious. And justified. Even so, she hadn't been prepared for how the disdain in his eyes would affect her.

Gia couldn't deny she was drawn to him. The moment she'd set eyes on him, something inside her had stirred. Some primal part of herself that she'd never known existed had been shaken to life. This strong attraction was ridiculous—she barely knew him—and yet in the wake of what she'd done, she felt a great sense of loss. And guilt.

Her purpose for staying here was to help him, not hurt him. How strange. She was marrying him to save his life, and yet she was ruining the life he had. Did everything connect? Like a tumbling line of strategically placed dominoes, did each action affect the next? It was all so confusing.

Landen would marry her, but he'd never forgive her. He'd made that clear with his threat to be the husband she deserved. His opinion of her had been shattered beyond repair. As was Clara's, no doubt. And Alice's.

"In the meanwhile, Gianna, you and I have much to discuss," Clara said.

Alice finally glanced up at Gia, and she knew at once the girl was privy to what had happened. The wounded look in Alice's eyes conveyed what she was thinking. That Gia had come under the guise of helping her, only to help herself to her brother.

Gia had betrayed Alice just as the girl was beginning to trust her. If possible, Gia sunk lower. She had to say something. "Alice, I—"

"Excuse me, please." Alice tossed down her napkin and shot to her feet. "I must tend to my roses," she said as she strode stiffly from the room.

Clara continued as if nothing were amiss. "Now, about your family. They must be notified at once."

Gia shook her head. "I have no family."

Clara narrowed her eyes. "No one?"

"They're all deceased," Gia said. The lie sounded smoother than she had expected. Perhaps it was practice, or the raw truth in it. After all her parents had done, they were, in fact, dead to her. The threats of having her committed, the forced tonics, the way they looked at her, were the nails in their coffins.

Their apathy toward Gia before the accident had always pained her. They'd favored her brothers and never pretended otherwise. Three of their children had fallen through the ice, but the one they'd loved least had been the only one to survive.

Clara studied Gia closely. "I see." The small acknowledgement seemed as close to a condolence as the woman had to offer. "Well, you have a new family now," she said. "I married into it, and soon you shall too. Albeit under quite different circumstances," she muttered, as though unable to help herself. "Since the invitations for the garden party you and Alice planned have already gone out, we will announce the engagement then."

The woman had managed to spin a proper twist on what might have been the scandal of the season. Gia couldn't help being impressed.

"The wedding will take place one week from Sunday," Clara said.

Gia's heart lurched. "So soon?"

"Not soon enough, if you ask me, but more talk with ensue if my nephew were to marry before announcing an official engagement." She released a quick sigh. "But at least it's not May."

Gia hadn't considered a woman like Clara to be so superstitious. *Marry in May and rue the day.* The old adage seemed more than appropriate to this particular occasion.

"The fourteenth of July will suffice." Clara fixed a stern gaze on Gia. "The two of you fell madly in love during the weeks since you arrived. That's to be the story of the marriage."

Gia said nothing. What could she say?

"The wedding ceremony will take place here, at the house, followed by a simple cake reception."

Clara rambled on about details of the wedding, but Gia focused instead on more important issues. She had to stop Landen's death from happening. Putting this feat to the forefront, she pushed thoughts of marriage from her head and tried to concentrate on the details of the vision and what might lead to it happening.

Unlike anything she'd ever felt during previous visions, the pervading sense of malice that had gripped her at the sight of Landen's lifeless body in the water led her to suspect foul play. Was there someone out there who'd want to hurt him? He hadn't amassed a fortune by being reckless or stupid, but perhaps he'd entered into some business dealings that had gone bad. This seemed the most likely direction in which to follow.

There were so many lakes in the area. Gia was no expert in the field of limnology, but she knew enough to deduce there'd be several creeks flowing in and out of them. Gia would scope out all of them in search of the scene of her vision. She would walk until her feet bled, but she would find the creek in which she'd seen Landen floating. What she'd gain from locating the site of the vision, she didn't know, but she had nothing else to go on. Perhaps her presence at the site might prompt another vision that would lead to a clue.

"You haven't touched your breakfast," Clara said, snapping Gia back to attention.

"I'm not very hungry." That was an understatement. The physical effect of her predicament suddenly became such that the mere smell wafting up from her plate made her queasy.

"Eat," Clara said. "You must keep up your strength, Gianna. There is much to be done over the next week, and you'll need it."

The reminder did little to help. But Clara was right. With a nod, Gia picked up her fork. She forced down a mouthful of poached eggs, and her stomach roiled in protest. Fearing she might retch, she reached for her coffee cup and took a deep sip. The warm brew did little to settle her tremulous nerves. She felt Clara watching but paid her no heed. Gia had all she could handle at present; she couldn't worry about Clara's scrutiny. Gia pushed away the breakfast plate as the thought of eating another bite made her feel ill.

Almost as ill as marrying a man who despised her.

* * * *

Upon entering the house, Landen had been summoned to the parlor where Aunt Clara had been waiting for his return from Troy. He was hungry and tired as hell. The last thing he felt up to was a conversation with Aunt Clara.

"You have to speak with Gianna, Denny," Aunt Clara said. "The girl isn't well."

He shrugged off his coat, then sank to a chair. "That makes two of us," he muttered, running a hand through his hair.

She frowned. "I am serious. She's barely eaten in three days. And from the look of her, she hasn't slept either. She puts up a brave front, but I can see plainly her fear."

"And what am I to do about that?"

"She is frightened of you."

Good, he thought as he stretched out his legs. The little liar had planned this from the start. He hadn't set eyes on her since that day in the parlor when she'd sprung her trap, and he'd had three long days to think. To ponder how he'd make her pay for what she'd done to him.

He would be a terrible husband to her. He'd carouse and cheat. Perhaps he'd start back up with Charlotte. That is, if she'd have him. Charlotte had been upset when he'd broken it off with her, but she'd be furious when she found out Landen was marrying another woman.

Although he'd made clear to Charlotte at the start of their affair he had no inclination to marry, he knew she'd hoped to change his mind. Her mother's incessant pushing had only made matters worse. Charlotte began appearing wherever Landen happened to be, even going so far as to take a suite at the Misty Lake Hotel for the summer, hoping he might propose. Instead, he'd broken it off. And now he was marrying Gia.

He cursed under his breath. For years, he'd lived his life as he'd dictated, as master of his own fate, only to be led to the altar by a scheming chit he barely knew. Oh, yes, he would make Gia suffer. He would avoid her by day, and by night he would make love to her until she begged for mercy.

The pleasure he derived from the thought of this particular form of retaliation made him angry. Despite his loathing for Gia, he remained physically attracted to her. His weakness at harboring any feelings other than hatred toward his future bride disgusted him almost as much as what she'd done.

"She's an orphan, you know," Clara said.

"If that information is intended to soften my opinion of her—"

"For goodness' sake, Denny, stop acting the martyr."

"Your immense enjoyment of the situation makes that difficult," he ground out.

With a huff, she waved off his observation and pressed on. "She's your fiancée now. You must reassure her that you've accepted the marriage and will treat her kindly."

"I'll do no such thing."

Clara drummed her fingers on the arm of her chair. "Then we may be forced to postpone the wedding until she adjusts to the situation. In the meantime, we'll announce the engagement and hope that's sufficient to quiet the talk."

Landen considered this for all of a moment. He refused to accommodate Gia in any way. If he had to adjust to the situation, so should she. "No. We marry as planned."

Clara nodded triumphantly. "So, you'll speak with her, then?"

He frowned. It was bad enough Gia had tricked him into marriage, now he had to make her feel better about it? Ridiculous. "She'll come around without my assistance."

"No, Landen. She will not." Aunt Clara leaned forward. "We are announcing the engagement at the reception on Saturday. How will it reflect on you if your future bride appeared looking despondent? Have you given thought to that?"

He hadn't.

His aunt's targeted strike hit with expert precision. His mother's erratic moods and chronic bouts of melancholia had affected them all. His chest clenched at the painful reminder of his childhood with a mother who had turned him and his father inside out.

"Come, now, you are a charming man," Aunt Clara said. "Use that charm on your fiancée. If not for her sake, then for your own." She patted his knee. "For your family."

* * * *

Gia stared out the window at the carriage parked in the drive. Landen was home. After a three-day reprieve from having to face him, her heart now flapped more wildly than a bird sprung from a cage.

She wrung her hands as she paced in circles, then stopped at the mirror. Tired eyes stared back at her. She sighed, feeling as wretched as she looked. She'd allow herself this final evening to ferment in her predicament, but come morning, she'd pull herself from the mire of self-pity and get on with things.

Had she even the slightest doubt in her prophetic ability, her first order of business tomorrow would be fleeing this place and the man she dreaded facing again. It wasn't too late. She could still run, still save herself from this marriage. But then Landen would die. As Prudence had died when Gia had taken the coward's way out.

Besides, she had nowhere else to go. As Clara had said, this was Gia's family now. And unbeknownst to them all, they needed Gia to keep it intact.

The distinctive sound of Landen's heavy footsteps in the hall gave her a start. It was well past ten o'clock—he wouldn't possibly consider disturbing her at this hour.

The solid rap on the door proved otherwise. She sprang to her feet. Primping at her hair in a desperate attempt to better her disheveled appearance, she walked to the door.

"You're back," she uttered as he strode past her.

He turned to face her, his gaze trailing up and down the length of her.

She shifted her weight to shore her weak knees against his inspection and her blasted attraction to the rude man.

"My aunt was not exaggerating." His lips gnarled with disgust. "You look like a dishrag."

Gia lowered her eyes.

"I wish to speak with you," he said.

"I'm sure you do."

"My aunt is concerned about you."

"There's no need for concern."

"My sentiment exactly," he said. "But just in case you're having second thoughts about the scheme you've hatched, let me remind you that there's more than your reputation at stake."

"I don't care about my reputation."

"I care about mine," he said. "And Alice's. Not that you give a damn about the girl you were hired to help."

"I do care," she shot back. "I care immensely."

Tilting his head, he eyed her skeptically. "Your acting skills are remarkable," he said. "If I didn't know better, I might almost believe you." His tone sharpened. "But unlike my aunt, I don't trust a word that comes from your scheming lips."

"I never intended for this to happen."

His jaw tensed at her pathetic defense. His narrowed eyes were devoid of emotion, empty and dark as a bottomless pit. She stared into her future and the endless eternity that would be their marriage until he spoke again. "Be that as it may, you've proved yourself to be a convincing liar, and now we will both pay the price for your deceit."

"I wished only to stay for the summer."

"Why?" he demanded.

For a moment, she was tempted to tell him the truth and be done with him. Life on the streets seemed a better alternative to life with this man. But the desperation in his plea and the trace of vulnerability behind the anger on his handsome face fortified her determination to protect him and finish what she'd started.

Gia had vowed when she came here to do what she must—to go where her visions led her—she'd not retreat now. She'd survived thirty paralyzing minutes in the freezing water beneath the ice; she could survive an unhappy marriage to Landen Elmsworth and whatever retribution he'd inflict upon her for what she'd done. She didn't have to like him to save him, but she couldn't live with herself if she didn't try.

He frowned at her silence, glancing toward the untouched supper tray on the small table by the window. "Have something to eat. Starving yourself will gain you no sympathy."

"I'm not seeking sympathy." She lifted her chin against the slight tremble in her voice.

"Perhaps not, but you're after something." He stepped toward her.

Her pulse skittered at his nearness and the carnal heat in his eyes.

"You've reaped more than you bargained for, Gia," he said, moving closer. "Because you've made your bed, and now you will sleep in it." She recoiled, turning away, as he leaned close to her ear. "With me."

Chapter 6

Gia kept to herself as much as possible over the next few days. Alice was barely speaking to her, and Landen was avoiding her completely. The only one who seemed able to tolerate her presence was Clara, whose sole focus was on getting her nephew properly married as soon as possible.

Dressing quickly, she donned the new dress that had been delivered this morning. She and Alice had been fitted for their dresses for the garden party days ago, and they'd arrived in the nick of time. Though the sapphire gown felt a tad loose, the color suited her nicely. She fluffed at the skirts, hoping no one would notice her slight weight loss.

Her appetite was returning slowly, and she was doing her best to stay well nourished. Shards of memory pierced her mind, jagged pieces of her shattered life back home. After Gia had refused the powders and tonics prescribed to alleviate her "hallucinations," her parents had stooped to concealing medication in her food.

Her favorite breakfast of scrambled eggs and hot chocolate became her daily dose of opiates. By the time she'd realized their treachery, she was spiraling down a tunnel of nothingness. Each day she'd fallen deeper and cared less. But somewhere during her drug-induced descent, she'd salvaged a thread of volition. She'd clung to that thread, all but starving herself as she'd wormed from the foggy depths of her shame and her parents' betrayal until she was lucid enough to formulate a plan of escape.

To this day she seldom ate more than a biscuit for breakfast, and the thought of consuming scrambled eggs or hot chocolate fairly caused her to gag. She gulped back the bitter pain of her past. She couldn't afford such distractions. Today was too important. She took a long breath, primping stiffly at her hair.

Clara would announce the engagement this afternoon at the garden party. Gia intended to use the opportunity to learn all she could about each and every guest in attendance. The affair would give her the chance to finally observe Landen in public. Being cooped up in the house with only the family was getting Gia nowhere in her effort to save his life. With any luck, today she'd glean some shred of insight during Landen's interactions with the people of Misty Lake that might aid her in discerning who might want to hurt him.

The small gathering that they'd originally planned to ease Alice into society had turned into something else, and Gia's sorrow for her part in pushing Alice to the wayside was palpable. She had to smooth things over with Alice. The girl would be a bramble of nerves at having to attend the party and in need of reassurance.

After finding Alice's room empty, Gia sought her out in the next likely place. Small tables had been arranged on the garden patio, each covered in crisp white linen and adorned with a sprouting vase of lily of the valley. Clay pots of all sizes displayed lush ferns and other greenery. Alice sat on a bench in the corner, claiming the spot she, no doubt, intended to occupy for the duration of the afternoon.

"May I join you, Alice?"

The girl shrugged in reply.

"The garden looks lovely," Gia said.

Alice sat in stiff silence, as Gia took a seat next to her.

Gia sat for several moments, contemplating what to say. "I can only imagine what you must think of me."

Alice turned to face her. "No. You cannot."

Gia sighed. "No, perhaps not." Alice was not making this easy, but Gia couldn't blame her. "I never meant for this to happen. Truly, I didn't." Gia shook her head. "I honestly don't know what else to say."

"You owe me no explanation," Alice said. "You owe me nothing." She lowered her gaze. "I didn't want a companion, anyway."

"I know you didn't. But I am hopeful that, in time, we might be friends instead."

Alice eyed her warily. She obviously didn't trust Gia any more than Landen did.

"Be a good wife to him."

Gia blinked at Alice's candor.

"He's my brother, and I love him. Promise me you will not hurt him." Alice's voice dipped so low Gia barely heard her. "I could not bear to see him hurt again."

"Again?"

Alice fidgeted with her hands. "He was jilted on the eve of his wedding day."

Gia stared, speechless. "He…when?"

"It happened several years ago," Alice said. "Her name was Isobel Harrison, and Denny met her while away at school. On the night before the wedding, Denny received a message from her parents informing him that she'd married another man. Denny never speaks of it and would hate that I'm speaking of it with you, but I felt you should know."

The depth of Alice's sorrow and love for her brother ached through the hollow void in Gia's soul. She missed her own brothers so much. Their smiles and laughter, their lively eyes filled with all their hopes for the future. She stiffened against her rising grief. "Thank you for telling me, Alice."

"We'll be sisters soon," Alice said. "And although I've no choice in the matter, I am willing to give you a chance, so long as you're a good wife to Denny. My brother is not perfect. Even under the best of circumstances, he's loathe to show it, but he does have a heart. A good heart." Alice straightened her spine and met Gia's eyes. "If you do anything to hurt him, Gia, I shall never forgive you."

The fire in her eyes proved she meant it. Alice had a bit of her aunt Clara in her, and her warning to Gia hit home.

"Alice! Gianna!" Clara's voice grew louder. "Where are—Oh, there you are," she said as she poked her head between the open glass doors. "Come inside now, ladies. Our guests are arriving."

Alice blanched, clasping her hands as though about to unravel.

"You'll do fine, Alice," Gia said with a smile of reassurance. "I'll be right at your side." Gia stood and held out her hand.

Alice remained firmly planted.

Gia's heart sank. Even now, in the throes of her crippling shyness, Alice spurned Gia's aid. "Alice?"

With a huff, Alice finally took Gia's hand.

But the girl's desperate act did little to close the awkward distance between them as they walked inside to receive their guests.

* * * *

Landen watched Gia from across the patio. On the outside, she seemed perfect. Gracious and lovely and chaste. He frowned. Unlike the fools she was charming, he knew better.

She sat with Alice on a bench in the corner, engaged in conversation with one of the young men loitering around them. Alice remained as stagnantly silent as the potted plant on the table beside her, but the look of stark terror she'd worn earlier had diminished to an expression of acute discomfort. A definite improvement for Alice.

At least Gia's presence would be good for one of them.

The male attention Gia was drawing might be a benefit to Alice, and yet Landen found he didn't like it. For all he knew, Gia was a cheat as well as a liar. The fear of being humiliated again by a cheating woman clenched in his gut.

Recollection of his last meeting with Gia fueled his unease. That she had appeared so distressed about marrying him confused him. Vexed him. Made him want to marry her just to spite her.

"She's lovely, Denny."

Landen turned, surprised by Charlotte's presence. He'd broken the news of his engagement to Charlotte the other night, and she'd taken it as well as expected. He'd ended their affair prior to being caught in his room with Gia, but reiterating this detail to Charlotte had done little to soften the blow.

While he'd taken a risk by trusting Charlotte with the truth of the matter, he felt he owed her that much. She'd never struck him as a vindictive woman, and despite her obvious disappointment about his upcoming marriage, he knew her well enough to know she'd maintain a dignified silence for her own sake, as well as his.

"I didn't think you'd come," he said.

Charlotte shrugged. "My curiosity got the best of me," she said. "Besides, my mother will want to know all about her, and I'll have to tell her something."

Landen stiffened at the reminder. Charlotte was understandably upset, but her mother would be furious. Maude Devenshire wanted Landen to marry Charlotte and had made no secret of this desire to anyone who would listen. Maude's aspirations for her widowed daughter were a force to be reckoned with. The only thing Landen had dreaded more than the bane of marriage was the bane of a mother-in-law like Maude Devenshire.

He glanced to Gia, stung by the irony he'd dodged one bullet only to be struck by another.

But Gia had no mother—no family—and Landen couldn't help pitying her for that. A woman alone in the world was a vulnerable target. He feared to imagine his sister's plight in the absence of his protection. Yet even in the most desperate of circumstances, he couldn't image Alice would trap a man into marriage as Gia had.

"Cheer up, Denny," Charlotte said. She placed a hand on his arm. "If I can manage a smile today, so can you." She tilted her head. "I'm looking forward to meeting her."

Landen frowned. Introducing his former mistress to his fiancée was not a task that he relished. While he had faith in Charlotte's diplomacy, their affair had been no secret, and people talked. He wondered how much Gia had heard. Not that he gave a damn. She'd schemed to marry a total stranger and would have to live with the consequences. He took a breath to manage his spiteful emotions. He wasn't a cruel man by nature, which, at present, seemed more than Gia deserved.

With any luck, she'd atone for what she'd done to him by maintaining propriety. The illusion of it, at minimum. If nothing else, he hoped to be spared the endless melodrama his father had endured. His mother's erratic behavior, the tirades and rants that had punctuated her public appearances and caused terrific sensations, had nearly destroyed his father. And still the man had loved her more than he'd ever loved his second wife.

Landen thought about his own past. After all these years, the memory of Isobel's face had become as vague and intangible as his love for her had. All that remained of that infatuation was self-loathing and the brutal reminder that he'd been a fool.

He inhaled a sharp breath, arming himself to the teeth with the truth. Marriage was not the ruination of men. Love was.

* * * *

Hours later Gia was still reeling with what Alice had confided to her about Landen's past. He'd been jilted. No wonder he hated Gia for trapping him into marriage. Gaining his trust would be a daunting feat, but she'd not dwell in hopelessness now.

She scanned the assembly of people around her. The suspects. Some were summer guests in town, others year-round residents of Misty Lake, but all were the upper echelon of society. Clara had introduced her as a dear friend of the family, preferring to wait until all the guests had arrived before making the engagement announcement.

As Gia sat planted with Alice in the corner, she watched Landen closely and kept her attention well honed. She quickly discovered she wasn't the only one who was drawn to Landen. There wasn't a moment since the party began that he didn't have someone at his ear. Presently, that someone was a pretty woman with an affinity for touching his arm.

"Who's that woman with your brother?" Gia asked.

Alice followed her gaze. "That's the Widow Filkins." Alice turned from the pair, but Gia saw past the girl's coyness.

Was it Landen's intention to flaunt his mistress beneath Gia's nose? Did he actually think she might care? She straightened her spine, bristling at the sight of the couple in the secluded spot near the rose trellis on the outskirts of the assembly. Landen turned from the woman, then headed in Gia's direction. Despite her best effort to remain unaffected, her heart hammered as he approached. He looked especially appealing today dressed in his fine clothes with his dark hair brushed back from his handsome face.

"It's time," he said, extending a stiff arm to her.

Gia glanced to Alice. "I won't be long."

Alice gave a nervous nod.

Gia took Landen's arm. The firm muscle beneath her fingers tensed as though repelling her touch.

"I hate leaving her alone," Gia uttered.

"It can't be helped." Ushering her briskly through the crowd, he led her toward Clara, who was waving furiously for them to hurry along.

"As you can see, my aunt is eager to bask in the triumph of publicly securing my noose." He turned to Gia. "Your triumph."

Gia swallowed hard, fearing she might never acclimate to the loathing in his eyes. Or the strong desire he stirred in her blood.

"If I may have your attention, everyone," Clara said. "I have an announcement to make."

The crowd quieted beneath Clara's request. "Thank you all for coming today. My husband Howard and I have always held a deep fondness for Misty Lake." Clara pressed a gloved hand to her chest. "Some of the happiest days of my life were spent here, with my family, amid the splendor of the lake and the mountains, and returning each summer to those cherished memories fills my heart with such joy. As does my exciting announcement," she said, eyes aglow. "It brings me enormous pleasure to announce the engagement of my nephew, Landen, to Miss Gianna York."

The party lapsed into silence. Stunned faces gaped at the couple as Clara gave her surprised guests a moment to absorb the news before continuing. "Please join me in congratulating them on this joyous occasion."

Everyone applauded, and to Gia's surprise, Landen bent to kiss her on the cheek. The brief press of his lips on her flesh lingered long after he turned away from her and into the crowd of well-wishers that surrounded them.

When the din of the excitement faded, Landen left her with the women while he joined the men for a drink. From the corner of her eye, Gia spotted Charlotte Filkins strolling toward her. The dreary-brown mourning color of her gown did nothing to detract from her loveliness. Sunlight glimmered on her auburn hair. Charlotte's smile faltered as the two women chatting with Gia excused themselves quickly and hurried away. Their abrupt departure left Gia standing awkwardly alone and unsure of what to say.

"My name is Charlotte Filkins, Miss York. I hope you don't mind my introducing myself, but I feared growing old before Denny got an opportunity to do so."

Gia's cheeks flushed at the confirmation Charlotte knew Landen intimately enough to call him by the name his family did. "Of course not," she said. "It's nice to make your acquaintance."

"I wish you and Denny all the happiness in the world." Charlotte's brief smile was weighted with sorrow. She tossed a forlorn glance toward Landen, and Gia all but felt the woman's heart splintering to pieces.

From across the patio, Landen was watching their exchange, looking as miserable as Charlotte. Gia's status as interloper had never felt as painfully strong as in that moment. Her insides twisted into knots at the fear she was altering the fate of these lovers—interfering with something that was supposed to be.

Charlotte recovered quickly, reclaiming her charm. "He's a fine man."

Gia couldn't help herself. "You care for him."

Charlotte tilted her head, her defensive expression softening. "Very much." She lifted her chin. "But I shall get over it."

With those simple words, Charlotte started away, but the strain in her voice left Gia doubting this would be quite so easy.

Chapter 7

Alice worked like an artist, face set in concentration, as she applied the finishing touches to Gia's hair. She stepped back from the dressing table, admiring her handiwork. "Finished," she declared in a rare tone of pride.

Gia gazed at her reflection in the mirror in front of them. Shimmering pins secured each perfectly arranged tress in place. She turned her head from side to side. A long lace veil hung from the garland of orange blossoms encircling the intricate twists of hair piled at her crown. She looked like a princess. She looked like…a bride.

The memory of the dream she'd had before leaving Boston waltzed into her head. A haunting sadness followed. During the darkest hours of her excruciating recovery, from the tatters of her unraveling life, a beautiful dream had been woven.

Perhaps it wasn't merely a dream but a vision. She'd been so addled from the opiates she couldn't be sure. But as vivid as it was vague, the dream had ensconced her in warmth, and she'd wrapped herself in the hope it had provided when she'd needed it most.

A maelstrom of emotions welled inside her, spewing forth in a rush of uncontrollable tears she couldn't contain.

"You don't like it?" Alice asked, clearly alarmed.

Gia blinked, wiping furiously at her eyes. "I do," she said, trying hard to compose herself. "Forgive me, Alice. I'm just being foolish." She forced a smile through her tears. "This is not how I pictured my wedding day."

Alice tilted her head, regarding Gia in the mirror. "I suppose not." The pity in her eyes made Gia feel worse.

"May I tell you something silly?"

Alice stepped to Gia's side to face her directly.

"Before I left Boston, I had a dream. One of those dreams that make you so happy you're disappointed when you wake up."

Alice nodded. "What was your dream?"

"I stood on a hill, watching the sunset. With a man."

Alice set down the brush, her lips pursed tight. "You've forced my brother into this marriage, so please forgive me for not sympathizing with you for your last-minute regrets."

Gia lowered her eyes, abashed. "You are right, Alice," she said. "I've made my bed. I know that." Feeling a fool for seeking comfort from the girl, she willed back her tears and shook off the stinging rebuff. Several awkward moments passed before Alice spoke again.

"So, who was he?"

Gia glanced up, surprised. Alice regarded her with more curiosity than judgment, and Gia inhaled a small breath of relief.

"That's what's so silly," Gia said. "I don't know. All I know is the love that filled my heart as I stared down at our interlaced hands felt so wonderful. So real." She shook her head. "So much so, I can't help wondering if he's out there somewhere. This mysterious man who leaned on a cane and made me feel loved."

Alice cast her gaze to the floor.

Gia couldn't blame her for her awkward response. In light of Landen's contempt for Gia, hearing the words out loud sounded pathetic to her own ears.

"I told you it was silly."

Alice shook her head. "It's not silly at all." Not a hint of reproach marred the girl's face. Alice had the makings of a true friend, and Gia's heart swelled with growing fondness for her future sister-in-law. "It was a beautiful dream." She reached for a handkerchief and dabbed at Gia's tears. "That's why it's so difficult to let it go."

The dream was the only good thing Gia had left home with. She'd tried so often to finish the dream, to return to it—to him. With a heavy heart, she endeavored to put it aside, but she'd never discard it.

The door flew open, and the sound of Clara's voice flooded the room. "See to it the champagne is properly chilled, and the flutes are sparkling," she said to the harried maid she left in the hall as she swished into the room.

Dressed to the nines, Clara looked radiant. Despite her seventy-plus years, her energy was relentless. As was her attention to detail. For the past week, the stout woman had barreled through the house like a loaded cannon, firing preparation orders at every turn. Get this, get that, do this, do that. And everyone from the gardener who'd trimmed the hedges to the pastor, who would perform the ceremony, had scurried to accommodate, including Landen, which had surprised Gia the most.

"I have something for you, Gianna," Clara said, her face aglow with excitement. She opened the small box in her hand, then placed it on the dressing table in front of Gia.

Gia glanced down at the cameo nestled inside the velvet-lined box. "It's lovely."

Clara puffed her ample chest. "That broach has been in the family for generations. Every woman in the Elmsworth family has worn it during her wedding ceremony."

"My mother wore this?" Alice asked, leaning in for a closer look.

"Yes, of course," Clara said. "Landen's mother wore it as well. God rest her pitiful soul," she muttered with a shake of her head.

The grim comment piqued Gia's interest in the story of Landen's mother. Something told her there was an intriguing tale to be told, but Clara's solemn expression during the heavy silence that followed deflated Gia's urge to prompt for more.

"It's tradition to wear something borrowed for good luck," Clara said with a renewed lilt in her voice. She patted Gia's shoulder. "I've a feeling you'll need it." She started from the room. "Come, Alice. I need you to help me with my rhinestone headpiece."

Alice rolled her eyes. "One might think she were the bride."

Gia smiled, nodding in agreement. "Thank you for helping me get ready, Alice."

"You're welcome." Alice kissed Gia's cheek and then hurried after her aunt, who'd rushed off at lightning speed.

Lifting the cameo carefully from its velvet bed, Gia caressed her thumb over the regal profile of aged ivory. It was a lovely piece, made more priceless by its history. A history she was about to become a part of. Clara's surprising comment about Landen's mother echoed in her head.

Gia would enter this family dragging a dark past with her, but she'd been so engrossed in hiding her secrets it hadn't occurred to her that the Elmsworths might have a few secrets of their own.

She opened the clasp to pin the broach to her collar. The sudden heat in her palm signaled a warning. Her flesh prickled. Her breath hitched. Closing her eyes, she surrendered to the unstoppable force, as the vision emerged from the darkness, sucking her in.

The smell of bourbon filled her nose. The air became stiflingly hot. Clara lay in bed, her face deathly white against her disheveled gray hair. Clutching the sheets, she moaned, writhing in pain. Her eyes bulged with fear.

With a gasp, Gia opened her eyes. Blood pulsed at her temples. Slumping back in the chair, she sank against the crush of her veil behind her, too drained to move. She unfurled her clenched fist, staring down at the cameo in her palm until her racing pulse slowed.

Still trembling with the dread the image had induced, she shot to her feet. She paced the room, trying to gather her wits. Somehow she had to warn Clara. But how? How could she possibly warn the woman about something that would happen—something she had no logical explanation for knowing? She pictured herself, kicking and screaming, as Landen carted her off to the asylum.

She paced faster, skirts swaying over the hoops beneath. Lost as to what she should do, she knew she had to see Clara. While she had no idea what she'd say, perhaps something would come to her.

She hurried to Clara's room, where she found her alone, still fussing with the fancy headpiece sparkling on her head. "What do you need, Gianna?" she asked as she primped in the mirror.

Gia's eyes fixed on the bed. Recognizing the massive carved headboard as the one in her vision, Gia scrambled for words, her mind reeling. "Clara, are you feeling all right?"

"My nephew is finally getting married," Clara crowed to her own reflection. "I feel wonderful." She narrowed her eyes and turned from the mirror. "Why do you ask?"

Gia fumbled for an adequate answer. "You're pale."

Clara frowned. "I'm old." She gave a sharp fluff to her royal blue skirts. "But unlike Bea, I refuse to use my age as an excuse to dwell on every ache and pain."

Gia stiffened. "So, you're not feeling well?"

"I'm fine." Her hands shot to her hips. "And I'm busy."

"Too busy," Gia offered. "With all the wedding preparations, you've had little time to rest."

Clara waved her away. "I'll get plenty of rest in Saratoga."

Or she'd contract a terrible illness there. "Perhaps you should consider postponing the trip."

"Nonsense," she said. "Tonight is your wedding night. Since Landen refuses to take you on a proper honeymoon, you should at least be allowed the privacy of the house." She pursed her lips in a disapproving manner that made Gia's cheeks flush. "Not that privacy matters to the pair of you," she muttered. "But Alice and I will depart after the wedding, never the less." She slipped on her gloves. "Two days should suffice."

Two entire days—alone—with Landen. The sudden shift in Gia's focus could not be reined. Despite her trepidation about the upcoming night, an unbridled excitement coursed through her blood at the thought of sharing Landen's bed. Her stomach lurched as her mind veered wildly with imagined scenarios. With the thought he might kiss her as he had that night in his room, touch her as he had. Heat flooded her face and swirled in her belly. She blinked hard, reclaiming her focus.

"But, Clara—"

"Enough, Gianna." Clara took an impatient breath. "All brides are nervous on their wedding day." She clasped Gia's hands in hers, and Gia appreciated her attempt to put her at ease. "There's no knot so tight as the bond of marriage." Clara let go of Gia's hands and spun away. "But we all manage to survive."

So much for gentle reassurance.

"Now stop dawdling, and go finish getting ready."

Biting back the urge to blurt out everything, Gia did as directed. At the moment, she had no other choice. Trying to explain the vision would be fruitless, especially now, when Clara's attention was so otherwise engaged. The highly anticipated marriage of her nephew would commence come hell or high water, and nothing anyone could say would distract the woman from seeing Landen's wedding went off without a hitch.

Once back in her room, Gia contemplated what she might do. Picking up the cameo, she held it tightly, trying to prompt another vision that might determine Clara's fate. When nothing happened, Gia pinned the piece to her collar and tried to force her fears from her mind.

Clara seemed fit as a fiddle. While Gia's vision had offered no inkling as to when the woman would fall ill, the bed in the vision told her she'd fall ill in this house. This detail, when coupled with the current sound state of Clara's health, led Gia to conclude that Clara was safe for the time being.

Gia had to believe this if she hoped to get through this day. Once Clara returned from Saratoga, Gia would keep a keen eye on her. In the midst of placating herself with this reasoning, she heard a knock on the door.

"The pastor has arrived," Alice said as she peeked into the room. "Everyone is ready."

Gia took a calming breath and followed Alice out the door. Landen stood in the hall at the bottom of the stairs. Her heart fluttered. Wearing a dark morning coat and gray cravat, he looked so handsome. And unhappy.

While she'd thought herself prepared to bear the burden of his misery in exchange for saving his life, looking at him now, shoulders slumped, head bowed in defeat, she wasn't so sure. She preferred his anger to this.

When he spotted her on the stairs and his eyes turned to blue ice, she welcomed his contempt and disdain like a pair of old friends.

He would never forgive her for ruining his life. The memory of Charlotte Filkins's pained face flashed in her mind. She blinked it away and descended the stairs. With each careful step, she grew more conscious of the heavy hoops and petticoats beneath her full skirts. The beautiful lace and silk trappings were made heavier by her doubts and the sight of the stranger she'd wed.

She knew nothing about him. All she knew was his anger. The anger she'd caused by forcing him to this moment. And his kiss—the heat that burned in his eyes when stoked by desire. Anger and desire. Hardly the stuff upon which to build marriage.

The distance to her groom closed, and her heart pounded faster. To her pleasant surprise, Landen's sharp frown eased as she neared. He straightened at attention, his features unmoving, except for his eyes. The flicker of heat in his gaze told her he liked what he saw. The deep swallow he took confirmed her suspicion.

Despite everything, he still wanted her. Her heart leapt. The thought sent her soaring. Not that she was so foolish as to hope he might ever love her. But if his desire for her could somehow thaw his glacial hatred, perhaps he might grow to tolerate her. Even care for her.

This hope blossomed as he stared at her, speechless. His lips parted as though he were about to speak. She stared up into his handsome face, waiting for some words of reassurance. Anything that might help her believe she wasn't about to make the biggest mistake of her life.

Instead, he offered only his arm when he said, "Let's get this over with."

Chapter 8

An hour later Landen found himself married. To his surprise he felt no differently than he had before reciting his vows. The sky hadn't come crashing down upon his head, and the world went on as if nothing had changed. And yet, nothing would ever be the same.

He felt so damn foolish. All these years he'd focused on securing the futures of his siblings. While Alice suffered from crippling shyness, Alex was afflicted with the condition of chronically falling in love. Landen had set his sights so firmly on the challenge of assuring they'd marry well, he'd never imagined, for one moment, he'd be the one entering into a dubious union.

Alex, especially, would appreciate this irony. Just last year, Landen had to intervene by talking Alex out of proposing marriage to a tavern maid, who was clearly after his money. Alex was currently in Syracuse and in love yet again. He'd written Landen of their plans to marry after Alex's graduation, but Landen doubted the relationship would survive that long. Alex was bringing his fiancée to Misty Lake to meet the family, but even if Landen disapproved of the woman, there'd be little he could say. He had lost all credibility when it came to advising his brother on marriage matters, and whatever this woman's circumstances, Alex was certain to throw this fact in Landen's face.

He swallowed this bitter pill along with the last gulp of his second glass of champagne. Watching Gia from where he stood by the fireplace, he still couldn't believe she was his wife. The champagne had loosened the tense knot in his stomach, and now he stood, merely numbed by his marriage to a woman whom he barely knew.

Gia sat in the corner of the room, Alice at her elbow. Despite everything, he had to credit Gia's unwavering loyalty to Alice. She didn't flit about, the center of attention, as most brides usually did. Rather, people flitted toward her. A damn flame drawing the doomed moths.

And draw them, she did. Men swarmed around her, as they had at the garden party, vying for the attention of Misty Lake's newest beauty. All harboring the same admiration in their eyes. Aunt Clara and Alice had done a fine job with Gia's bridal array. And he, the most foolish moth of them all, found it difficult to take his eyes off her.

Gia spoke something to Alice and then walked toward the table that held the punch bowl. She took a long sip from her glass, then headed outside to the patio. Craning his neck toward the window, he noticed she stood alone in a rare moment he could not pass up.

He crossed the room, then stepped out to the patio. Unaware of his approach, Gia stood at the stone wall, fiddling with the ring on her finger.

"My aunt insisted I purchase a ring."

She stiffened in surprise but didn't look up. "It's the most beautiful thing I've ever seen," she uttered more to herself than to him.

The sincerity in her voice fell over him like a spell. He stiffened, shaking off the rush of satisfaction spurred by her approval. "As I said, my aunt insisted."

That much was true. But his plan to purchase a simple gold band flew out the window the moment he'd spotted the yellow diamond ring in the jeweler's glass case. For some inexplicable reason, he'd wanted Gia to have it. Not solely because he could afford it, but because it had reminded him of her. Vibrant and brilliant. Infinite facets, one upon the other, so blindingly beautiful. Yet hard enough to cut glass.

How easy it was to forget the dazzling gems were merely stones at their core. Despite the analogy, despite everything, he wanted this woman. His wife. Anger prickled inside him. Her citrus scent drifted toward him on the breeze. That damn dress, stark white and buttoned up to her ears. Knowing what hid beneath the frilly layers of her skirts only enticed him more. The unforgettable curve of her hips through the sheer night rail she'd worn to his room, the warmth of her body pressed to his, left him stalled in a memory he didn't want to escape.

"A ring such as that one will be difficult to ignore," he said. "I thought it a perfect reminder."

"Reminder?"

"Every time you look at it, you'll be reminded that you're a married woman."

She stared, perplexed. "You expect I might forget?"

"I expect a faithful wife."

She bristled at his insinuation. If possible, the crimson flush of her cheeks made her prettier. She lifted her chin. "And may I expect the same faithfulness from my husband?" She crossed her arms. "Or shall I pose that question to Charlotte Filkins?"

She was too damn bold for her own good. He frowned, more because she'd caught him off guard. "Do not insult Charlotte in my presence."

"Are you in love with her?"

He blinked, surprised, once again, by her boldness. And the unmistakable distress in her eyes. While the answer to her question was a resounding no, he found himself withholding any reply.

Gia shifted her weight. As a newly married woman, he could see how this might hurt her, and oh, how he wanted to hurt her. Marrying a man who did not love her was one thing—marrying a man who was in love with another woman was quite another.

She swallowed hard at his silence, averting her eyes. With a toss of her head, she recovered quickly. "Not that I care a whit. Feel free to carry on with whomever you like."

He shook his head, smiling at her blunt retort. "While your permission is appreciated, you are my wife now, Gia. And as such, I promise I shall bestow all my carnal desires upon you."

* * * *

Gia gritted her teeth, detesting him now as much as he so obviously detested her. Why on earth was she bothering to save the insufferable man's life? Why on earth did she care?

Perhaps, she'd turn out to be the culprit responsible for his floating in the creek. The horrible thought shamed her, but she could not stop herself. The man vexed her beyond reason.

The damn smirk on his lips told her this was the reaction from her that he sought. To unnerve her with his endless reminders of the intimacies she was now expected to share with him. Resenting his attempt to exert some husbandly power over her, she refused to give him the satisfaction of playing into his hand.

Inhaling a quick breath, she met his smile with one of her own. Placing a firm hand on his arm, she rose to her toes. "I look forward to it," she whispered into his ear before she strode away.

She glanced over her shoulder, enjoying his stunned expression as he watched after her. Somehow, that expression was worth lowering herself to his level. She hated to admit it, but rattling him was also great fun.

Once inside the house, she felt differently. Liar, wanton, manipulator. She had no idea who she was anymore. Her thoughts meandered to her parents. How shocked they would be if they knew she was married. More likely, they were well past caring. She had no doubt they were relieved to be rid of her. They'd proven this by not coming after her.

Gia shook away thoughts of the past. She should have held her tongue about Charlotte. Had the man any honorable feelings toward his former lover, he wouldn't have kissed Gia the way he had in the first place. But nothing about Landen Elmsworth seemed honorable at the moment.

Gia turned toward the sound of giggling girls huddled in the foyer just outside the room. She listened for the sound of Alice's voice, hoping she might be among them. To her chagrin, she heard something else.

"Alice Elmsworth is pretty enough, but she possesses the personality of a mouse," one of the girls said. "I don't think she's uttered a word all day."

"There's nothing unnatural about that," another girl replied. "Since mice can't speak."

They all laughed, and Gia's temper rose to new heights. Had Alice happened upon this conversation, she'd be destroyed. Tears of anger burned Gia's eyes. Alice was a sweet person, who would never hurt anyone. She deserved understanding for her social anxiety, not ridicule.

Gia charged into the foyer, hands on hips. "Or perhaps Alice has the good sense not to waste words on spiteful girls who have no manners," she snapped. "Alice might be shy, but she's also smart and generous, and kind. Any one of you would be lucky to call her a friend."

The girls cringed, shamed by the reprimand. Their eyes widened like startled deer as they stared over Gia's shoulders before bolting from the room. Gia turned to watch them scurry away, and saw Landen in the doorway.

She blinked back the remnants of her shaky emotions, lacking the stamina to deal with him now. "Excuse me," she said, attempting to pass.

He caught her arm.

She froze, her heart still pounding in anger at the girls. If he said anything to rile her in her current state, she was certain she'd box his ears. She glanced up at him, ready to pounce, but the empathy on his face told her he'd overheard the exchange.

"Well done."

Gratitude shined in his eyes, and she couldn't look away.

"It's time to cut the cake!" Clara called to them.

Gia blinked and started away. Landen caught up to her, and together, they made their way through the crowded room to the cake table. With Clara's enthusiastic guidance, Gia cut the first piece of cake.

"Now pack this away," Clara told Florence. "It's to be enjoyed on their fifth anniversary."

Everyone applauded. Five years… If only Gia could share their optimism. Presently, she couldn't see past the next five days—could see nothing past her ominous visions of Landen and Clara.

The thought prompted Gia to make one last-ditch attempt to keep Clara home. After they enjoyed their cake, people began to depart. Clara seemed perfectly well, laughing and seeing off the guests.

Gia took this opportunity to seek out Landen. The man with whom he spoke excused himself with a smile as Gia approached.

"I wish to speak with you about your aunt," she said.

"She's your aunt now too."

She sighed at the sarcastic reminder. "Yes, of course."

"What is it you'd like to discuss?"

"I fear she's overexerted herself this past week."

"She's a tough old bird."

"Even so. Perhaps you could persuade her to postpone the trip to Saratoga until she's adequately rested."

Narrowing his eyes, he glanced toward his aunt, who was laughing heartily with the pastor. "She looks fine to me."

"She looks very pale." The lie got his attention.

His smug look faded. "I hadn't noticed."

"Go see for yourself," Gia said.

Landen turned from Gia, then strode to his aunt. Clara's dismissive wave ended their brief conversation, and before Gia knew it, he was back at her side.

"She's fine," he said. "She'll have a good soak in the baths at Saratoga. And we'll proceed with our wedding night as planned." He smiled. "I'm looking forward to it as well."

* * * *

Florence helped Gia undress. Slipping into a light robe, Gia was grateful to finally be free of the suffocating skirts and undergarments now heaped on the bed.

"Mr. Elmsworth had me prepare a bath for you in his room," Florence said.

Gia nodded. "Thank you."

"He's waiting," Florence added when Gia made no attempt to move.

Gia fastened her robe securely, fingers trembling as she headed down the hall to Landen's room. "Aunt Clara and Alice have left?" she asked as she stepped inside.

"They're well on their way. Except for Florence, the house is ours." He removed his coat and placed it over a chair. "Now stop stalling and come have your bath."

Gia glanced at the steaming tub in front of the fireplace. "You needn't have gone to the trouble. I bathed this morning."

He smiled. "This bath is for my benefit, not yours."

Her breath hitched, and she peered at the floor.

"Don't be shy. We are husband and wife now."

"Yes, I am aware," she said as evenly as she could manage.

He sat, still fully clothed except for his coat, in a chair facing the tub. He waved his arm. "Proceed."

She lifted her chin. His smug enjoyment of the power he thought he had over her was infuriating. Inhaling a deep breath, she resolved to thwart his control. She moved toward the tub. Slowly. Raising the hem of her robe, she lifted her foot over the rim of the tub, testing the temperature of the steaming water with her toes. She dangled her leg, her calf a pendulum, toes skimming the water. She shot him a glance to gauge his response. He watched, mesmerized, gripping the arms of the chair.

Her confidence soared. Opening the robe to expose her shoulders, she sank her foot lower. She let the robe fall to the floor, then stepped into the tub. She stood naked before him, firelight at her back. Holding her breath, she resisted the instinct to cower in shame. He swallowed hard, and his arousal overpowered her modesty. She straightened her spine. Staring into his eyes, she lowered herself carefully, then slid into the sudsy water.

Submerged in the heavenly warmth, she closed her eyes to her pounding heart. Fire burned in her belly as the heat of the water—his eyes—consumed her. "Satisfied?" she asked through the silence.

"Oh, I am far from satisfied." His voice was husky and deep as he walked toward the tub. He knelt at her head, his face a mere inch from hers. He reached for the sponge and dipped it into the sudsy water. Squeezing the water over her shoulders, he let the sponge roam with the downpour. She squirmed inside her flesh beneath the trail of the sponge. He repeated the sweet torture, over and over, until she was trembling. "All in good time," he whispered into her ear.

She melted beneath his words, the water, the brush of his breath on her skin. He eased her forward. Water lapped at her breasts, teasing her nipples. He caressed her back in small circles, and she moaned, tension draining from her muscles but building elsewhere.

His lips met her neck, and her head tilted toward him. After dropping the sponge, he clasped her face between his wet hands and kissed her. Hard. She drove her tongue madly against his, her emotions reeling with the awe of discovery. The pleasure. In this moment it all seemed so right. Her core ached, wanting more. Her plan to thwart his control was lost to her bliss. Her sheer want for this man. Clutching his shirt, she pulled him closer. The only thing stronger than her want was her need, and, oh, how she needed him.

As though reading her thoughts, he lifted her from the tub and carried her, dripping wet and sudsy, to the bed. The cool air opposed the heat of the water, her scorching blood, and her skin. Grasping his neck, she absorbed the warmth of his clothing.

They fell to the bed, and she welcomed him into her arms, kissing him fiercely. He tasted of champagne and cake, a delicious combination. The answers to all her girlhood questions would soon be revealed. With him… It all felt so natural and so meant to be. Eager to experience anything and everything Landen had to offer, she swirled her tongue against his, diving deeper.

With a groan, he pulled his mouth from hers. The hot kiss to her breast set her aflame. She arched her back as he sucked her nipple between his lips, his tongue driving her wild. She moaned, lost in the sensations and pleasure. She tore at his clothing, their shadows in the firelight dancing on the ceiling and walls.

A sudden knock sounded on the door.

They froze where they lay, both panting for air.

"Mr. Elmsworth."

It was Florence.

Landen released a long sigh, head hung in irritation. "What is it, Florence?"

"Please, come quickly. Your aunt has returned home. She's in very bad shape."

Chapter 9

Landen raced down the stairs, Gia at his heels. Aunt Clara sat slumped on a chair in the foyer, clutching her stomach.

"What happened?" he asked.

"I don't know." Alice's voice trembled. "It came on so suddenly. We were almost to Saratoga when she started complaining of pain in her stomach. I wanted to get her to the hotel, but she insisted on turning around and coming all the way back home."

"Do not speak about me as if I weren't here," Aunt Clara scolded. "I'll die in my own bed, not in a hotel room."

"You are not dying," he said.

She keeled forward from the force of her pain, and he wasn't so sure this was true. For as long as he could remember, Aunt Clara had never been ill. Uncle Howard had always been the sickly one. Landen's aunt was the last of his elder relatives, and his chest tightened at the thought of losing her too.

"I'm going for the doctor." He started for the door.

"Get me to my bed," Clara said, attempting to rise.

Gia rushed to assist her. "Let's get her upstairs first," she said, grasping Clara by the arm.

Landen nodded. Trying his damnedest to remain calm, he helped Gia get Clara to her feet. Together they started the mountainous journey up the staircase, inching at a snail's pace as they moved Clara along.

They finally managed to get her to her room, and Clara collapsed on the bed.

"I'll be back soon with the doctor, Aunt Clara," he said.

Clara reclined on the pillows, eyes closed. Whether she'd heard him or not, he couldn't tell.

"Hurry," Gia said.

He started for the door, hesitating at the sight of Alice. Tears welled in her frightened eyes as she hugged her arms to her chest. He faltered with the urge to console her.

"We'll be fine," Gia said. "Go."

The certainty in Gia's voice reassured him. While Alice might crumble in the crisis, Gia would take charge. Gia nodded toward the door, and he started away.

"Denny, wait." Clara struggled to sit upright. "Before you go, I must speak with you."

"Not now. You need a doctor. We'll talk later."

"There may be no later. This is my death bed, damn it, and I'll have my say in it," she said, sounding more like her old self.

Unable to argue her point, Landen obliged. With an anxious sigh, he took a seat in the chair beside the bed.

"We've always been at odds, but all I've ever wanted was what's best for you. What's best for the family. I know you blame me for what happened with Isobel," she said. "Just as you blame me for pushing you into this marriage, but promise me something."

"Aunt Clara—"

"Please, Denny," she said. "It's important."

He cradled her trembling hand in his. "What is it?" he asked. A lump of emotion rose in his throat. He swallowed his sorrow and regret at the possibility of losing this woman, who'd vexed him so often—and meant more to him than he'd realized until now.

"Take care of your brother and sister." She glanced over his shoulder. "And be kind to your wife. Howard and I were married for thirty years," she reminded him with a shaky smile. "You're married now and just beginning your lives together. I won't be here to help you along, but promise me…" Gripping his hand, she winced in pain.

He waited in the unbearable helplessness of her suffering until she was able to speak again.

"Promise me that no matter what happens, you will… You will name your first daughter after me."

Landen blinked in surprise. The vain request was true to form for Aunt Clara, and despite the somber circumstances, he couldn't help smiling.

"I promise," he said, patting her hand.

She nodded. "I'm so happy you're settled now."

"I know you are," he said honestly. He placed a kiss on her stark white cheek. "We'll talk more later. When you're feeling better." He stood. "I'll be back soon with the doctor."

She closed her eyes, dismissing him to the task, but he couldn't move, couldn't leave her.

"Landen."

Gia's soft cue nudged him from his frazzled state, and he swallowed hard. Without a word, he rushed from the room, dogged by urgency and fear. By the time he returned with the doctor, his aunt might be gone.

* * * *

To Landen's immense relief, Aunt Clara was still alive when he returned to the house with Doctor Reed less than an hour later. During his absence, Gia and Alice had managed to get his aunt into a nightdress. Tucked beneath a thick quilt, she moaned, clenching her teeth, as Gia applied a wet compress to her forehead. The bottle of brandy on the bedside table told him Gia had attempted to treat his aunt's pain on her own until the doctor arrived.

At Aunt Clara's insistence, he waited with Gia and Alice downstairs in the parlor while Doctor Reed examined his patient in private. Landen paced the carpet, his mind reeling in a dozen directions. "I don't understand how this happened," he muttered. "She looked fine to me, and now she's in this state." He shook his head. "I should have—"

"For goodness' sake, Denny," Alice said. "You're not responsible for everything. No one could have predicted this."

"She did." He flung a hand toward Gia.

She flinched, dark eyes flashing wide.

"She noticed Aunt Clara didn't look well this morning." He turned away, emotions tumbling inside him. Fear and anger and guilt balled into a massive knot in his gut.

This relative stranger had observed what he hadn't. Even after Gia had pointed it out to him, he'd given no real credence to her concern for his aunt's health. He realized now that he'd refused to see it—had not wanted to see it. He'd been so overcome by his eagerness to get Gia into his bed he'd practically pushed his aunt out the door.

He turned to Gia. "I should have stopped her from going to Saratoga as you suggested."

The tight purse of her lips told him that she agreed and wanted to say so out loud.

"No one stops Clara from doing anything," she said, taking the high road instead.

Her attempt to mollify him had the opposite effect. His anger tore off in every direction. At Gia. At himself. Even at his aunt for falling ill and interrupting his wedding night. The despicable truth stoked his anger and guilt.

But the memory of Gia's naked body, her silky wet skin, invaded his mind nonetheless. Her hair was still damp from the bath, tendrils curled at her temples. His desire for this woman who'd encroached on his peaceful existence and turned his life upside down would be his undoing.

"I'll ask Florence to bring coffee," Gia said.

"No," he said sharply. "Go on to bed." Already he was ignoring his aunt's advice to be kind to his wife, but he couldn't stop himself. "Alice and I will take care of our aunt."

"Denny!"

"It's all right, Alice." Gia gave a nod toward the door. "Please see to the coffee."

Alice obliged, looking grateful for the excuse to escape the tense scene.

Gia turned back to Landen. Anger flashed in her eyes, and he knew she was seething. He also knew he deserved it.

She took a step toward him. Her citrus scent was pure heaven. "We are all upset, and this is no time to quarrel," she said. "But your concern for your aunt does not give you the right to behave like an ass. Clara is my aunt too. You said so yourself." She tilted her head, awaiting his protest. "I'm a part of this family now, and like it or not, I'm not going anywhere."

Her gumption was as alluring as her scent. And as effectively taming. He took a deep breath, conceding the truth. Despite wishing otherwise, he did not want her to go.

* * * *

Gia glared at Landen, daring him to object. He was upset about Clara, but the blasted man made it difficult to sympathize with him. While Gia couldn't truly fault him for disregarding her warning about Clara, she was irked, nonetheless, that he had.

And now he had the audacity to be angry at her?

How unfathomable it seemed that this was the same man who'd held her in his arms and kissed her so passionately only hours before. She searched his eyes for any sign that he remembered. For any shred of proof that what had transpired between them had been real. That he'd felt what she had in that bed. Staring into his steely face, she felt foolish for her effort.

The doctor entered the parlor, surprising them both.

"What's wrong with her?" Landen said, nearly accosting the man.

The doctor held up a hand. "I believe your aunt is suffering with a bladder stone."

"Bladder stone?"

The doctor nodded. "Extremely painful. With any luck, the size of the stone is not overly large and will pass on its own."

"And if it is overly large?" Landen asked.

The doctor shook his head. "Given her age, surgery is out of the question. If the stone remains lodged, she will die."

"Christ Almighty," Landen uttered.

"We can only hope for the best."

"What do we do in the meantime while she suffers?" Landen asked.

"I'm afraid there's not much to be done. She must drink plenty of water to help flush the stone from her system. Continue to give laudanum to ease the pain. Other than that… Time will tell." He turned to Gia. "She's asking for you, Mrs. Elmsworth."

It took her a moment to realize the doctor was addressing her. That *she* was Mrs. Elmsworth. And that Clara had asked for her. She glanced to Landen, and he averted his eyes.

She hurried from the room and up the stairs. No doubt, Clara had noticed Alice was unraveling at the seams from the stress and had called upon Gia for assistance instead. With each step, Gia mustered the fortitude required to withstand Clara's misery.

Gia took a long breath, then opened the door. She stepped inside the room and into the scene of her vision. The carved headboard on the bed. Clara clutching the sheets, her face gnarled by pain. Gia's fear grew with every detail, every moment.

"Oh, Gianna," Clara uttered. "This pain…I've never…"

Gia rushed to the bed and sat next to her. "Shh. Don't try to speak."

The laudanum was quieting Clara some. Her eyes fluttered closed as she quickly complied.

Gia had never seen anyone die. Not of an illness, anyway. The deaths she'd witnessed had been caused by accidents. Sudden and without warning. No time for last words or good-byes. Lives torn from this world with a force so powerful it rendered those left behind reeling in the void. And in a chronic state of fear that life could end in a heartbeat.

Or in one step.

The horrific memory of that day gripped Gia by the throat and wouldn't let go. She could barely draw breath through the raw anguish of losing her brothers. Strong and healthy young men, who were laughing one moment and drowning the next. During that eternity beneath the freezing water, before it all went black, Gia's only consolation had been that she would die with them.

She glanced to the bottle of laudanum on the bedside table. The temptation to take a swallow for herself had never felt so strong. Just one taste to numb the brutal memories and help get her through whatever this night might bring would be all that she needed.

"Gianna." Clara poked Gia's arm.

Gia blinked. "Yes, what is it?"

"Get me my hair brush. I can't meet Howard in heaven looking like this."

"Clara—"

"Please." Clara closed her eyes.

Gia sighed. The poor woman was preparing to go, and Gia hadn't the heart to stop her. Clara was nothing if not dignified, and her desperate plea spurred Gia to tears. There was no harm in appeasing the suffering woman. Accommodating the request might even help her rest easier. Anything to lessen her suffering.

Gia walked to Clara's dressing table and picked up the silver hairbrush. She glanced into the mirror at Clara's reflection behind her. Clara's eyes were still closed, but the tense lines of her face marked her pain.

Gia's gaze moved from the reflection of Clara to her own. She glanced down at the brush in her hand, clutching it tightly. She'd never succeeded in summoning a vision, and she was petrified of what she might see, but she had to try. She had to know. While she could do nothing for Clara, she could help prepare Alice and Landen for whatever might come.

With a deep breath, she closed her eyes. Clearing her mind, she concentrated on nothing but the feel of the cool metal object in her hands.

The metal warmed in her palm, and she gasped, heart pounding. Releasing herself to the sensation, she welcomed the heat, inviting it in. The vision drifted through the darkness of her mind, drawing closer. Like an approaching lantern in the night, it neared, and she floated toward it—into it—until she was there.

Clara sat upright in bed, a breakfast tray on her lap. Dressed in the nightdress she wore now, she looked tired, but her eyes were bright. Her cheeks were rosy and flush as she bit with zest into a plump sweet roll.

Gia smiled, and the vision went dark. She opened her eyes, leaning forward on the table. Exhaustion gave way to jubilation as she turned to face Clara. "Shall I brush your hair for you now?"

Clara nodded. "Thank you, yes," she murmured.

Gia brushed Clara's hair. With each gentle stroke through Clara's gray curls, Gia's spirit soared higher and higher. For the first time, Gia had managed to summon a vision. She'd willed it to come to her, and it came. She'd controlled it.

This new aspect of her ability could change everything. She didn't know how or why this had happened, or if it would happen again, but of one thing she was certain.

Howard would have to wait.

Chapter 10

The clock on the mantel ticked away minutes that felt more like hours as Gia and Landen sat alone in the parlor. Doctor Reed had given Clara some private instructions to follow throughout the night. Until his return in the morning, Clara insisted on suffering without an audience.

Frazzled and exhausted, Alice had retreated to her own room a half hour ago, after Landen promised to wake her if there was any change with their aunt's condition. Gia had dismissed Landen's suggestion that she go to bed, too, opting instead to follow him downstairs.

The room darkened around the glow of the single lamp in the corner as their solemn vigil crept toward midnight. Even Gia's certainty that Clara would recover did little to console her during the poor woman's present misery. Gia glanced to Landen, which only made her feel worse.

Leaning forward on the edge of his seat, he sat across from her, elbows on his knees, rubbing his brow. He hadn't uttered a word since bidding Alice good night, and his silent worrying now bordered on unbearable. Gia wrung her hands, aching to dispel his fears with what she knew.

Not that telling him about her vision of Clara's recovery would ease his distress. The shock of learning his new wife clamed to possess some fantastic ability to foresee future events would merely compound his troubles. The last thing he needed was the added burden of discovering he'd married a mad woman.

"Clara is going to be fine," Gia said, slicing through the deafening silence.

He blinked, glancing up at her, as though he'd forgotten she was there. He gave a swift brush to his stubbled jaw. Despite the weariness in his eyes, he looked so handsome.

"Forgive me for not sharing your confidence." He reached for the decanter of brandy on the table between them. "Would you care for one?" he asked as he poured.

The heady aroma of liquor tempted her senses. She could barely breathe. The brandy flowed, rising slowly inside the beveled glass, rich and smooth. Liquid peace.

"No, thank you," she lied. Inhaling a breath, she reclaimed her focus. "Clara is a strong woman. She'll recover. Trust me."

His eyes pinned hers. Gia cringed at her poor choice of words. In his harsh expression, she saw he had no intention of trusting her—not now—not ever.

Averting his gaze, he took a deep sip of his brandy. The alcohol seemed to relax him, and he eased back on the sofa. "Aunt Clara and I have always spent more time locking horns than anything else."

Grateful he'd let her request for his trust pass without a retort, she straightened in her seat. "The two of you are a lot alike. It stands to reason—"

"We are nothing alike."

The stubborn denial was too childish to resist. Gia nodded in mock agreement. "That's precisely what Clara would say."

He shook his head in defeat, curbing the smile that twitched on his lips.

The tension between them lightened, as did Gia's mood.

"You and your aunt share the same determination to protect your family. You both do what you feel is best for those you love. Despite any resistance."

"If you're referring to my efforts with Alice, that's true. But I'd never force my siblings to do anything that might hurt them."

"And Clara would?"

His lips tightened. "Not intentionally, no." He reached for his drink and took another long swallow. Reclining into his seat, he rested his head on the back of the sofa. He closed his eyes. "She dogged me so relentlessly to marry Isobel," he uttered to the ceiling.

The brandy's tranquil effect on him was apparent, and Gia indulged in the state of his loosened reserve.

"Alice mentioned that you were previously engaged."

A sardonic smile stretched across his face. "Did she also mention that I was a fool?"

Gia frowned. "Of course not."

He opened his eyes, then stared at the empty drink he held propped on his knee. "I should have expected as much from Isobel."

Gia's pulse quickened at his candor. Since first hearing about his engagement to Isobel, Gia had so many questions about the woman who had broken his heart. "What do you mean?"

He leaned upright to refill his drink. "When I first met her, she was engaged to another man."

Despite Gia's initial surprise, she concluded the outcome. Landen Elmsworth was handsome and smart. Wealthy. "And you stole her away?"

"Yes."

His tone was provoking and brutal. Devoid of regret. Armed with such innate self-assurance, he possessed the means to rob anyone blind.

"But the night before the wedding, another man stole her from me."

Gia regarded him closely. "That must have been very painful."

"Just deserts."

A note of contrition strained his sharp tone. Perhaps he rued his transgressions after all. This contrasting aspect to his arrogant nature intrigued her. However misguided she might be by the prospect, her desire to learn more about him flourished through her veins. Like the fevered excitement she'd felt at his physical touch, the anticipation of knowing his mind felt just as potent. "No one deserves to be hurt."

He gave a snort of disgust. "I find that sentiment strange, coming from you."

She stiffened against his renewed disdain. "I never intended to hurt you."

His face turned to steel. "You intended to marry me. That's one in the same." He set down his drink, then shot to his feet. "I'm going to check on my aunt," he said as he strode from the room.

* * * *

The soft nudge to Gia's shoulder jolted her awake.

She sprang upright in the parlor chair, blinking hard. Alice stood over her with a beaming smile on her face. "Aunt Clara has passed the stone."

Gia exhaled in relief.

"She's resting comfortably now," Alice said. "She's even asked for something to eat."

"I'll have Florence prepare breakfast."

"She already has. It's waiting for us upstairs. Aunt Clara insisted we join her."

Gia followed Alice upstairs, rejecting any halfhearted attempt to straighten her appearance. She was too tired, too emotionally drained to expend wasted effort to gain Landen's approval.

Gia stepped into Clara's room, and as before, was greeted by a scene from her visions. Clara sat upright in bed, a breakfast tray covering her lap. Resembling a woman who'd just endured the labor of childbirth, she looked tired and exhilarated at the same time.

Clara waved Alice and Gia toward the breakfast table by the window. Landen waited until they were seated before dragging another chair from the hall and joining them at the table. To avoid sitting with his back toward Clara, he slid the chair next to Gia, then sat beside her.

Positioning the chair for a better view of his aunt, he moved closer to Gia. His knee brushed hers, but she didn't move. Neither did he. She glanced down at his knee, the muscular thigh resting against hers. When she looked up, he was watching her. The smirk on his lips matched the smug gleam in his eyes as he inched the chair closer.

She swallowed hard, doing her utmost to settle into his unsettling nearness. Clara prattled away between bites of breakfast, relaying the doctor's sound advice that she forgo thoughts of returning to Saratoga and remain close to home. Everyone agreed, and they ate and laughed and celebrated her recovery over two pots of coffee and a mountain of sweet rolls.

"The Westcott Ball takes place in three weeks," Clara announced. "Since my burial has been postponed, and you will not be in mourning, we shall all go together."

Alice groaned.

"You cannot deny me now, missy," Clara said, pointing the large roll in her fist. "I intend to use this family's collective relief at my recovery to my full advantage."

"Of course you do," Landen said.

"Any objections to that?"

He held up his hands in surrender. "No objections at all." He leaned toward Alice. "It's going to be a long summer."

"Very long." Alice hung her head in her hands.

"Wretched imps." Clara waved them off with a huff, but amusement danced in her eyes.

Despite all their bickering and underlying discord, it was now plain as day that the siblings truly loved their domineering old aunt. Perhaps this crisis might serve as a reminder to how truly blessed they were to have been given a second chance with her.

Gia thought about her brothers, and her heart felt as heavy as her bulking guilt. What she wouldn't give for a second chance with them. For the opportunity to hug them, to make up for every instance she'd been annoyed or angered by them. To tell them she was sorry for killing them…

"Gia?" Alice asked. "Are you all right?"

Gia blinked. "Yes, I am fine."

"You're exhausted," Landen interjected. "You've been up most of the night. Go get some rest."

Whether his directive stemmed from concern or his wish to be rid of her, she didn't know. She was too overjoyed by Clara's recovery to care.

* * * *

When Gia awoke later that day, the sun was setting. She sat at the window, staring out at the lake. Beneath the pink and orange horizon, water rippled on the breeze. Despite how tired she'd been when she'd fallen into bed, she'd had trouble falling asleep. To her surprise, once she succumbed to her exhaustion, she'd slept soundly for hours. Now that she was awake, all her troubles stirred to life too.

Clara's recovery reinforced what Gia had always known, but had lately forgotten. Landen was in danger. She felt lost and alone. Afraid.

"You're awake."

She started at the sound of Landen's voice.

"How is she?" Gia asked as he stepped into the room.

"Sound asleep," he said. "I've no doubt she'll be out until morning."

Gia nodded. "You must be exhausted as well."

"On the contrary. I feel wide awake."

He yanked his shirt from the waist of his trousers. The disheveled result caused a hitch in her throat. The intimacy of seeing him this way, in this room where they'd come so close to consummating their marriage, took her by storm. Had that been only yesterday?

Memories flashed through her mind. The charge of excitement that followed made it feel like a lifetime since he'd carried her naked to the bed. She rose to her feet, though she wasn't sure why. Her breasts tingled with arousal. The heat flushing her cheeks pooled at her core.

"Are you hungry?"

She shook her head, summoning her voice through her lust. "Not at all."

He stepped toward her, unbuttoning his shirt as he moved. "Did you get enough sleep?"

"Yes."

His blue eyes brimmed with need, not hatred, and she all but melted into a hot puddle at his feet.

"Are you certain?"

She nodded, heart pounding as he moved even closer.

"Good." He stripped off his shirt. "Now get back into bed."

Chapter 11

Gia's surprised expression turned coy. "Are you sure you wouldn't prefer getting some sleep instead?"

Eyeing her intently, he shook his head at the memory of the body beneath the thin night rail. Making love to her was the only benefit to this marriage, and one he intended to use to his full advantage.

"I would prefer to proceed with where we left off yesterday." He reached to touch her hair. The stray wisp at her temple felt like silk between his fingers. His lust for his new bride grew stronger with each passing moment. "I can refresh your memory in case you've forgotten. I had just carried you to the bed—"

"I remember."

The flush of her cheeks made him smile. There was no room for modesty between them now. Not anymore. He'd had a sampling of the passion inside her. The passion he planned to fully unleash.

"So long as you feel up to—"

Clasping her face between his hands, he stifled her words with a kiss. The citrus scent of her flooded his senses. Desire channeled hot blood through his veins. He devoured the softness of her lips, the sweet taste of her mouth.

She looped her arms around his neck. With a sultry sweep of her tongue, she joined in the dance, boldly taking the lead.

The pace of the kiss slowed to a rhythmic motion of stroking tongues and mounting pleasure. The woman kissed like fire. Like a demon. A wanton goddess in his arms. His good fortune enflamed his libido. A groan emerged from deep in his chest as he thrilled in the burn.

Growing rock hard against the soft curves of her body, he melded his tongue to hers, delving deeper. Harder. Faster.

He drew away, heart pounding. She blinked, looking dazed as she awaited his move. Mired in the moment, in her carnal beauty, he could barely breathe. A gust of air and base need swelled his lungs as he scooped her into his arms. He carried her to the bed, then dropped her onto the crumpled sheets.

She stared up at him, breathing hard through parted lips. He removed his trousers, her gaze following his every movement. Swallowing hard, she licked her lips and opened her arms. The effect of her invitation, her want for him, bolstered his fervor. He clenched his teeth against his excitement and climbed over her.

The fabric of her silk night rail between their bodies might as well have been wool. He had to get her naked. Drawing her up, he felt dazed by the flush of desire on her face. He lifted the garment over her head, then flung it aside. Her breasts rose and fell with each breath as she pulled the loose ribbon securing her hair. With a shake of her head, the fragrant mass tumbled free.

Leaning toward him, she grasped his shoulders, kissing him urgently as though she feared, as he suddenly did, they might be interrupted again.

He lowered her to her back, and she opened her legs, welcoming him into the warmth between her trembling thighs. Her breasts teased his chest as he hovered above her, his hard shaft pressing against the heat at her core.

He kissed her ear.

"Ohh," she uttered.

The smooth flesh of her neck tasted as sweet as her mouth. She turned her head from side to side as he trailed his lips along her throat, her shoulders, and breasts. God, her breasts.

He cupped the firm mounds, the perfect weight and feel, sucking a taut nipple between his lips. Arching her back, she clutched at his hair. Each small sound of her pleasure, every ardent response, heightened his arousal. His need.

Aspiring to touch and taste every delectable inch of her, to extend the pleasure of making love to her well into the night, became a lofty ambition. But they were married now, and there'd be plenty of nights in which to indulge in prolonged pursuits.

He nudged his hardness against the dewy warmth at her center. She lifted her bottom and moaned in his ear. Memories of their past and the night she'd snuck into his room infused with the heat of the moment. She'd wanted this from the start. Schemed to get it. And, Christ, he would give it to her.

He pushed between her legs, then thrust inside her. She gasped, eyes flashing wide.

He froze, burying his head in her hair. In the wake of her prior deception and the cunning required to spring such a dubious trap, he'd doubted she'd be a virgin.

Once again, she'd surprised him.

Breaths of pain filled his ear. Surrendering to the proof of her virtue, he was overcome by a rush of tenderness. He did his best to be gentle, moving slowly as she adjusted to the feel of his body in hers.

"It's all right," he uttered against her hair.

She gave a stiff nod, eyes tightly closed.

"Open your eyes," he said softly.

She complied, staring up at the ceiling.

"Look at me."

Her eyes met his, and a tear slipped from the edge of her lashes.

"Good girl." He kissed her forehead, pressed his lips to her tear-stained temple. His tongue teased her ear.

She sighed, her body slackening beneath him.

Encouraged, he dragged his mouth down her neck, an exploit she seemed to enjoy. Lingering at the sensitive spot on her throat, he began to move inside her again. To his delight, she began to move with him.

He exhaled in relief. Ecstasy. She kneaded his back as he moved faster. Her hips rose to each thrust. With each thrust, he drove deeper. Her abandon told him she was feeling it now, the winding bliss and soaring pleasure. Her ardent response reeled him closer. She clutched at his shoulders. Small gasps of pleasure became lingering moans that lured him to the edge.

She cried out, her body pulsing against his, and not a moment too soon. The sound of her climax echoed in his ears as he finally let go. The force of his release shuddered through him again and again as he clung to her, coasting on the ride of his life.

His heart was still pounding when he finally rolled away and collapsed next to her on the bed. Several minutes passed before he could speak. "Are you all right?"

Nestling into the pillows, she stretched her arms above her head. "I'm wonderful," she said, closing her eyes.

He smiled at the luminous look on her face. "It gets better, you know."

Her eyes flashed open. "Truly?"

He laughed at her honest surprise. "Truly." He traced his finger along the curve of her jaw, and her eyes fluttered shut.

Absorbing the sight of her, lounged so contently, so exposed, he couldn't help being perplexed. She'd lied her way into his bed, but there was nothing deceptive about her now. All he saw was the glow of her bliss, the soft curves of her bare shoulders and breasts. His shaft twitched with restored arousal.

So much for his hope that once they'd made love, his maddening lust for her might be sated. He'd been driven to a state of rapture by a virgin. Christ, if her first time produced results such as this, he was done for.

"Are you hungry?" he asked.

"Ravenous." She propped up on her elbows. "Shall I get us something?"

"I'll go," he said, bolting upright.

He could use a few minutes to himself. Fumbling into his clothes, he felt as giddy as a drunkard with a head full of booze. His lack of sleep had obviously caught up with him.

Downstairs in the quiet kitchen, he prepared a tray laden with cold roast beef, a loaf of bread, and a bottle of wine. Gia hadn't eaten since breakfast, so he added a thick wedge of cheddar to the fare.

He started from the kitchen, slowing as he eyed the cookie canister on the counter. Recalling Gia's fondness for sweets, he smiled, then opened the lid and piled two gingersnaps on the tray.

Ascending the stairs, he realized that while he still loathed the idea of having a wife, having Gia in his bed was something he could get used to. The thought brought him no solace as he returned to their room.

The erotic sight of her stilled his heart. She lounged on her side amid a sea of tangled sheets, one hand cradling her head, the other resting on the curve of her hip. Tousled hair framed her face in the candlelight.

Although she now wore her night rail, she may as well have been nude in the mesmerizing effect. She smiled at the sight of the food—or him—and the inside of his mouth turned to dust.

Steadying his hands, he placed the tray on the bedside table, then fixed her a plate. She sat up on her knees, biting into a hunk of bread as he poured two glasses of wine.

"Oh, no, thank you," she said, waving him off.

"You don't enjoy wine, either?"

She tilted her head, looking baffled.

"You refused to join me in a brandy last night, and you never touched your champagne at the reception."

She stared down at her plate. "I don't care much for the effect of alcohol."

He considered this skeptically. "Most people care quite a lot for it," he said, raising his glass.

She shrugged. "In that regard, I am unlike most people."

"In many regards," he uttered truthfully. He'd never known a woman like her.

Charlotte had been as transparent as glass in her motives for their affair. So had Isobel, had he had the good sense back then to see it. The women of his past were romantic creatures, who'd charmed him with claims of love and devotion to get what they'd sought.

Gia was different.

She'd wormed her way into his life and under his skin with her wits and her wile. He'd never seen it coming. Her reasons for manipulating him into marriage remained a mystery, not that those reasons mattered now. But he couldn't get a grip on what made her tick, and it irritated the hell out of him.

That he desired her as he did irritated him as well. He could barely wait to have her again. While the first time for a woman was always painful, she'd managed to enjoy a good part of it. Her next time would be better.

She ate heartily from her plate, looking no worse for the wear. Still he rued not being gentler with her.

"You might have warned me that it was your first time," he said.

The stricken look on her face took him aback.

Dropping the cookie she held to her plate, she swallowed hard. "You had assumed otherwise, of course." Her lips pursed in disgust, her eyes twin pools of disdain.

He stiffened at her sudden hostility. She'd misinterpreted his remark. His concern for her. But, hell, yes, he'd assumed otherwise. What the devil did the woman expect after what she'd done to him?

"You cannot possibly fault me for doubting your virtue."

Her pretty mouth opened, but nothing came out. The fire dimmed inside her glistening eyes.

He was right, and she knew it. But his shallow victory wasn't enough. He was doing his damnedest to adjust to their situation, and she seemed hell bent on making it impossible.

"I've accepted this marriage, but the fact remains." He fluffed at his pillow, restraining the urge to pound the feathers out of it. "You connived your way from employee to wife." Slumping back on the pillow, he closed his eyes. "One good romp between the sheets with my virginal bride has not made me forget that."

Chapter 12

Gia lay in bed, staring through the darkness toward the moonlight outside the window. Whether it was the long nap she'd taken earlier that kept her from falling asleep despite the late hour or the aftereffect of making love for the first time, she felt wide awake.

She glanced at Landen's still form lying so peacefully only inches from hers. How strange it felt to have a man sleeping beside her. The deep sound of his breathing filled the darkness as she lay there with her whirling thoughts. After being awake for twenty-four hours straight, he'd no doubt expended the last of his energy driving her into ecstasy.

It was difficult to believe the man who'd made love to her with such passion was the same man who'd insulted her so callously a mere hour later. While she could not blame him for his low opinion of her, it hurt just the same.

She had hoped that the intimate act of consummating their marriage might diminish his anger toward her and they might forge a new start. Unfortunately, she'd been the only party swept into oblivion, as he'd made it perfectly clear he had no intention of forgetting a thing.

Despite the evening's terrible ending, she would remember this night forever. Making love with him had been heaven. Replaying the scene in her mind made her smile. There'd been no obstacles between them—no troubles or fears. Not even secrets and mistrust had stood in the way of their bodies' desire for each other. When they were naked, life was simple and pure. The sweet thought prompted her to tears. Tears of a bride's joyous discovery mixed with tears of sadness for what had ensued. And tears of fear for the future.

What if he never looked at her that way again? Never touched her that way?

Already she yearned for more. His hands and mouth on her flesh, his body entwined and trembling with hers. The dull ache of longing grew stronger. Heat flushed her face. She turned onto her side, flipping her pillow as she moved. With a frustrated sigh, she pressed her cheek into the pillow, but the cool linen did nothing to temper her lust. How could she desire a man who could barely tolerate her? A man who'd promised to never forgive her? Perhaps her parents had been right after all, and she truly was addled.

She blinked, staving off memories too distressing to relive. Nestling beneath the sheets, she found a strange sense of comfort in the warmth of the strong presence behind her. She'd spent so much time on her own. Despite Landen's feelings toward her, she was no longer alone in the world. She belonged to him now, and Landen protected what was his.

For the first time in years she felt truly safe. Tucking the sheet to her chin, she closed her eyes and let the soft steady sound of her husband's breathing lull her to sleep.

* * * *

Gia reveled in the throes of the wonderful dream. Melding into the heat of the firm body against her back, she welcomed the onslaught of sensations, the hand caressing her breast, the lips nuzzling her neck.

She pressed her bottom against the prodding hardness behind her, indulging in the vividly erotic dream. The sound of her moans stirred her awake. Opening her eyes, she discovered she hadn't been dreaming.

Landen's warm breath fanned her neck. Arousal trumped animosity, it seemed, and she smiled to herself as she realized the hem of her night rail was riding her waist. He trailed his hand from her breast to her hip. Still drowsy, she arched like a cat against the source of her pleasure. The press of his lips on her nape sent tingles down her spine, and she all but purred in delight.

As though impelled by her blatant lack of resistance, he nudged his knee between her thighs. The sheet that covered her disappeared as her legs fell open to the dawning sunlight and the wonderful things he was doing from behind her.

Her heart pounded and her limbs trembled with the sweet torture of anticipation. Biting her lip, she awaited his move, grinding back against his thigh. He clasped her aching core, and she gasped in delight. He held her, cupping her so possessively, so intensely, the pleasure radiated from her flesh to her heart.

With an audible sigh, she surrendered completely to his masterful hand. His fingers moved slowly, then faster, and then slowly again. Gusts of ecstasy lifted her higher, and she clutched at the sheets.

"Oh, yes," she murmured, unable to silence the hysteria of pleasure erupting inside her. Not since the opiates had anything made her feel so utterly mindless—so good. Landen's touch might prove to be as addictive, but she wouldn't fret about that now. She would savor every moment they shared in this bed and regret not a one.

She writhed against the strum of his fingers, wondering how he'd learned all that he knew. Sensations flooded her veins as she grew wetter and wetter.

With one firm thrust he slipped inside her. The sound of his pleasure rumbled through her ear, and she delighted in the proof of his bliss. He pushed deeper. His hand moved in circles between her legs and she arched toward the pressure, the friction of his shaft sliding in and out of her. The tension wound tighter and tighter. She cried out in in exquisite release, splintering in a dozen different directions as it all came undone.

With a ragged groan, Landen came quickly behind her, crushing her to his chest.

His tight grip on her slackened as they descended to earth. He released her completely, and the chill of his absence made the summer morning feel as cold as December.

He rose from the bed, and she closed her eyes, heard the rustle of his clothing as he dressed. Without a word, he crossed the room to the door, then closed it quietly behind him.

She lay there alone, her body still trembling.

So this was to be their marriage. All they would share.

A bed, wordless passion, nothing more.

She shook off her chagrin. As difficult as it might seem at the moment, she had to stay focused. So much had happened since arriving in Misty Lake, there'd been so many distractions. Her body still hummed from the latest, but she did her utmost to channel her thoughts to her task. She'd married Landen for one reason and one reason only. To save his life. Once she accomplished that feat, once he was safe, she'd try to fix things between them.

Her other visions had come to life shortly after experiencing them. The vision of Landen had depicted the season was late summer, but she had to be sure.

Rising from the bed, she glanced around the room for an item to touch. She strode to his dresser where all his private things sat. She touched the coins he'd emptied from his pockets, then concentrated on a pair of fine cufflinks. Nothing.

She walked to the washstand. A comb and a hair brush were arranged neatly next to the basin. She touched the comb and the soap dish with no results. Sighing, she reached for the porcelain cup that held his shaving brush and razor.

Grasping the cup in her hands, she closed her eyes. Her breath quickened with her pulse as the cool glass started to warm. She followed the sensation through her fingers, through the glass. The vision appeared, and she was in a clearing in the forest beneath an old gnarled tree. She shivered with a chill of foreboding and the sickening sound of pained grunts.

Landen lay on the ground, hands raised in defense against the booted feet kicking his ribs, his face. Blood oozed from his mouth and nose.

Gasping for air, she opened her eyes. Her knees trembled. She clutched at the washstand for support, heard the sound of glass shattering against wood.

"What happened?"

She started at the sound of Landen's voice behind her, but she couldn't move. He strode toward her, his reflection in the mirror looming closer.

The sound of glass crunched beneath his boots. "Gia?"

She turned slowly to face him, hoping she didn't appear as frazzled as she felt. "I…"

"You're bleeding." His eyes widened in alarm. He yanked a towel from the rail on the side of the washstand, then pressed the towel into her palm. "Come sit down." He took her gently by the arm. "Watch your step."

She nodded, soothed by his genuine concern. She blinked, feeling foolish. Of course he'd display concern—one had no other option when there was blood involved.

He led her to a chair, then knelt beside her.

She couldn't bring herself to look into his face for fear she'd blurt out some futile warning about what she'd seen in her mind. Her body trembled in her fears for him, and the urge to slump against his chest and sob into his shoulder overwhelmed her. She fought to pull herself together as she opened the towel to inspect the cut. "It's not bad at all," she said in as cheery a tone as she could muster. "See."

He winced at the sight of the injury; his face turned stark white.

"Are you all right?" she asked.

He shot to his feet, swaying.

"Landen!"

His eyes fluttered briefly before rolling back in his head, and then he fainted dead away.

* * * *

Gia's heart pounded. "Can you hear me?" she asked, kneeling over him.

He blinked hard several times, then sat upright. "Yes, I am fine."

She helped him to his feet. "Are you sure?"

"I am fine." He pulled from her hold and any further attempts to assist him.

She rushed to pour him some water, and he guzzled it down.

"Thank you," he said, running a shaky hand through his hair.

She nodded, relieved the color had returned to his face.

"We should have Florence tend to your hand," he said as though nothing out of the ordinary had happened.

She eyed him, amazed, as he toed the broken glass by the washstand.

"What were you doing with my shave kit?" he asked.

His attempt to change the subject was dreadfully effective. "I was just moving it to tidy up a bit. I was clumsy. I'm sorry." Her voice skittered on the lie. The memory of her vision. Landen fainting in a heap at her feet.

"It's not your job to tidy up," he said. "We have help for that."

She nodded. "Are you sure you're all right?"

He sighed at her prodding, looking more embarrassed than irked. "I don't react well to the sight of blood."

Moved by his humble admission, she smiled. "No, you don't."

To her relief, he smiled too. "I'll send Florence up."

He stepped from the room, leaving Gia alone with her poignant thoughts. The surprising discovery that this proud, virile man possessed such a frailty touched her deep down. The swell of warmth in her chest intensified, budging loose something burrowed inside her.

She cared for him now…

She had to warn him about her visions. She had to do something with what she knew. Landen wouldn't end up in the creek as a result of some mishap. He wouldn't fall or be tossed from a horse. The vision foretold what she'd suspected all along.

Someone was going to kill him.

Chapter 13

They had just finished luncheon when Florence announced that Landen had a visitor awaiting him in the parlor. Clara paused her prattling long enough for Landen to excuse himself before resuming her oration on every tiresome detail regarding the upcoming weekend and the highlight of the season, the Westcott Ball.

Gia was more interested in who Landen's visitor might be. In the two weeks since she'd experienced the horrible vision of Landen being beaten, she'd resigned herself to the disheartening fact that everyone he knew was now a suspect.

While she'd met several people at the garden party, reception, and a handful of other small affairs in town, the Westcott Ball would provide her with introductions to everyone.

As though reading her thoughts, Clara said, "Everyone will be there. The hotels are nearing full capacity already. Several eligible young men will be in attendance as well." She directed a nod at Alice, who rolled her eyes in return.

Gia shook her head at the poor girl's unenviable position. Now that Landen was finally married, it seemed Clara had set her sights on finding a husband for Alice.

"Don't roll your eyes at me, missy," Clara scolded. "It's high time you cease this wallflower nonsense. You're a lovely young woman and must act before losing your bloom."

"My bloom?"

Clara waved off her niece's derision. "You know what I mean. And you'd do well to follow my guidance. I listened to my mother's advice and was engaged during my very first season." She puffed her ample bosom. "I don't need to remind you that your Uncle Howard was the most handsome, sought-after bachelor in Albany when we met."

"So you've mentioned," Alice muttered.

Before Clara had a chance to respond, Landen returned to the room. His somber expression conveyed something was wrong.

"What's the matter?" Gia asked.

"Tom Bidwell had some distressing news," he said. "The Toomey boy is missing."

"Missing?"

"He went fishing alone yesterday morning and never returned home. His family searched all night. They found his bait can and pole on the shore. His line was snagged on a log in the water, and they fear he may have drowned trying to retrieve it."

"Dear Lord," Clara uttered.

Gia gulped. She clutched her skirts to combat a surge of panic as she recalled her brothers' drownings and the memory of being trapped beneath the ice, the water flooding her lungs.

"I'm going up to the Toomey house as soon as I load the boat in the wagon. The current is strong at the lake's outlet, and as many boats as possible are needed for the search."

Gia summoned her voice. "I'll go with you."

Landen shook his head. "There's no time—"

"I am coming." She stood, turning to Alice. "May I borrow your wrap?"

"Of course." Alice handed Gia the wrap on the back of her chair.

"Gia, no," Landen said, stopping her in her tracks. "I am going alone."

"Your wife should be with you," Clara said with a pointed stare. "As a show of support for the Toomeys."

Landen sighed, turning to Gia. "All right. You can stay with Edna Toomey while we search. Tom told me the woman is beside herself."

"Understandably so," Clara said in a pitying tone.

"You'll be all right here with Alice?" Landen asked Clara.

"Yes, yes," she said, waving them toward the door. "Go."

With the boat soundly secured in the back of the wagon, Gia and Landen departed for the Toomey house on the other side of Misty Lake. The silence between them seemed to lengthen the miles, as did Gia's fears for the missing boy.

"Sam and Edna are good people," Landen said suddenly. "The boy is their only child."

He stared straight ahead as he spoke, his profile tense. His concern for his friends ached through her veins. Her fingers twitched with the urge to touch his hand. To acknowledge his worry and the compassion that dwelled in his heart.

"They will find him."

He turned to face her, looking incredulous. "Are you always so blindly optimistic?"

The question stemmed from her positive affirmations during Clara's illness, so she took no offense. How could she? From his perspective, her certainty that Clara would recover had probably seemed naïve at the time. But Landen had a tendency to expect the worst, and Gia couldn't resist the opportunity to remind him of this.

"Are you always so pessimistic?"

He frowned. "Optimism leads to disappointment. Eventually."

"And pessimism leads elsewhere?" She shook her head. "Without hope there is nothing." She lifted her chin against any rebuttal.

Tilting his head, he studied her closely. "Well then, I *hope* you are correct regarding the Toomey boy."

Gia hoped so, too, and she uttered a prayer to this end as they journeyed along.

They ascended the steep hill through the pines, and the small cottage overlooking the lake finally came into view. A throng of people overflowed from the porch and into the small clearing that served as a yard.

Gia gazed around as she waited for Landen to unload the boat. The crowd consisted of several familiar faces, many of whom Gia recognized from the garden party and wedding reception. But there were no cheerful greetings today, no smiles or sounds of laughter in the air.

"Go on into the house and see what you can do for Edna," Landen told Gia. "I may be a while." With a nod, he urged her toward the house, then joined with the men preparing for the search.

Gia made her way across the yard, past a large collection of lanterns and rakes. Her stomach turned as she imagined the little boy's lifeless body being buoyed to the water's surface on the end of one of those rakes.

Swallowing hard, she stepped onto the porch and through the open door. She shimmied through the crowd in the hall to the parlor. Edna Toomey sat on the sofa, barely visible inside the circle of woman attempting to console her.

Gia inched toward Edna, whom she'd met only once, then knelt in front of her. "Mrs. Toomey?"

"Oh, Mrs. Elmsworth." Tears welled in her swollen eyes. "He's only seven years old. Where on earth can he be?"

"They'll find him." Blinking back tears of her own, Gia patted Edna's hand, hoping they'd find him alive.

"They think he drowned," Edna said, as if reading Gia's mind. "But my Georgie knew better than to go into the water alone." She dabbed her tears with a handkerchief. "He's a good boy."

Gia's heart wrenched at the woman's inconsolable anguish. Gia staved back tears as the memory of her mother's grief over the loss of Gia's brothers pervaded her mind. Her head filled with the echo of the tormented sobs, the pointed silence—the unspoken accusations that plagued Gia the most.

"Such a good boy." Edna sniffed.

"Let me get you some water," Gia said, as if more water might help.

The woman nodded, and Gia left on her invented errand. On the way to the kitchen, she scanned the empty corridor that led to the rear of the house.

No one would notice if Gia disappeared for a few minutes. She summoned her nerve, then backed from the crush of bodies in the hall. Inching down the narrow corridor, she gazed into the first room, then the next until she found the boy's bedroom.

She slipped inside the small room, closing the door quietly behind her. Stepping onto the worn rug, she meandered past the open toy chest, sidestepping a wooden horse and toy train. She sat on Georgie's small bed, caressing the pillow upon which he rested his head each night.

When the pillow produced no results, she set it back in its place, then grabbed the stuffed bear next to it. Hugging the raggedy thing to her chest, she took a deep breath. The din at the front of the house began to fade.

Her ability had never felt more under her control, as though it were just below the surface, awaiting release. Closing her eyes, she emptied her mind, unleashing whatever might come.

Her ears buzzed as a vision materialized in the distance. The temperature dropped. Gooseflesh formed on her skin. She followed the sound through the darkness, steeling herself against the fear of what she might see. The musty smell of dirt clogged her throat. The sound of frightened whimpers filled the darkness around the small form huddled in the dirt.

Gia gasped. The boy hadn't drowned. He was trapped.

She opened her eyes, heart pounding. The urge to race from the room to relay her news gave way to exhaustion. She tossed the bear aside but was too drained of strength to do anything more.

After breathing deeply for several moments, her pulse finally began to slow to an even tempo. Unable to rein her excitement, she shot to her feet, then hurried back to the parlor. Shoving her way into the room, she addressed anyone who might listen.

"Is there a cave nearby? Or a mine shaft, perhaps? Someplace where Georgie might be trapped?"

The women stared, surprised by her outburst.

"Is there?" Gia asked of the startled faces.

"He could be trapped," Edna uttered. She considered the prospect, her weary eyes brightening with life. Hope.

...Optimism leads to disappointment... She brushed off Landen's grim words. The boy was alive.

"Is there a mine shaft? Does anyone know?" Gia pressed.

The ladies looked to one another for answers, shaking their heads.

"I think there's an old well on the White property," Edna said as she stood.

Gia nodded, encouraged. "We must find out."

She hurried outside, Edna and the other women on her heels, to where Landen and the last group of men were just embarking on their search.

"Landen!" she called, fairly breathless with excitement.

He strode toward her, brows raised at the clutch of chattering women behind her. "What is it?"

"It just occurred to us that the boy may be trapped somewhere. In a cave or deep hole." She paused briefly for breath. "Edna says there's an old well on the White property."

"They searched the White property last night," he said. "They've searched every inch of the area. They didn't find or hear anything."

"But the boy may have been sleeping or unable to call out for help," Gia said.

Landen frowned, glancing over her shoulder. Taking her arm, he led her a few steps away. "The boy was at the lake. His fishing gear—"

"Edna said Georgie was not allowed to go into the water by himself."

"Children don't always do as they're told." He lowered his voice, leaning closely. "Gia, please. This is difficult enough for Edna without you making it worse."

"I'm not trying to make it worse. You don't know for certain he drowned."

"And you don't know that he hasn't."

But she did know. She lifted her chin. "I—"

"We're searching the lake," he said sternly.

"But—"

"And you are doing the woman no good by giving her false hope."

"There is no harm in hoping."

"And when the boy's pulled from the lake?"

"If he has drowned, she can mourn then. Until that time, she can hope."

"Elmsworth!" Tom called. "Let's go!"

"Take Edna back to the house, and let us conduct the search of the water before it gets dark."

Gia tossed a glance at the group of impatient men watching their exchange. "Fine." She straightened her spine. "We women will conduct our own search."

"You will do no such thing," he ground out through clenched teeth. "That woman has been up all night. She's in no state to go traipsing through the fields after vain hopes you've sowed in her head. Now take her back to the house and wait for us there."

While he might be right about Edna, Gia refused to submit to his commands. She'd vowed to never again allow anyone to control her—to stop her from doing what her visions led her to do. Had she not succumbed to her parents' browbeating, Prudence would still be alive.

"The other women can stay with her. I will go on my own." She started away.

He grabbed her arm. "Listen to me—"

"No." She yanked free.

He stared, stunned by her defiance.

Disapproval circulated among the men who watched on. Ignoring their grumblings, Gia said, "We are wasting time. If Georgie is in the water, we're already too late to save him. But if he's trapped somewhere..." She'd felt the boy's fear during her vision, felt his pain. He was hurt. She swallowed a sob, tears welling in her eyes. She had to trust her ability, no matter the cost. "Please, Landen." She clutched his arm. "Please."

* * * *

Despite his vexation at his wife's obstinate behavior, Landen felt himself caving beneath Gia's desperate plea for his help. Tears shimmered on her lashes, and it took all the strength he possessed not to pull her into his arms to calm her hysterics.

Staring into her dark eyes, he felt his throat tighten. He'd never seen her like this. He'd brought her here hoping she might help comfort Edna. She'd been such a comfort to Alice during Clara's illness. Truth be told, she'd been a comfort to him, too, although it pained him to admit it.

He took a deep breath. "All right," he said. "Wait here."

Embarrassed and frustrated by his certainty they were wasting time, he strode toward the waiting men to explain the situation. With each step, he rued succumbing to Gia's appeal, but she'd left him little choice. Edna and the other women seemed convinced Georgie had fallen into a hole, and Landen had no doubt Gia was responsible. Edna's fragile state had her teetering on the edge of reason, and there'd be no way around investigating their unlikely theory now.

For Edna's sake, Landen persuaded Henry Whalen and Tom to join him on a quick search of the White property before heading out on the lake.

"Tom confirmed there's an old well on the White property," Landen murmured to Gia. "Henry and Tom will go with me there before we head out on the water."

Exhaling in relief, Gia nodded, looking grateful for their assistance. At least she had the good sense to realize the men were better equipped to rescue Georgie than she was.

Despite Landen's directive, Edna refused to remain at the house. Flanked by her friends, she clung to their arms as tightly as she clung to the hope they'd find her son, safe and sound, as they crossed the field to the abandoned White property.

Tall weeds ensconced the crumbled stone foundation on the hill that once supported a house. A crow squawked from its perch atop the dilapidated fireplace.

Henry pointed. "The well is somewhere over there by that stone wall."

"Georgie!" With renewed strength, Edna ran toward the wall. "Georgie!"

Landen ran after her, and the others followed. He grabbed Edna's arm, until Tom took hold of her.

"Wait here," Landen told her, reaching for the lantern Henry had lit.

Landen waded through the weeds, searching as he walked. He spied the ring of stones marking the well in the distance. Narrowing his eyes at the sight a few feet away, he quickened his pace. His breath caught in his throat. A hole gaped through the wide plank that served as the well's cover. His heart lurched, and he sprinted to action. He tore off what remained of the splintered wood, heart pounding.

Dangling the lantern before him, he gazed down into the dark depths below. The anxious chatter of the crowd behind him fell deathly silent. Focusing his eyes, Landen searched for signs of movement as he followed the beam of light over pieces of splintered wood to the boulder on floor of the well. His shoulders slumped with disappointment. Swallowing hard, he turned to face the crowd. "He's not down here."

Edna sank to her knees, sobbing.

"Are you sure?" Gia asked.

Landen stood, wiping his sleeves. "He's not here."

The sound of Edna's grief howled through the grim silence. Landen's chest tightened at the thought the worst was yet to come. The woman had some dark days ahead, and he bit back a curse at the extra pain this wild goose chase had caused her.

He strode toward Gia, teeth clenched. "Satisfied?"

She shook her head, lips quivering. "He could still be trapped somewhere else. He—"

"Enough!" She was tenacious as hell, but he was her husband. He'd be damned before he let her forget this. He pointed his finger. "Do not speak one more word."

She flinched, clamping her lips.

He took a deep breath, glancing to Edna. She cried into her hands at Tom's feet, her endurance clearly at its end.

He turned away from the pitiful sight, furious. He must have been out of his mind to have listened to Gia and her improbable notion. She'd weakened his resolve when he'd needed it most, and he was as much to blame as she was for this ugly debacle. "Let's head back to the lake," he called to Henry and Tom as he started away.

"Listen!"

They all turned to Henry.

"I hear something. Listen!"

The air stilled. Beneath the sudden silence, Landen heard something too. A small sound in the distance.

"Georgie?" Edna's eyes widened as she scrambled to her feet.

Landen listened hard, glancing around. The sound was coming from the old foundation on the hill. "Up there." He strode toward the ruins, the sound growing louder. "Here!" he called to the others as they raced to join him. "There's a root cellar!"

"Georgie!" Edna yelled.

Landen struggled to lift the heavy door of the root cellar, and Henry rushed to assist. Together they finally pried the door open. Light shined into the dark hole below.

The little boy lay huddled in a ball, unmoving. A kitten mewed loudly at his side.

"Georgie!" Edna called, gazing down at her son.

Landen descended the dirt stairs, and the kitten skittered away. Crouching in front of the child, Landen took a deep breath, then gave a tap to his shoulder.

The boy stirred, then rolled to his back. "My ankle hurts."

Landen blew out a gust of relief. "He's all right!" he called over his shoulder. He patted Georgie's knee. "Let's get you home."

The kitten mewed at them from the darkened corner.

"Friend of yours?" Landen asked.

Georgie nodded. "I followed him here."

Landen lifted the boy carefully. "We're coming up!" He carried the little boy up the stairs and into the sunlight. "His ankle may be broken," he warned Edna.

"Oh, Georgie!" Edna cupped the boy's face and smothered him with kisses. "What happened?"

Georgie blinked, breaking free of her grasp long enough to speak. "My pole got stuck on a log, so I was on my way home when I saw a kitten."

"And you followed it here?"

He nodded. "The cellar door was cracked open, but when I slid under it, it fell closed, and I couldn't get out."

"Oh, my poor darling," Edna cooed.

"Shadow kept me company," he said, glancing at the kitten now nestled contently in Gia's arms. "Can I keep him?"

Edna laughed, and the others laughed too.

"Yes, yes of course you can."

Landen watched the uplifting reunion, feeling drunk with relief.

"Brilliant thinking, Elmsworth!" Tom said with a slap to Landen's shoulder.

Landen shook his head, overwhelmed with emotion. "It wasn't my brilliance, I assure you." He glanced to Gia. Rejoicing with the others, she smiled through tears of joy, the kitten cradled in her arms. The pride that swelled in Landen's chest knocked the air from his lungs. "The credit belongs to my wife."

Chapter 14

By the time Gia and Landen boarded the wagon and departed for home, it was well past dark. Gia breathed in the crisp night air as they drove beneath the starry sky, tired but exhilarated by the day's events.

"The boy was lucky only to have suffered a sprained ankle," Landen said. "He might have died down there." He turned to face her. "If it weren't for you."

Gia stared into his handsome face, basking in his recognition. "And you," she said. "Thank you for investigating our idea."

He cocked a brow. "As I recall, you gave me no choice in it."

She smiled at his flimsy reprimand. "No, I suppose I didn't. But Edna was adamant Georgie wouldn't go into the water by himself. Her trust in the boy convinced me he had to be somewhere else."

"And you were right."

Gia was too elated by Georgie's safety to rue her duplicity. After all, there was a kernel of truth in her explanation of how she'd formed her conclusion to his whereabouts. The boy was in the bosom of his family now, and that's all that mattered.

"I was overly harsh with you earlier," Landen said.

His tone carried an apology she didn't deserve. She'd challenged him in front of his friends—not exactly a wifely behavior a man could condone.

"You were concerned for Edna."

"Yes. And you were determined to help." He turned to face her. "And you did."

The approval in his eyes left her speechless. A rush of warmth flowed through her veins. She started and ended each day in the bliss of his physical passion that, until now, had been all she could ask for. As premature at it might be, his heightened regard had kindled a spark of hope for something more.

"I am simply happy he is safe and back with his family," she said. The bona fide affection Edna had displayed to her son tugged at Gia's heart. "He's one well-loved little boy." A twinge of envy ached through her. The same shameful envy she felt toward her brothers as she recalled her parents' favoritism and their treatment of her after the accident.

For two days, Gia had lain upstairs in her bed, recovering and waiting for them to come to her. But they were too bereaved to exert the effort, too depleted to summon gratitude for the daughter whose life had been spared. The daughter who could never replace the beloved sons they had lost.

They'd had to deal with her eventually, but with each vacant glance at her, she'd heard the words they were thinking. *It should have been you.*

"Not all children grow up feeling loved by their parents." The words fell from her mouth before she could stop them. She squirmed in her seat, abashed by the slip.

"Are you speaking from experience on the matter?"

Too beset by memories to pretend otherwise, she didn't bother to try. "Yes." She took a deep breath. "I don't mean to imply my parents were intentionally cruel to me, but indifference can feel that way. Especially to a child. My parents favored my brothers, you see."

"You have brothers?"

"They died," she said quickly. "Mark and Miles fell through the ice of a frozen pond." She lifted her chin against his surprise, against the tears that always welled up inside her when she thought about that horrible day. Strangely, the tears didn't come.

She hadn't spoken her brothers' names aloud in years. And yet, it felt so natural to speak them now. To Landen. "My parents loved those boys to distraction. Unfortunately, I was spared such adoration." She shrugged, feigning a smile. "Enduring disparity is a common fate for daughters."

"And for sons from first marriages."

Gia stared, surprised by his candor. Was he confiding in her? She tilted her head, intrigued by this unpredictable man and the childhood ghosts that had haunted him. *I am the product of my father's first marriage*, he'd told Gia on the day they had met.

"My stepmother was a good woman," he said. "And yet…"

"When she looked at you, there was something missing in her eyes. Something that was present when she looked at your siblings."

He gauged her intently. "Yes."

She nodded. "It must have been difficult adjusting to your father's second marriage. Seeing him with a woman other than your mother."

His face tightened. "My mother was ill for most of her life. Too ill to care for me as a mother should."

"And your father?"

"He had his hands full with my mother." He straightened. "At any rate, the course of events resulted in Alice and Alex. And for this, I am grateful."

"You never felt envious of them?"

He blinked at her bluntness, shaking his head.

"Did you?" she pressed.

The affronted look on his face faded as he considered her query. "At times."

Like a soothing balm, his reluctant admission helped lessen the sting of her festering guilt. While she'd loved her brothers with all her heart, she still hated herself for coveting what they'd had.

"I wouldn't have thought it possible," she said, fiddling with her hands.

"Wouldn't have thought what possible?"

"That you and I might have something in common."

This garnered a smile. "Nor I," he said, turning his attention back to driving.

The moonlit road stretched between the tall pines. Fireflies blinked all around them.

"Speaking of siblings, I've received a letter from my brother. He'll be arriving in Misty Lake soon."

"Oh, that's wonderful. Alice must be thrilled. She talks so fondly of him. I'm surprised she hasn't mentioned it."

"I haven't told her yet," Landen said. "My brother is not the most dependable man. I wanted to be sure his plans were set before I told her."

"Well, I look forward to meeting him."

"And we'll all have the pleasure of meeting his latest mistake."

"What do you mean?"

"It seems my brother is in love. Again."

She sighed at his disheartening cynicism. "And you assume this is a mistake?"

He frowned, turning to face her. "You don't know Alex." He turned back to the road, his tense profile relaxing. "He intends to marry this woman," he said. "At least he's promised, this time, to let me meet her before he does anything rash."

"Such as?"

"Such as he's prone to do."

"I see," she said, suppressing a smile. Landen's frustration with his brother was obvious, and she could hardly wait now to meet the man who'd managed to rankle him so.

"The young woman's cousin will be accompanying them."

"Will they all be staying at the house?"

"Bea is due back from Saratoga this week, so the house will be full. Alex's guests will stay at the hotel in town."

"Will they arrive in time for the Westcott Ball?"

"The following weekend."

"That's too bad. I'm certain Alice would feel more comfortable among such a large crowd with Alex in attendance. According to Aunt Clara, this ball is the highlight of the season." A cool breeze brushed Gia's cheeks, and she tightened the shawl around her shoulders.

The vision commenced with the usual warning. Gia stiffened in dread. Landen sat only inches away, but the deafening buzz in her head disregarded the unfortunate timing. Her pulse quickened. Helpless to stop the inevitable, she closed her eyes. Darkness ascended like a stage curtain introducing a scene.

Beneath a crystal chandelier, Alice danced, whirling through a crowded ballroom in the arms of a man. The pink gown she wore matched the ribbons flowing from her hair and the pretty blush in her cheeks. Gia's spirit soared on the melody of the orchestra and the sight of Alice's beaming smile. Then, just as suddenly as the vision had appeared, it was gone.

Gia slumped back in her seat. Recuperating in a warm glow of elation, she smiled. She'd become so accustomed to the ominous visions, she'd almost forgotten the joyful promise in the good ones. Strangely, this happy vision had come from out of nowhere. She'd held nothing in her hands to inspire—and then she remembered she'd donned Alice's wrap.

"Gia? Did you hear me?"

"Hmm?"

"Are you cold?" Landen asked.

Before she could respond, he pulled on the reins and the wagon rolled to a halt. He reached beneath the seat and produced a blanket. "Here." He draped the blanket around her, ensconcing her inside the soft wool.

Nestling into the blanket, she gazed into his face, his eyes gleaming in the moonlight. She swallowed, looking forward to the warmth of their bed and all the wonderful things that awaited her there.

He closed the blanket beneath her chin, and she shivered again, but not from the chill. Her breath hitched as he touched his thumb to her jaw, caressing the corner of her mouth. The rapt yearning in his eyes made her insides flitter as he traced a light path across her bottom lip. She trembled, felt her tongue brush his finger as he dragged it so slowly, so exquisitely over her lip.

He drew the blanket gently toward him, then kissed her. Right there in the wagon. In the moonlight. In the middle of the road.

It was heaven.

She sank against his mouth, the familiar taste and smell of him, and a spark fanned to flames in her belly. The fiery yearning blazed between them as always, and yet, something was different. Perhaps her perception had been skewed by the emotional day and their prior exchange, but there was something more than lust behind the press of his lips.

Or perhaps the feeling was more hopeful than true. Either way, they shared childhood demons, and this mutual part of their pasts made her feel closer to him. She wrapped her arms around his neck, wanting more. Deepening the kiss, he moaned, that sinfully delightful sound that curled her toes, as he melded his tongue against hers.

He drew away, breaking the kiss much too soon. Disappointment tempered the race of her heart.

"We should be going. I want to get home." He readjusted the blanket around her shoulders. "And into bed."

She smiled at his lusty words. "That makes two things we have in common."

He laughed, turning back to the reins.

Feeling daring, she scooted toward him, then rested her head against his firm shoulder. Half expecting he might shrug her away, she savored the spicy scent of him for as long as she could. To her relief, he remained as he was, and she smiled contently as they rode toward home.

* * * *

The sound of Gia's distress jolted Landen from sleep. He shot upright, the scene beside him rousing him fully awake. Gia writhed in her sleep, limbs flailing in the midst of a dream. He poked her shoulder. "Wake up."

To his surprise, his touch made her more frantic. She let out a shriek that could wake the whole house. Kicking free of the sheets, she gasped, spewing feral sounds more beastlike than human. She clawed at the air.

Grasping her shoulders, he shook her hard. She struggled, shaking her head and gasping some more. His alarm heightened to fear. He'd never seen anyone in such a state while asleep. The memory of his mother's violent fits hit full force. "Gia!"

She lashed at him, and he winced as her nails raked his neck. His heart thundered. Dodging the onslaught, he shook her harder. "Wake up!"

Her eyes flashed open.

"Wake up!"

Terror filled her wide stare. Her chest heaved as she struggled to catch her breath. Disorientated, she blinked several times, her gaze darting around.

"Calm yourself. It was a dream."

She shook her head as though she didn't believe him.

"A dream," he said firmly.

"I'm sorry." Her voice quaked. "I-I…"

"Shh." He gathered her damp body into his arms. She clung to him, trembling against his shoulder. "Shh." He petted her disheveled hair, the citrus scent of her calming his own racing heart.

Easing from her grip, he endeavored to rise. "I'll get you some brandy."

"No!"

He flinched at the vehemence of her outburst.

"I don't want a drink."

He nodded, settling back on the bed. "Do you want to tell me about the dream?"

"I… It was awful."

"So I gather." His attempt at humor went unnoticed as she seemed miles away.

"I was drowning."

He nodded in understanding. "You'd been talking about your brothers today. It's only natural—"

"I was with them when they drowned."

He blinked, uncertain he'd heard her correctly. Absorbing her words, he stared, dumbstruck by the horror of what she'd witnessed. No wonder she'd had a nightmare. He thought of Alice and Alex and could barely draw breath through the vise of pain that gripped him at the mere thought of losing them.

The same pain Gia lived with each day.

In a pitiful attempt to console her, he reached for her hand and gave it a squeeze.

She clasped his fingers, and the slight gesture gave him hope that he'd helped in some way. She'd been through so much, and he so wanted to help. But just as he'd thought her ordeal couldn't have been worse, she stunned him again.

"I fell through the ice too."

His sharp intake of air nearly choked him. His mind spun in disbelief—in the images he could not force from his head. Gia plunging into the freezing-cold water. Gia flailing for her life. He swallowed, feeling sick to his stomach. And angry as hell at the cruel unfairness of it all.

The despair on her lovely face tore his insides to shreds. He gazed at her, lost for words but desperate for something to say. "Christ, Gia," he uttered lamely.

She lowered her head, and tears rolled down her cheeks.

Unable to bear the sight of her misery for one moment more, he pulled her into his arms once again. She had no one—no parents or siblings—only him. Cradling her in his tight embrace, he vowed to himself to protect her with his life from this moment on.

"It's all right," he cooed in her ear. "You're all right."

She shook her head against his chest. The anguish in her muffled words sent a chill down his spine.

"I will never be right."

Chapter 15

The Westcott Ball was a grand affair, crowded with more people than Gia had encountered in one place in years. She stepped inside the beautiful ballroom and into her memories of Boston and all the familiar sights and sounds of a lifetime ago.

The sound of music and exuberant conversation wafted through the splendid room beneath sparkling chandeliers. Gia smiled through a flood of introductions and requests for dances. By the time Landen led them to the chairs lined up against the wall, her dance card was fairly filled.

Settling into her seat between Clara and Alice, Gia watched as Landen departed to join a group of men who'd invited him for cigars out on the patio. The urge to keep him in sight was so strong she could barely resist abandoning her seat—and Alice—to follow him. There were so many people in attendance, and the person who wanted to hurt Landen might very well be among them.

"Several of the guests are summer residents," Clara said. "Very affluent people from the city." She fanned her face. "Of course, many year-round residents are here as well. The Westcott Ball is a public affair, always has been for as long as I can remember."

"The Westcotts seem like nice people," Gia said of the couple who'd greeted them at the door.

"They are dear friends," Clara said. "I've known Virginia and August for years. Not a bad bone in their bodies."

"Good evening, Clara."

"Speaking of bad bones," Clara murmured as a tall woman approached. "Good evening, Maude." Clara waited until Maude was seated, then lifted a hand toward Gia. "I don't believe you've had the pleasure of meeting my nephew's new bride." Clara smiled graciously, presenting Gia to the stylish woman. "Maude Devenshire, this is Gianna."

Maude pursed her lips, her tone as frosty as the look in her eyes. "How do you do?"

The polite smile Gia offered did nothing to sweeten Maude's sour disposition. "It's a pleasure to meet you," she said, wondering what she might have done to earn this woman's obvious dislike.

"Maude is Charlotte Filkins' mother," Clara said.

Mystery solved.

Landen's sudden marriage to Gia had hurt Charlotte, which in turn, had hurt Maude. Understandable, given Charlotte's relationship with Landen prior to Gia's arrival in town. Gia's feelings as interloper between the couple returned full-force as Maude appraised her intently.

"My daughter told me your last residence was the Troy Female Seminary. Is that true?"

Something in her question was meant to intimidate Gia, but she refused to be cowed. Gia had worked hard at the school, and her position there was nothing to be ashamed of. She lifted her chin. "I was employed there, yes."

"My Charlotte spent several years at the Female Seminary," Maude said. "As a student, of course." She turned to Clara. "You must be greatly relieved your nephew is finally settling down. Despite the circumstances," she muttered.

Clara's smile conveyed no reaction to Maude's snide remark. "The circumstances are trivial when they produce results such as this. They're a fine match, don't you agree?"

Gia cringed.

Maude straightened her spine. "I suppose I must take your word for it," she said.

"Yes, I suppose you must." Clara's triumphant smile broadened. "We all look forward to their blissful future together," she said with an affectionate pat to Gia's hand.

"Let's hope you may one day celebrate a blissful future for your niece as well." Shaking her head in a pitying gesture, Maude glanced to Alice in the corner. "Such a shame."

The deep breath Gia took to steady her temper failed miserably. A vile response filled her mouth, but Clara's squeeze to Gia's fingers deterred her from voicing it. Gia clamped her lips as she leaned back in her seat.

"Speaking of hopes for the future," Clara said, "where is your daughter?"

Maude narrowed her eyes. With an affronted lift of her chin, she said, "She went for a glass of punch."

"Oh, that sounds perfect," Clara said. "All this chatting has left me parched." She turned away from Maude. "Would you care for some refreshment, ladies?"

"Yes, very much," Gia said.

Clara stood. "Please excuse us, Maude," she said as she swished away.

Gia and Alice followed after Clara, past the rows of chairs. Maude's remark about Alice echoed in Gia's ears with each step she took. Alice's crippling shyness had cost the girl dearly, there was no way around the truth of the matter.

Since they'd arrived, only one man had requested an introduction to Alice. That poor fellow had been chased off by Alice's awkward lack of input to the conversation he'd tried to initiate, and now he was nowhere to be found.

Gia's vision had foretold Alice would accept a dance, here in this room, and despite however improbable the scenario seemed at the moment, Gia held fast to her patience as they made their way through the ballroom.

The long walk to the refreshment room seemed endless in the face of Alice's palpable self-consciousness. The girl moved stiffly, head bowed in her attempt to deflect the notice of the grand audience she imagined was watching her.

Clara, on the other hand, welcomed attention. She strode like a queen through the room, her gloved hands clasped at her waist, tossing nods and greetings to everyone they passed.

Gia took Alice's hand and gave it a squeeze. "Are you hungry?"

"Alice doesn't eat in public," Clara muttered over her shoulder. "She ate at home in her room before dressing."

"I'm not hungry either," Gia said. "Unless there is cake."

"There's always cake," Alice said.

Gia smiled. "I know."

Alice's nervous smile made Gia feel better.

The refreshment room housed tables of delectable treats. Cakes and biscuits, cold tongues and sandwiches. Clara enjoyed a cracker-bonbon with her coffee while Gia and Alice indulged in cool punch and cake.

"The flower arrangements are magnificent," Alice said, clearly impressed. "I wonder who designed them."

Gia glanced at the tall sprays of flowers and ferns. "We can ask Mrs. Westcott when we see her again."

"*If* we see her again," Alice said. "There are so many people."

Henry Whalen appeared in the doorway, looking dapper in his fine suit. He smiled brightly at Alice as he approached, and Gia's heart lifted as she anticipated a forthcoming dance invitation to Alice.

"I think I'd like another glass of punch," Alice uttered before scurrying in the opposite direction.

Gia gaped at the girl's hasty departure.

Henry's smile dimmed as he watched Alice make her escape to the punch bowl. The wounded look on his face explained the reason for Alice's empty dance card.

"Good evening," he said with a nod.

"Good evening, Henry." Gia smiled, hoping to soften the brunt of Alice's snub. While Gia understood the extent of the girl's anxiety, those who didn't know her might, quite understandably, mistake her evasive behavior for rudeness.

"Would you do me the honor to dance with me, Mrs. Elmsworth?" he asked Gia.

"She'd be delighted," Clara answered for her. "I believe you're unengaged for the next set."

"Yes, you're correct on both counts," Gia said. "I am delighted and unengaged."

"Alice and I will see you back at our seats," Clara said, waving them off.

While Gia wanted nothing more than to join Alice in her haven in the corner, a dance might help Gia summon some much-needed words of encouragement for the chat she intended to have with the girl after this dance.

Gia took Henry's arm and headed out to the ballroom.

* * * *

The Westcott Ball was a maddening crush of people. After enjoying a cigar on the patio in the fresh air outside, returning to the ballroom felt stiflingly hot and uncomfortable. Adjusting his cravat, Landen shrugged in his waistcoat as he made his way through the room, taking notice of Gia dancing with Henry Whalen. He wasn't surprised. Several men had already clamored for dances with Gia, and Landen had no doubt several more men would follow suit before the night ended.

Landen sidled through the clusters of people to the outskirts of the assembly. To avoid Maude Devenshire and Charlotte, he took the long route to his destination. Coward that he was, he had no wish to subject himself to the snide words behind Maude's contemptuous glances.

He approached their seats, where Aunt Clara stood chatting with a group of women. Alice sat where he'd left her, in the deepest corner of the room, fiddling with the fan in her hands.

A mix of sympathy and frustration twisted in his gut as he took a seat beside her. She was a beautiful young woman, funny and smart. Her baffling lack of confidence hurt him as much as he knew it pained her. Hoping to put her at ease, he said, "That color suits you nicely."

Alice fluffed at her skirts. "You're the third person tonight to tell me as much," she said, glancing up. "I had planned on wearing my white gown, but Gia insisted I wear the pink instead." She glanced around the room. "I feel as though I'm sticking out like a sore thumb."

"You always feel that way," he reminded her.

"I can't help it," she said.

He sighed. "Well, Gia was right about the pink," he said with a smile. "She should be keeping you company, though."

Alice glanced toward the dance floor. "She hasn't had the opportunity to sit. Every time she starts to head my way, she's dragged out for another dance."

Landen craned his neck toward Gia. Dancing with Morgan Bidwell, she looked radiant. So at ease. So unlike his poor sister, whose brittle nerves were so frayed by the crowd he could almost hear them rending inside her gown.

He turned his attention back to Gia. She smiled up at Bidwell, charming him with small talk as they moved. In her partner's arms, she danced gracefully, royal blue skirts flowing around her. One would never guess so much pain and tragedy hid inside the pretty package she presented to the world.

While Landen had had his fair share of misfortune, the hell of what Gia had endured made him feel small. He spent so much time wallowing in self-pity and the pain of his past. His mother's death and the deaths of his father and stepmother. Isobel's betrayal.

Dark times and dark memories that still shadowed his days. But through all the misery, he'd never been alone. He'd had his family to share in his grief—Aunt Clara and his siblings—to help him go on.

Gia had no one.

He could almost understand what had driven her to insinuate herself into his life and his family.

Almost.

"She looks lovely, doesn't she?" Alice asked.

With a curt nod, he averted his eyes.

"Oh, for goodness' sake, Denny, she's your wife now. Would it kill you to admit she looks lovely?"

In that moment, in that confidence, Alice conveyed the woman she was. The strong, intelligent—although irritatingly perceptive—woman he wished the world to see. If only she could apply this assertiveness with others, she'd be out on the dance floor and not hiding in the corner frittering time by vexing him.

"What is it you want from me, Alice?"

"I like her." Alice's eyes brimmed with admiration. "And I believe that, deep down, you do too."

"Cease baiting me."

"Why should this bait you?" She shook her head. "Poor Denny." She tsked in that annoying way Aunt Clara often did. "Married to the most beautiful, charming woman at the ball."

"Am I the only one who hasn't forgotten that she bamboozled me into marrying her?"

"As Aunt Clara pointed out, it takes two to tango." She shrugged. "That's all in the past, anyway. You are married now and must look to the future. Besides, I honestly don't believe Gia intended to *bamboozle* you."

His temper spiked at her words—at being forced into a conversation he'd rather not be having. Especially with Alice, a chaste girl who knew nothing of such matters and the degree to which some women would stoop to get what they wanted. Or needed.

"Are you taking her side against mine?"

"Of course not," Alice said. "I'm not taking sides at all. I'm merely trying to tell you that I don't believe Gia intended for this marriage to happen any more than you did."

"Please enlighten me as to what would possibly lead you to believe that."

"She didn't wish to marry you, either."

He stared, speechless. Although Gia spoke more bluntly than any woman he'd ever known, her relaying this bit of information to Alice surprised him. For some reason, it also rankled him even more than discussing with his sister the subject of his marriage.

"She told you that?"

Alice shook her head. "No. But like most women, she'd dreamt of the man she thought she'd marry."

He quirked his brow. "Most women?"

Alice blushed.

He smiled, encouraged by his sister's dreams of marriage, despite her lack of ambition toward the pursuit of finding a husband. As for Gia...

After witnessing one of her nightmares, he was relieved, at least, to learn she experienced pleasant dreams as well as terrifying ones.

Unable to resist his curiosity, he leaned in close. "Who did Gia dream of marrying?"

Alice shrugged. "I don't know. She doesn't know, either."

He eyed her skeptically.

"She dreamt of him, though," she assured him. She sighed, succumbing to the romantic notion with the same whimsical look she'd worn as a child after he'd read her a fairy tale. "A man who loved her and leaned on a cane."

He blinked.

"That's what she told me," Alice said.

While most women dreamt of marrying Prince Charming, Gia had dreamt of marrying a man with a cane. "Women," he uttered, shaking his head. "Ridiculous creatures, the lot of you."

"Nevertheless, it proves my point."

"What point?"

"The man of Gia's dreams was not you."

His chest tightened. The statement struck him like a solid punch, knocking him off balance. He straightened in his seat, annoyed by his surprising reaction. Annoyed at Alice for devoting such focus to his life, instead of her own. For rousing feelings inside him he'd rather not feel.

He glanced back to Gia, and his chest clenched again.

As though sensing her words hit their mark, Alice reached for his hand. "But fate had other plans for you both, so you must let go of the past and make the best of what you've been handed." She nodded toward Gia on the dance floor. "Just as your wife is trying so hard to do."

Chapter 16

When the dance ended, Gia made her way from the dance floor, surprised to find Landen waiting for her.

"Would you care for something to drink?" he asked.

She glanced toward their seats.

"Aunt Clara is with Alice," he said.

She nodded. "I could use a glass of punch," she said, taking his arm.

He led her from the ballroom. The cooler air felt wonderful as they crossed the foyer. Unfortunately, the refreshment room was more crowded than it had been earlier. And much warmer.

Landen went for their drinks while Gia attempted to cool herself with her fan.

"Here's your punch," he said.

"Thank you." She drank the delicious punch, glancing around. "How is Alice faring?"

"As well as usual." He took a sip of his drink. Brandy from the smell of it.

"She must be bored to tears."

"I kept her entertained." Amusement danced in his eyes. "Or perhaps I should restate that. She kept me entertained."

"Oh?"

"She enlightened me about something," he said.

The smirk on his face warned Gia that she would not like what she was about to hear.

"She told me that women have dreams about the man they wish to marry."

Gia blanched. "I cannot believe she told you about that."

"I must admit I am crushed."

"No, you're not. You're amused."

"That too," he said with a smile.

There was nothing malicious in his teasing, only a good-natured humor she found herself enjoying, despite her embarrassment. She shrugged.

"As Alice told you, it's common for women to have dreams about the man they might marry."

"Yes." He tilted his head. "But I imagine it's fairly uncommon for women to dream of marrying a man who leans on a cane."

Her smile faded, but not in anger. A month ago she'd refused to abandon the dream that had meant so much to her. The dream she'd held like a fragile butterfly between her palms. But somehow, in the time that had passed, in her shifting feelings for Landen, she'd accepted reality. She'd opened herself to what stood in front of her, reached for the promise in the depths of his eyes, and in doing so, she'd unwittingly set the dream free.

He glanced over her shoulder. "I think the man of your dreams just arrived," he said.

She turned, following his gaze. A gray-haired man who appeared to be in his late seventies inched into the room, cane in hand.

"He's a tad old for you, though, don't you think?"

She scolded him with her fiercest glare for making fun of her. Then she burst out laughing. "You are a wicked man, Landen Elmsworth."

He waggled his brows. "And I can give that oldster a run for his money." He leaned closer. "If you know what I mean."

"I've no doubt of your meaning. Or the truth in it."

He smiled at her brazen admission. "Perhaps I should call him out for holding my wife's heart hostage." He started away in a mock attempt at acting on his ridiculous threat.

She grabbed his arm, pulling him back. "Stop it now," she said, laughing some more.

He laughed too. The sound of his laughter reverberated around her, warming her from the inside out. She so enjoyed this playful side of him.

"Wait until I get a hold of that sister of yours," she said, wanting to strangle Alice for breaking her confidence.

"Don't fault Alice." The amusement slipped from his face. "She only told me because she cares for you."

Gia's heart stilled. His defense of his sister touched her like a sweet caress. His steadfast devotion to his family extended far past duty. And miles past the treason afforded by her parents. She averted her eyes to hide the emotion welling inside her. Unfortunately, her gaze landed on Maude. All evening she'd felt Maude watching her. Hating her. Gia sensed Landen noticed it too.

"Let's collect Aunt Clara and Alice and head home."

"We can't leave yet. Alice hasn't danced."

"Alice never dances. Unless it's with me or Alex, and even then, it's like pulling teeth to get her on the dance floor."

"Well, she will dance tonight," Gia said.

"Pushing her will not work. You've told me as much."

"I will not have to push her. She will dance of her own accord. Because she wants to." To cover her overconfidence she added, "There are so many young men here; one of them is bound to ask her. You'll see."

"Care to wager on it?"

She gaped. "You're proposing a wager on Alice? Your very own sister?"

"If you're afraid…"

Armed with her secret advantage, she accepted his dare. Gambling on her visions could prove an interesting pursuit. "Name your bet."

He smiled. "If I win… You must draw me a bath." He leaned to her ear. "And then bathe every inch of me."

His warm breath in her ear flowed through her body. A hot spring bubbled in her belly at the memory of their wedding night, when he'd bathed her that way.

"All right," she agreed. "And if I win, you must draw your own bath." Leaning toward him, she rose on her toes. "Before I bathe every inch of you."

Her counter offer pleased him immensely. She saw it in the hitch of his breath, in the way his throat moved as he swallowed. Their eyes met and held in a moment of shared desire so strong she ached from the force of it.

"Good evening, Elmsworth."

Landen let go of her hand, nodding to the tall man who'd approached.

"Good evening, Whithers."

The man turned to Gia. "This must be the lovely Mrs. Elmsworth."

"Gianna, this is Kenneth Whithers," Landen said.

Gia smiled. "I'm pleased to make your acquaintance."

"The pleasure is mine, dear lady," he said with a bow. "May I have this dance?"

Gia glanced to Landen, who nodded politely as Mr. Whithers led her to the dance floor.

Mr. Whithers was a competent dancer, and Gia followed his lead. The music floated through the room, but a strange humming tone rose over the tune. She blinked, trying to stave off the buzz in her ears as it grew louder and louder.

She closed her eyes. A picture flashed in her mind. Mr. Whithers, eyes bulging in fury, red faced and yelling over a desk. At Landen.

Gia opened her eyes, unsure how long she'd ceased moving. Her legs buckled, and she gasped in dread as she sank. Mr. Whithers caught her, supporting her weight while she fought to steady herself.

"Are you all right?" Mr. Whithers asked.

She blinked, feeling faint. She'd never had a vison prompted by touching someone. Random objects, yes, but people, never.

"Mrs. Elmsworth?"

She nodded, regaining her footing. "Yes, I am fine."

Landen appeared from out of nowhere.

"Gia?" He reached for her, clearly concerned.

"I feel a tad warm suddenly," she said, fanning her face.

"Let's get you some fresh air." Landen took her arm and led her carefully toward the open doors.

Once outside and away from Mr. Whithers, she felt better. Landen sat her on one of the benches outside the door. She took in the fresh air, trying to calm her racing pulse and frantic thoughts. Kenneth Whithers… "How well do you know him?" she asked.

"Who? Whithers?" Landen shrugged. "A few weeks. He's earned a solid reputation in in the city. I'm considering making some investments with him."

She shook her head. "Don't do it."

"Pardon me?"

"There's something about him I don't like."

Landen's brows narrowed. "You've known him for all of five minutes."

"That's all it took for me to know he's bad news."

He eyed her warily.

"I am serious. Trust me on this."

Landen stiffened, and she saw in his face that she tossed the word trust around far too often for his liking. She rubbed her temples to soothe her nerves.

"Are you feeling better?" he asked.

"Much better, thank you."

"Are you certain?"

"Yes, I am fine." She smiled. "Let's go check on Alice."

* * * *

Gia held Landen's arm, enjoying the crisp scent of him as they reentered the ballroom. She willed herself to stay calm, to file away until later the vision she'd had of Mr. Whithers and Landen until she could process it privately, and not in the middle of the Westcott Ball.

"I don't believe it," Landen said.

Gia followed his gaze across the room. Alice stood as a young man led her to the dance floor.

"Who is that fellow?"

"That's Mr. Shanley's son, Ben."

"Shanley? The gardener?"

Gia nodded. "Virginia Westcott pointed him out to me and Alice. She told us Ben designed all the floral arrangements for the ball tonight. He's quite an artist."

"You arranged for this, I suppose?" he asked, tipping his head toward Alice.

"I arranged nothing. It's merely nature taking its course."

Landen's frown faded as he watched his sister, looking radiant on the dance floor as her partner twirled her around.

"I've never seen her looking so at ease in public."

Gia watched the couple, smiling. "They have a lot in common.

"Are you feeling well enough for one more dance?" he asked.

"With you?"

"It's the Westcott Ball, and the Westcotts make their own rules," he said.

She glanced around, noticing several married couples dancing together.

"I can keep a closer eye on Alice from the dance floor," Landen said as he led her into the crush of other dancers.

Gia sighed at his reason for asking her to dance, yet her heart pounded, as it always did, when he was touching her.

"Besides, we're in the country, remember?" He grimaced over her shoulder. "Although you'd never know it from some of the fashions."

She stifled a giggle at Mrs. Birch's tall, feathered headdress.

"Please promise you'll never wear such a ridiculous thing in my presence," he said.

She laughed, gazing up at him. He looked so handsome. Her heart stilled with longing. And fear. "Promise me you'll never wear a red scarf."

He cocked a brow.

She tried her best to make light of her odd request. "I detest the color red," she said, clasping his arm more firmly.

He led her toward the dance floor. "You needn't worry. I detest scarves."

She smiled, feeling like the weight of the world had lifted from her shoulders. While she wasn't foolish enough to believe he was safe based on his hatred of scarves, could the omission of this one minor detail change everything?

They stepped onto the crowded floor and into a furnace. She didn't care. Alice was dancing. And Landen was holding Gia in his arms.

From the corner of her eye, she spotted Maude watching them. The chill of Maude's icy eyes had not thawed in the least. The adversarial exchange between Clara and Maude had only heightened Maude's dislike for Gia, she was certain of it. But it felt nice to have Clara defending her. Nice to have people who cared.

Dismissing Maude and Mr. Whithers, and all the other negative thoughts that nagged at her mind, Gia focused instead on the moment. The music was lovely. The room was grand. And Landen was a fine dancer. She followed his lead as if she'd danced with him all her life. She glanced up to find him staring down at her.

"What?"

He shook his head. "Nothing."

She smiled up at him. "I'd think you'd have something to say to me for winning our bet."

"Congratulations," he said. "But in all honesty, given the conditions you presented, I've never been so happily resigned to losing a wager."

She smiled, pressing her body ever so slightly to his. "Nevertheless, as winner of said bet, I'll demand prompt and full payment."

His dark eyes glimmered beneath the chandelier. She could feel his want for her in his look, in his touch, in the rhythm of his breath. She swallowed her own eager desire. As much as she was enjoying the moment, she could not wait to get home and away from the crowd, away from Kenneth Whithers and Maude Devenshire.

She longed for the bliss of their room, where nothing else in the world mattered.

And Landen was safe.

Chapter 17

Over the next few days, the household buzzed in anticipation of Alex's pending arrival. The excitement was contagious, and Gia looked forward to meeting Alex, whom Alice had described as charming and handsome with a heart of pure gold.

His visit would coincide perfectly with Landen's birthday and the special family supper she and Alice were planning. After spending the day shopping for birthday gifts in Troy, Gia and Alice enjoyed the leisurely carriage ride home, laughing and chatting like true sisters.

Alice had confided to Gia how much she'd enjoyed dancing at the Westcott Ball and how much she admired Mr. Shanley, her dancing partner. It warmed Gia's heart to see the girl expressing interest in something other than her rose bushes.

"Aunt Clara insists on referring to Ben as a mere gardener, but he's so much more," Alice said. "Did I mention he's designed several of the most beautiful gardens in Misty Lake?"

Gia nodded, suppressing a smile. "You mentioned it, yes."

"You will try and persuade her and Denny to allow Ben to call on me, won't you, Gia?"

"I'll do my best, I promise," Gia said, patting her hand.

Despite their misgivings about Ben Shanley, Clara and Landen saw Alice's rare willingness to spend time with anyone outside the realm of the family as a welcome change that might open the door for other more suitable young men.

Of course, Gia kept this bit of information to herself. There was no point in disappointing Alice with their mindset on the matter, so long as they granted Ben permission to call upon Alice. Fate would take it from there.

Fate. The word echoed through the dizzying swirl of confusing thoughts in Gia's head. Since meeting Mr. Whithers at the Westcott Ball and the vision she'd experienced while dancing with him, Gia now deemed him her sole suspect in wishing Landen harm. She had to keep Landen away from Whithers, and from entering any dealings with him, but how? How could she convince Landen of the man's nefarious intentions without offering any logical proof?

Time was running out, and Gia needed to find the site of the vision that had brought her here. The place she feared most…

"Are there any creeks around Misty Lake?" Gia asked.

Alice regarded her with an inquisitive look. "There's a creek in the woods next to the estate," she said. "Why do you ask?"

"I thought I might try my hand at painting. A flowing creek would make a pretty subject."

"I suppose," Alice said. "But why not paint a scene of the lake instead?"

Gia shrugged. "I'd prefer to capture the effect of moving water." The more lies Gia told, the easier they seemed to come to her. She sighed at the disheartening realization that her mysterious ability had fated her to a lifetime of lies and manipulation. She shook off her shame and the helplessness of what she could not control. Her actions were motivated to help, not harm, but reiterating this fact did little to assuage her guilt.

She turned toward the window. She'd take a walk in the woods tomorrow morning. Perhaps the site of the vision might provide her with a clue or another vision. Anything that might aid in her quest for answers.

By the time Gia and Alice arrived back in Misty Lake, it was almost time for supper. The four of them dined at the large table that would be full by this time tomorrow evening when Alex arrived with his guests.

"Now, let's see." Clara ticked off the mental list in her head. "The menu for this week has been set, and Florence readied Alex's room this morning." She took a sip of her wine. "Landen you must have the badminton net set up. You know how much your brother enjoys badminton."

"You mean how much he enjoys besting Denny at badminton," Alice said. She turned to Gia. "They are ridiculously competitive."

"They are men," Clara said.

"Guilty on both charges," Landen said. "But let it be known, I best him at archery every time."

"Let's hope the boy has time for such sports during this visit," Clara said. "From his last letter, he seems quite enamored with Miss Richardson. Since he's arranged rooms for her and her cousin at the Lakeside Hotel, I suspect he plans on spending a good deal of his time there."

"I'm certain Alex will spend enough time at the house to please even you, Aunt Clara," Landen said.

"To insure it, I shall insist Miss Richardson stay here with us. Since Bea decided to spend a few weeks at Saratoga, the girl can have that room. Alex and her cousin can share Alex's room." She shook her head. "A man acting as chaperone." She tsked. "Obviously the family is not much for convention." She shook her head some more. "Thank goodness we're in the country," she muttered. "At any rate, Miss Richardson shall stay here at the house. We'll all be together, and Gianna and I can properly chaperone."

"Two birds with one stone," Landen said. "Resourceful, as always."

She waved off his teasing. "This wine is delicious, Denny. We must be sure to get more."

Landen reached for his wineglass. "Rest assured, the task is at the top of my list."

A smile passed between Landen and Alice as he sipped liquid fortitude, but Clara prattled on unoffended. Gia admired Clara's propensity for indulging her family's amusement at her expense—for allowing the small quips that bound the siblings together.

The meal passed in a pleasant evening that left Gia realizing how much she'd come to enjoy being with this family and how much she'd come to care for them all. She actually felt as though she were a part of them now. A feeling swelled inside her, a feeling so foreign, so forgotten, it took her a moment to discern what it was.

Happiness.

* * * *

Later that night, Gia nestled into the warmth of her favorite place in the world. In the crook of Landen's arm, she felt safe and protected. But more importantly, when he was with her, she knew he was safe. Deliriously spent by their lovemaking, she let her fingers play lazily over his chest, through the fine curls of hair, the taut plane of muscle and ribs.

"I have something for you," she uttered.

His left brow rose in that wickedly seductive expression that made her quiver inside. "While I'm uncertain I'm up to it again so soon, I will do my utmost to rise to the occasion."

She slapped at his chest, and he laughed, cowering from her playful assault. "I mean I have a birthday gift for you." She leaned to the bedside table, then opened the drawer. "Here."

His smile faded as he sat up to take the small box she held out to him. "This was unnecessary." The surprising modesty in his voice was endearing.

"Of course it was necessary. I couldn't let your birthday pass unnoticed."

"Unnoticed? As though you and Alice haven't been planning a celebration all along."

She gaped at him. "Alice will be so disappointed that you know about the supper. You must pretend to be surprised."

"I pretend to be surprised every year. I can manage to do the same this year." He tilted his head. "It's just us, correct? Just family?"

She nodded, thrilled he'd included her in his definition of family. "Yes, just the family. And Alex's guests, of course. Alice mentioned you wouldn't want us to fuss, so we've planned a simple evening." She waggled her finger. "I will not, however, divulge what Florence is preparing for your birthday supper."

"Will there be cake?"

"Of course there will be cake. A rich cake with creamy—" She narrowed her eyes at the grin on his face. "What?"

He shook his head. "Your mouth is watering from merely speaking of cake."

She smiled too. "Obviously, you've noticed I possess a slight sweet tooth."

"Slight?"

"All right," she admitted as she fluffed her pillow. "An enormous sweet tooth." She sprawled on her side to watch him open her gift.

With a grin, he reached toward her bare leg. "When something is good, it's hard to resist." He touched the box to her knee, slowly trailing it up to her thigh.

She inhaled at the contact, the simmering look in his eyes as his gaze followed the box to her hip. She felt her nipples harden, the tingling heat between her thighs.

He leaned toward her, but she halted him with a palm to the chest. "Stop it now and open the box."

He drew back his hand in surrender. "All right, you win." He opened the box, then lifted the silver chain from the velvet lining.

"It's a medal," she said, springing upright. "Saint Christopher."

Cradling the medal in his hand, he inspected the engraved image closely. "Saint Christopher… The saint of safe travels."

"Wearing it will protect you." She tilted her head. "You will wear it, won't you?"

He nodded, his humble gaze soft and warm. "Yes." He slipped the chain over his head. It shimmered in the lamplight against his broad chest, and she smiled, liking the effect immensely.

"Thank you." He regarded her with a tender affection she hadn't thought possible. Her heart leapt in her chest.

"You're welcome."

His gaze slid down the length of her body, and his tone deepened. "Now come here. I have something for you."

* * * *

Gia glanced to the clock on the mantel. "It's almost midnight," she said. "Almost your birthday."

"Actually, I wasn't born until two in the morning."

Her thoughts wandered to her own birthday—the last one she or anyone else had ever acknowledged. She'd lost her brothers, and nearly died herself, on the very day—the very hour—of her birth. The eerie coincidence had always plagued her. From that horrible day forward, her birthday had become a day reserved for grieving the death of her brothers, nothing more.

She blinked away dark memories of the past and returned to the moment. "Two in the morning," she said. "That was inconvenient."

"I also was a large baby. Just shy of ten pounds." He smiled proudly, as though claiming credit for the accomplishment.

"Oh, my," she said, wide eyed. "Your poor mother."

His smile dimmed as he averted his eyes.

The tension in his countenance should have kept her from pressing, but she longed to know more about the woman he'd never spoken of. "Tell me about her," Gia said.

He turned to face her. "What have you heard?"

The memory of Clara's grim words echoed through Gia's ears. *God rest her pitiful soul.* Gia shook her head. "I haven't heard anything, really," she said truthfully. "That's why I'd like you to tell me about her."

"She was ill." He ran his hand through his hair. "Mentally unstable." He watched her closely, as though to gauge her reaction.

"Oh," she uttered, unable to hide her surprise.

"For as long as I can remember, she behaved erratically. Calm and serene one moment, restless and aggressive the next."

"That must have been difficult for you."

Dark memories shadowed his face. "For my father, as well. I'm told they were happy for years before things started changing. Before she began hearing those damn voices."

"Voices?"

"In her head," he said with a tap to his temple. "Voices that told her to do things."

Gia swallowed hard. "What kind of things?"

"Irrational things, inappropriate things. Violent things."

"How awful." Gia's heart ached as she imagined his painful childhood and what it must have been like to grow up with an unstable parent. To grow up trying to make sense of something so difficult to understand. Something so scandalous. Society had little tolerance for the mentally disturbed, and for a brief moment, Gia almost pitied her parents for their frightening belief that their daughter was insane.

Her heart stilled. What might Landen think of her if he knew her secret? If she told him of her visions? Even worse than deeming her insane, he'd deem himself doomed to relive the misery of his past. The thought sent a chill of cold fear down her spine.

"Through it all, though, my father loved her. He never gave up hoping she'd wake up one day and be well."

"That was admirable."

"It was foolish."

She flinched at his sudden hostility.

"He should have accepted her condition. Prepared for it." He gave a thump to his chest. "Prepared me for it." His dark eyes glazed with anger. "She hanged herself."

Gia's breath caught in her throat.

He shook his head. "My father never told me outright that she took her own life, but I overheard the help talking. I was nine years old at the time and didn't want to believe it. I never asked him about it, but years later, Aunt Clara confirmed it."

"I'm so sorry."

"My mother ended her life with no thought to me and my father."

"Oh, I'm sure that's untrue."

"She left us. No warning, no good-bye. Nothing."

Gia stared, not knowing what to say.

"I will never forgive her for that."

"She was ill."

"Yes. But somehow reminding myself of that fact does little to temper my anger."

Gia blinked back her welling emotion.

"Some say mental illness is passed on through the bloodline."

She glanced up in surprise. "Is that something you fear?"

"Wouldn't you?" He took a deep breath, and his taut features softened. "I fear it not for myself."

She assumed he referred to his siblings, but then she remembered they shared only a father. "For your children?"

"Yes."

Although she dreaded hearing the answer, she asked anyway. "Is that why you avoided marriage for so long?"

"One of the reasons, yes. I didn't learn the truth about my mother until after Isobel broke off our engagement," he said. "But our situation, yours and mine, left no choice in the matter." He shrugged. "Not that I gave a damn about sparing you from the truth at the time."

She nodded, lowering her eyes in the face of his bitterness. Her shame.

"But I thought it fair to tell you now," he said. "About the risk."

His heartfelt fear for his children, his blunt honesty, touched her deeply. She swallowed hard, understanding suddenly how much she had forced upon him with her trickery.

"Thank you for telling me." She placed her hand atop his. "The best things in life are often well worth the risk."

She stared into his handsome face. While he might not ever trust her enough to believe this, beneath all the pain and resentment in his troubled eyes, she could see that he wanted to. His fingers splayed, entwining with hers. The simple move became the grandest of gestures. With the clasp of his hand, he'd accepted her comfort with no intent to seduce—no approach to his lust.

She glanced down at their interlocked hands, and she knew that she loved him.

* * * *

On her way to breakfast the next morning, Gia noticed a message addressed to Landen on the tray in the foyer. She stopped in her tracks, her mind coursing with more than simple curiosity. Could the note be from Mr. Whithers? Disregarding the prick of guilt she felt for snooping into Landen's private correspondence, she snatched up the message. She opened the envelope carefully, then pulled out the page folded inside. She glanced around quickly, then scanned the bold print.

Dearest Denny,

I must see you at once. I'll be walking at Sandy Cove this morning. Please meet me there.

Charlotte.

Gia's heart sank to her feet. She'd rather the note be from Whithers than Charlotte. Angry at herself for the bitter thought, she returned the note to the envelope, then dropped it back onto the tray.

The memory of Landen and Charlotte together at the garden party scraped like thorns against her tattered pride. Jealousy bled from her pores. Was it Charlotte he thought of when he made love to Gia? Charlotte's face he saw when his eyes closed in that moment of rapture—in that moment he clung to Gia's body, unleashing everything inside him?

The thought sucked the air from her lungs, and she stiffened against her painful insecurities. Her fear she was merely a substitute for the woman whom Landen truly wanted. For the woman he could not have because of Gia's interference.

Gia bit back a curse. Landen was her husband, and Charlotte had no right to make demands upon him. No matter what had transpired between the couple before Gia and Landen married, the fact remained, they were married now, and Charlotte had no claims to him.

Smoothing her skirts, she did her utmost to compose herself, then started down the hall. The sound of footsteps heading toward her quickened her heart as she hurried on to the dining room.

"Good morning, Mrs. Elmsworth," Florence said as she rounded the corner.

"Good morning, Florence." Exhaling a breath, Gia passed quickly, tossing a glance over her shoulder as Florence went about her daily task of collecting the messages.

Gia continued to the dining room, then took a seat at the empty table.

A few minutes later, Landen joined her. She poured him a cup of coffee as Florence entered the room, message in hand.

"You received a message, Mr. Elmsworth."

"Thank you, Florence." Landen read the message.

Gia sipped her coffee, doing her best to act nonchalant.

He stood. "I have to go into town."

"Is everything all right?"

"Yes," he said, stuffing the message into his coat pocket. "I have some business to attend to."

She gazed at him, hoping he'd say more. Hoping he'd tell her where he was going. That this "business" with Charlotte was perfectly innocent.

He didn't.

"I'll be back soon."

Gia nodded, swallowing a thick lump of disappointment. Charlotte had requested to see Landen, and he was all but running from the house to oblige.

Tears burned in Gia's eyes, but she blinked them back. These past few weeks had led her to believe she and Landen were getting closer, and he was opening his heart to her. After last night, she'd felt sure he was beginning to care for her. She was a fool.

Lifting her chin, she staved off her tears as the man she loved turned his back on her, then hurried off to meet his mistress.

Chapter 18

Landen rode toward town, fighting the urge to turn his horse around and go back to the house. He couldn't imagine what was so urgent Charlotte had to see him immediately, but he was more consumed with thoughts of Gia.

The medal she'd given him had surprised him. A gift he'd wear every day, beneath his clothing, where no one but she knew it was there, no one but she would ever see it, was an intimate choice that roused intimate feelings.

He inhaled a long breath, but the crisp morning air failed to clear the intoxicating memories of last night from his head. The more time he spent with his wife, the more time he wanted to spend with her. Not that this was necessarily a bad thing. They were bound together for eternity after all. But it was a confusing thing. He may not believe he could ever truly forgive her for forcing him into marriage, but over the past weeks, he'd discovered he could live with what she'd done. He could care for her.

How could he not? Everything about her aroused him. The feel of her skin, the scent of her hair, the sounds she made when he touched her—when he carried her over the edge. He'd never experienced such an insatiable desire for a woman. Never felt from another woman Gia's insatiable desire for him.

And it wasn't just in bed that she captivated him. She was compassionate and smart with a keen sense of humor. She made him laugh. Made him think. Made him feel.

Which led him to his current dilemma. He was sneaking off to meet his former mistress behind his wife's back. Not only did Landen feel guilty for meeting Charlotte, but truth be told, he didn't want to meet her. He'd barely given the woman a thought since he'd married Gia, and he couldn't deny the reason for this.

His mind had been occupied with thoughts of Gia.

"Denny!" The man in front of the Lakeside Hotel waved his arms.

Landen squinted against the sun. "Alex?" He slowed the horse, craning his neck for a better look. Smiling, he snapped the reins and turned the horse into the drive of the hotel. He hopped from the horse, greeting his brother with a bear hug.

"When did you get here?" Landen asked.

"Less than an hour ago." Alex smiled. "It's good to see you, Brother." He slapped Landen on the shoulder. "How are Alice and Aunt Clara?" He waggled his brows. "Your wife?"

This last question was aimed to provoke some expected response, but Landen refused to be baited. He was too pleased by his brother's arrival to be miffed at him already. There'd be plenty of time for that, as Landen was certain Alex's incessant need to goad him hadn't waned during the months since they'd parted.

"They're all well. Looking forward to seeing you."

"I'm looking forward to seeing them too. Where are you headed?"

"I have business in town."

"For a minute I was afraid Aunt Clara got wind of our early arrival and sent you here to deliver us straight to the house."

Landen laughed. "You have the entire day to settle in. Though I must warn you, Aunt Clara wants Miss Richardson to stay with us at the house."

Alex nodded. "I'm sure Sissy would prefer that as well. I'd better inform her of the change of plans before she finishes unpacking the tower of trunks piled in her room." He shrugged. "She wants to make a good impression," he said with a smile that made him look as young as a schoolboy. "Wait until you meet her."

Landen could see in his brother's eyes his adoration for Miss Richardson. Of course, Alex had displayed this same lovesick expression before. Several times with several women. A part of Landen admired Alex's ability to live for the moment. To flit from one woman to the next like a bee buzzing through flowers in a garden. "We'll see you tonight for supper, then," Landen said, feigning interest in meeting Alex's latest rose.

"Before you go, come meet Sissy's cousin." Alex pointed across the lawn to a blond-haired man seated between two women on one of the large chairs facing the lake.

Landen started with Alex down the stone path that led to the sparkling water.

"He's a kindred spirit and the best of men," Alex said.

Shrugging off the childish sting of Alex's admiration for his new friend, Landen wondered, as he often did, why he and Alex weren't closer.

Something more substantial than the difference in their ages and mothers supported the wall that stood between them, Landen was certain of it.

Alex regarded Landen with equal parts of love and resentment, and try as he might, Landen failed to understand why. Perhaps Landen had been too hard on Alex after their father died, too autocratic. But Alex had been young and in need of direction, and Landen had done his best to step into his father's shoes and provide his siblings with the solid guidance he'd felt they both needed. Whatever the reason for the underlying discord between them, Landen doubted this visit would change things.

"Kit, here's my brother," Alex called to the man.

Kit turned to face them. Although Kit appeared older than Alex, he possessed the same striking good looks that made women swoon. Landen suppressed a smile as he imagined the trouble the pair could get into if given the opportunity to carouse about town.

With a tip of his hat, Kit excused himself to the ladies, then started up the stone path.

A memory flashed like a bolt of lightning through Landen's mind. He blinked, dumbstruck, absorbing the strange coincidence as the finely attired man made his way slowly toward them.

Alex stepped to Kit's side, placing an affectionate hand on his shoulder. "Landen, this is Kit Richardson," Alex said. "Sissy's cousin and my good friend."

Alex's introduction droned on, but in his distraction, Landen barely heard him.

"It's good to finally meet this rascal's brother," Kit said, displaying teeth as perfect as the other features of his face.

"And it's good to meet you." Despite feeling a fool for the preposterous thoughts roiling in his head, Landen couldn't temper his shaky reaction. His gaze dropped, fixing on the walking cane in Kit's hand. And suddenly Gia's amusing dream about the man she'd hoped to marry no longer struck him as funny.

* * * *

Gia decided to go for a walk. After obsessing about the morning's painful turn of events, she had to do something to keep from driving herself mad. She donned her most comfortable slippers, then headed out the back door in search of the creek Alice had told her ran through the woods along the estate.

Gia's heart raced with her rampant thoughts. If Landen thought Gia would stand idly by while he continued his relationship with Charlotte, he had another think coming, and she planned on telling him as much the moment she saw him.

Her heart panged with the humiliating thought of demanding he honor their vows. Vows she'd forced him to declare. How could she expect honesty from him when she'd been so dishonest? He would, no doubt, remind her of this fact, and now that she loved him, his defense of his ongoing affair with Charlotte would be too much too bear.

She blinked back her tears. While this was not the life she'd ever imagined for herself, this was her life. She shook off her self-pity. At least she had a life. Her brothers weren't so fortunate. Neither was Prudence. Lifting her chin, she charged toward the tree line in the distance.

Her imagination wreaked havoc on her as she walked. She swatted at a swarm of gnats as she entered the woods. What were Landen and Charlotte discussing right now at Sandy Cove? What were they doing? The scenarios weakened her resolve, and tears prickled her eyes once again.

If Gia stepped aside, the lovers could be together. The alternate option hit her like a slap to the face, but she had to consider it. She could still do what she'd come here to do—save his life—and then she could disappear. As she had when she'd fled Boston. Divorce was becoming more common, that was also an option. The only thing that was not an option was standing by and doing nothing to prevent Landen's death.

She needed another vision. She had to locate the place where she'd seen Landen floating in the water, and she had to prove the culprit was, indeed, Mr. Whithers.

She walked for what seemed like miles along the bank of the creek. Since arriving in Misty Lake, she'd kept her eyes honed for the site of her vision. Now that she'd located the creek, she hoped she'd recognize the place when she saw it.

Her feet were beginning to ache. Still she walked. She kept thinking about Landen and Charlotte together, and her anger and hurt kept her feet moving. The path she tread grew steeper, her feet sorer, but still she walked and she walked.

And then she was there. She knew it instantly. The row of towering pines. The narrow trail that widened into a flat ledge high above the water. The old, gnarled tree. Her skin prickled. She stared down the embankment at the shallow water flowing over the bedrocks.

This was it—the place where Landen would die.

* * * *

Landen drove down the road, unable to loosen the tense knot in his gut. While Alex's presence usually caused a subtle tension in Landen, it was meeting Kit Richardson that had him on edge. Kit Richardson, the man Alex worshipped and Landen's wife had dreamt of marrying. Landen shook the absurd thought from his head. He was being childish and irrational, and he knew it.

Pushing thoughts of Kit from his mind, he rode through the arched wooden structure that marked the entrance to the park that led to Sandy Cove. After dismounting, he walked the horse down one of the several worn paths toward the bench where Charlotte waited. He glanced around the park at the other people picnicking on the lawn and strolling about, feeling guiltier with each step he took.

He bit back a curse and quickened his pace. If word got back to Gia about this meeting, she'd be hurt. And Landen did not want to hurt her. How different from when they'd first married and he'd wanted to do nothing but hurt her.

Deciding he'd tell Gia about the meeting upon his return, he tethered the horse, determined to get this over with as quickly as possible.

"Good morning, Charlotte." He took a seat next to her, assaulted by the strong smell of perfume.

Charlotte's demure smile faded at the formality of his greeting. She filled the awkward moment by fluffing her burgundy skirts as he sat stiffly beside her.

"I know this must seem strange, my asking to see you, Denny, but I have something to tell you."

"What is it, Charlotte? What's wrong?"

She sighed, her forehead creasing with worry beneath the wide brim of her hat. "It's my mother."

"Is she ill?"

Charlotte shook her head. "No, nothing like that." She fiddled with her gloved hands, acting as nervous as Alice did in a crowd. "She is very angry about your marriage to Gianna. I know it's ridiculous that she harbors such a grudge, but she harbors one, nonetheless."

Landen knew all about Maude and her grudges. Her smear campaign against Charlie Harding, the poor handyman she'd hired to paint her house in the city, had served as a lesson. When the color Maude had selected didn't do her house ample justice, Charlie refused to repaint it for free. Maude had destroyed the man's reputation and business, and all to avoid honoring a debt she could well afford to pay.

"What has she done?" Landen asked.

"She went to visit Mrs. Amery at the Female Seminary," Charlotte said. "They are old friends, you see, from when I attended there as a girl."

Landen stared at her, baffled. Mrs. Amery was the same woman who'd recommended Gia for the position of Alice's companion. The same woman who'd assured Landen of Gia's fine work at the school. "And?"

"And Mrs. Amery disclosed some information to my mother about Gianna. Information my mother was planning to divulge to anyone and everyone who might listen."

Landen sighed.

"I'm sorry, Denny. Truly I am."

Landen studied her face, sensing a small part of her was not sorry at all. Considering how abruptly he'd ended their relationship, he supposed he couldn't blame her. "What information?"

"Before I tell you, I want you to rest assured that my mother will keep silent about what she's learned."

"Like hell she will."

"She will." Charlotte nodded furiously against the force of his doubt. "I can promise you that. I swore to her that if she told a soul, I would never speak to her again." She glanced down at her hands on her lap. "And I meant it."

His anger cooled as he gazed at her, not knowing what to say. "I appreciate that, Charlotte."

She smiled a sad smile. "I would do anything for you, Denny. Surely you know that."

He hadn't, but he did now. Until this moment, he hadn't realized the extent of her feelings for him. Or how badly he'd hurt her. His stabbing guilt thrust deeper. After the intimate relationship they'd shared, he could not even recall the taste of her kiss, let alone the heat of her body.

"I'm only telling you because I feel you should know."

"So, tell me."

"Gianna has not been truthful with you."

He narrowed his eyes, growing angry again. "What do you mean?"

"Her parents are not dead as she claims."

He inhaled sharply, shaking his head.

"They are alive and well and living in Boston."

"That's not true."

"It is. Mrs. Amery has no reason to lie about such a thing. Gianna told her that she ran away. That she fled her home in Boston to escape her parents."

He blinked. "Why? Why would she want to escape her parents?" He was angry as hell and taking it out on Charlotte, but he didn't care.

Charlotte sighed, taking his hand between hers. His stomach sank like a rock at the solemn look in her eyes and his fear of her reluctant reply.

"Because they were about to have her committed to the asylum."

Chapter 19

Gia made the arduous ascent up the tall staircase, her feet aching. She entered the bedroom, hung her wrap, and then plopped into a chair. Wincing, she pried off her muddy slippers, massaging her cramped toes. She'd walked for miles and all she had to show for her effort were ruined slippers and blistered feet.

Try as she had to summon a vision at the creek, she'd experienced nothing. Not so much as a flash or a flicker of anything. As blood flow returned to her throbbing feet, she decided the trek still had been worth it. At least now she knew the place she must ensure Landen avoided at all costs.

Landen took morning rides on his tall black horse, but he usually rode through the fields. When he fished, he did so at the lake. She'd never known him to go walking through the woods and couldn't imagine any plausible scenario in which he'd journey behind the estate to that secluded place high above the creek.

She wrapped herself inside the logic, but found little comfort in the flimsy reassurance. However improbable it might seem at this moment, Landen would somehow end up at the creek. And somehow, Gia had to stop him.

Her shoulders slumped beneath the weight of the impossible situation. Pushing her doubts from her mind, she dropped her foot to the floor, glancing at the clock on the mantel. Landen was still in town conducting his "business" with Charlotte.

Thoughts of the pair together consumed her. With each passing moment, Gia's jealousy grew stronger. Fiercer. A monster she fed with every insecurity she'd ever had about herself.

Charlotte Filkins was a respected, proper lady, while Gia was a liar with a scandalous past. A freak of nature with a weakness for opiates and parents who were glad to be rid of her.

The disheartening comparison sunk her lower. She stiffened her shoulders, shaking off the painful summation of her character. There was no changing the past, and she didn't have time to dwell in self-pity. Alex and his guests would be arriving in a few hours, and she still needed to bathe and dress for Landen's birthday supper.

She froze at the sound of Landen's distinctive footsteps outside the door. Shooting to her stocking-clad feet, she straightened her appearance, ready for battle. Although she couldn't very well admit she'd read Charlotte's message, Gia would pry from him the truth about his relationship with Charlotte, one way or another. She was his wife, and if nothing else, she deserved that much.

The door opened, and Landen strode into the room.

The sight of him sent a flutter through her belly. With an angry breath, she braced herself against the effect of his presence. "You're back," she said coolly.

He said nothing as he shrugged from his coat.

Miffed by his silence, she pressed onward. "Did you finish your *business* in town?"

He stiffened at the implication in her tone, avoiding her eyes. He flung his coat to a chair, then yanked at his tie. "I was with Charlotte."

She blinked at the unsolicited admission. The pinch in her chest spread outward, a massive wave that ached through to her bones. Deep down she'd hoped she'd jumped to some sordid conclusion about an affair. But here he stood, not confessing, but declaring his morning tryst to the woman he'd made love to last night. The man had no shame.

Without so much as a glance in her direction, he strode to the bureau. Clanking glasses and bottles, he poured himself a drink. She glared at his back, seething at his lack of remorse.

He tossed back his head and guzzled his brandy. The slam of the glass against the wood surface gave her a start. She knew in that moment, there would be no remorse. Gritting her teeth against her welling tears, she stood there, trembling with anger. His broad shoulders rose and fell on the deep breath he took before he finally turned to face her.

"Are your parents alive?"

Air caught in her lungs; blood rushed from her face.

"It's a simple question, Gia." He stalked toward her.

She took a step back. Her mind raced as he neared, and then it all became clear.

Maude Devenshire. It had to be Maude who'd unearthed Gia's past. The woman was angry about Landen's marriage, and Clara's goading her at the ball hadn't helped.

"Answer me," Landen said.

Gia hadn't prepared for this. She had no acceptable answer, mapped no route of escape through the maze of her lies. "Yes."

He winced in stunned silence.

"I can explain," she croaked out.

"With more lies?"

Anger blazed in his eyes, but there was hurt in them too. Her betrayal stared back at her through his pain and confusion.

"Don't bother. I cannot believe a word that comes from your mouth."

The disgust in his tone hurt more than his anger. She deserved nothing less. She lowered her head, mired in a swamp of regrets. She had come so close to gaining his trust. She had come so close to *him*.

"Please, Landen." She reached toward him, but he shrugged from her grasp.

"Your parents were about to have you committed?"

She heard the horror in his voice, felt the pain of his childhood ripping through him.

"I know what you're thinking, but I am not mad."

"They were going to commit you."

"Because I refused to stay medicated. They were afraid of my visions and—"

"Visions?" He stared aghast.

His mother had heard voices…

She shook her head furiously. "I am not insane. I see visions. Prophetic visions. But I am not insane."

"I cannot listen to this." He held up his hands. "I won't."

"You must." Tears streamed down her face, down her throat, drowning her. "My visions are real. You must believe me."

He shook his head, starting toward the door.

She started after him, desperate. "When I told Mrs. Amery that I fled Boston, she couldn't keep me on at the school. She arranged for my position here. That's when I had the vision of you."

He stopped in his tracks, turning slowly to face her.

"I was holding the card Mrs. Amery gave me," she said. "Your card. And I had a vision of you floating in a creek. I came here to save you." She pelted him with the truth, having no more to lose. "That's why I had to marry you, don't you see? Clara was going to send me away. I had to stay here to save you."

His mouth fell open as he took in her words. His eyes narrowed to slits as this registered. "Are you telling me that you tricked me into marriage because of this madness?" Disbelief gnarled his face; a vein emerged at his throat. "That you ruined my life based on some nonsense you imagined in your mind?"

She stared at him, struck by the hatred in his eyes. In the face of his anger, in the face of losing him forever, she realized how much she loved him. "Yes."

"You are insane."

The words stabbed through her heart, piercing her in two. She swallowed her pain and her pride. Her welling hopelessness. "Your life is in danger. I saw it, Landen. You were in the water, beaten and unconscious. You wore a red scarf."

He scoffed, repeating her words. "In the water. A red scarf." He shook his head, his voice growing louder. Angrier. "No one wants to kill me! I don't own a red scarf!" He raked a hand through his hair. "And I will not continue this conversation for one moment more." He pointed his finger. "You will keep quiet about your past. About these visions and everything else to do with this nonsense."

The demand sounded familiar. She'd heard it before. The memory of her parents' threats echoed through her head, and she shook them away. Her frantic attempts to warn them about her vision of Prudence had resulted in disaster. Gia had been promptly medicated, Prudence died, and the person Gia once was had died with her.

Gia lifted her chin. "And what about Charlotte?"

He tilted his head, his jaw twitching.

"She could not wait to tell you about my sordid past. She'll tell—"

"Do not speak to me about Charlotte," he ground out. "If it weren't for her, Maude would have destroyed you by now."

His defense of Charlotte hurt even more. Gia was the villain. The usurper. She hadn't asked for the visions that had led her to this—that had led her to falling in love with him—and she bit back a curse at the unfairness of it all. "I don't care about that," she shot back. "All I care about is you. Saving you."

The hard look on his face softened. He blinked, and the trace of tenderness in his eyes disappeared. "Say nothing of this to anyone, Gia. Or I swear to Christ, I will divorce you, to hell with the scandal."

She summoned her strength against his threats. Against his hatred, and whatever else might stand in her way. She would not back down. She would not surrender as she had in Boston. She would fight to save Landen, as she should have fought to save Pru.

"Believe I'm insane, if you must. But believe this as well. Someone wants you dead. I saw it as plainly as you're standing here now." Her body trembled, but to her surprise, her voice sounded firm. Almost calm. "So, you can divorce me, Landen. You can toss me to the street. But I will stay in Misty Lake until I know you are safe."

Chapter 20

Landen stormed down the stairs and straight out the door. He walked toward the lake, his chest heaving. What the hell had he gotten himself into with this woman?

She actually believed she had visions. Prophetic visions. And she'd forced this marriage upon him as a result of these delusions. He squeezed shut his eyes, but he could not block out the picture of her, tears streaming from her desperate eyes, begging him to believe the unbelievable.

She'd come to Misty Lake to save him. If he weren't feeling so damn sorry for himself, he might feel sorry for her.

He ran a hand through his hair, fighting the urge to yank a fistful from his head. He'd finally managed to accept their marriage and what he'd believed was her reason for tricking him into it. A young woman alone in the world and desperate for security had to do what she must to survive. That was understandable.

Gia's reason was insanity.

The hell of his childhood felt like yesterday as he stood there, staring at the lake. The sun was setting, casting an orange glow on the rippling water. The serene picture calmed his pounding heart. His racing mind slowed as jumbled thoughts fell into place. His wife was afflicted as his mother had been....

And yet, Gia was nothing like his erratic mother. Gia was dependable, rational, and sharp as a whip. Sensitive and confident, and so damn passionate he couldn't get enough of her. He snatched up a stone and flung it over the water so hard he nearly lost his footing. A splash sounded in the distance as he stumbled to catch his balance. Gia had seduced him into delusions of his own, into the fallacious belief there was something solid building between them—something more substantial than what they shared in their bed.

An avalanche of foolish hopes he hadn't known he possessed crashed down on him, burying him alive. Gia had survived a terrible trauma, which was, undoubtedly, the cause of her delusions. Her words in the wake of her nightmare screamed through his head. *I will never be right.*

His wife was broken, and he spat a loud curse, trying his damnedest to figure out what to do.

Her parents had medicated her to combat the problem. He'd ignore it. So long as she hurt no one else, he'd bury his head in denial for as long as he could. He sighed, deflated by the depressing irony of the situation.

Like father, like son.

* * * *

Gia made her way downstairs, dreading having to face Landen so soon. She'd thought about feigning a headache or some other illness to avoid the family dinner, but decided against hiding away. Instead, she'd get through the evening by appearing as though everything was fine. Landen believed she was addled, and she refused to foster that belief by looking distressed or isolating herself in her room. She'd taken great care arranging her hair and dressing in her favorite blue gown.

Confident she looked her best, she took a deep breath, then entered the parlor, where the reunion with Alex was well underway.

"Ah, here's Gianna," Clara announced to the room. She introduced Gia to Alex and Cecilia.

"It's a pleasure to meet you," Gia said to Cecilia.

"Please call me Sissy," she said with a smile that lit her stunning blue eyes. "Everyone does."

Gia turned to the handsome young man, who looked so much like Landen.

"And everyone calls me Alex." With a polite bow, Alex added, "Or Landen's kid brother."

Gia smiled, despite the tinge of sarcasm she'd heard in his words.

"It's lovely to meet you, Gianna," Sissy said. "And if you don't mind me saying so, your gown is divine." She turned to Alex. "Isn't it divine?"

Gia's cheeks heated at Alex's lengthy appraisal.

"Divine, indeed." He turned to Landen. "My heartfelt congratulations to you, Brother," he said with a wink.

Landen's lips tightened as his gaze met Gia's. Seeking shelter from the thoughts behind his cold eyes, she took a seat on the sofa. With a fluff of her skirts, she settled into the space next to Alice.

"This is such a lovely summer house," Sissy said, clearly impressed.

From the manner in which she soaked up her surroundings, gushing over the draperies and décor, Gia guessed Sissy was unused to such finery.

"On the ride here, we passed your home in Troy," Sissy said. "Is it as grand on the inside as it looks from the street?"

She posed the question to Gia, who could only shrug in return. "I'm afraid I can't answer, as I haven't yet seen it." Glancing at Landen, she was struck by the dawning possibility she never would.

Her lies had shattered any hope for a future with him. So intent was her focus on ensuring he survive the summer, she'd failed to consider the impact her actions might have beyond achieving that goal. She shook the worry away. First things first. She'd come this far to save him, and she would do what she must.

The hard lines of Landen's face softened as he turned to Sissy. "The house is quite comfortable," he assured her in a most humble tone.

"Yes, quite comfortable," Clara agreed. "Though I must admit a fond attachment to this old place." She gazed around as though collecting the memories. "Time passes so quickly," she uttered. "I can hardly believe that in a few short weeks it will be time to close this house for summer."

"I noticed during the drive that the leaves are beginning to change color already," Sissy said. "The views are so lovely."

"Is this your first trip to Misty Lake?" Gia asked.

"Yes. Until my cousin told me that Alex's family summered here, I'd never heard of it," she admitted with a sheepish smile.

"And would this cousin be the same one who escorted you to Misty Lake?"

"Yes." Sissy's smile dimmed as she considered Clara's question. "Kit promised he'd be here in time for supper," she said, glancing nervously toward the grandfather clock in the corner.

Gia smiled, hoping to ease her obvious embarrassment over her cousin's absence. "I'm sure he'll be here soon."

"I'm sure he made a few friends at the tavern," Sissy muttered.

"He'll be here," Alex said in defense of the man's inexcusable tardiness.

"When my chaperone fell ill, my cousin insisted I not cancel my trip. He volunteered to act as chaperone himself." She shrugged. "He is doing his best, but I'm afraid he's not very good at it."

"No matter," Clara said. "Tomorrow we will have your trunks delivered here, and you shall stay with us for the remainder of your visit. Your cousin too."

Sissy smiled. "That would be wonderful. Thank you."

With a nod, Clara sealed the deal, proving once again that the old woman always got what she wanted.

Florence entered the room. "Mr. Richardson has arrived."

The tall man appeared in the doorway, and Gia's breath caught in her throat. She glanced at Landen. He sat back in his chair, watching her, his lips drawn tight. She saw on his face that he'd read her reaction, but she could not hide her surprise.

Mr. Richardson entered the room, but it wasn't his dazzling smile that made her heart pound. It was the cane in his hand.

* * * *

Landen watched Gia closely. She sat, mouth agape, staring at the man. She stole a glance at Landen, looking as startled by the coincidence as he'd been. With a toss of her head, she straightened in her seat, gaining her composure as Alex made introductions.

"Please forgive my tardiness everyone," Richardson said, looking genuinely abashed. "Time got away from me." He pointed his cane toward the window. "The mesmerizing views of the lake held me captive on the hotel veranda. I've discovered a new appreciation for the soothing effects of the outdoors," he said. "No wonder so many people summer here." He glanced at Alice and then at Gia. "Although I see now that the views are picturesque indoors as well."

Landon restrained the urge to roll his eyes.

"I see we have a real charmer in our midst," Aunt Clara said. She patted the sofa cushion beside her. "Come sit here, beside me, Mr. Richardson."

The man obliged, resting his cane between his knees. "Please call me Kit," he said with a smile.

Gia smiled cordially at Kit, avoiding further eye contact with Landen. Not that he blamed her. The tension between them was already so thick he felt certain the others had noticed. She'd been so late to join them in the parlor earlier he'd begun to imagine she'd escaped through a window.

But after what had seemed like an eternity of engaging in small talk with Alex and Sissy, Gia had finally made her grand entrance. She'd breezed into the room like a gust of fresh air, stirring everyone's attention.

Even now, the sight of her, looking radiant in a blue gown, her dark hair piled high atop her head, still made Landen's head spin in confusion.

He didn't know what he'd expected after their confrontation upstairs, but he hadn't expected she'd appear so well put together. She'd carried herself through introductions with Alex and Sissy with the grace of a swan. Not so much as a ruffled feather had marred her perfect appearance and stoic demeanor.

Until the moment Kit had arrived.

Even then, she'd recovered quickly. She chatted with the group as though she hadn't a care in the world, as though she hadn't dreamed of marriage to a man who walked with a cane. As though she weren't hiding some secret lunacy beneath the pretty mask of normalcy she presented.

Her capacity for deceit angered him all over again, and he pulled his eyes from the sight of her to steady his temper.

Sissy cooed something to Alex, who cooed something in return. Landen had to admit—the pair seemed in love. To his surprise, the observation filled him with a feeling other than cynicism. He felt loss.

Would he never know what it felt like to be truly loved? He thought of Isobel, and the ridiculous feeling grew stronger. She'd claimed to love him enough to leave the man she'd been promised to, but she'd proved her true love was money. Being jilted on the eve of their wedding had shattered Landen's ego.

What Gia had done to him hurt so much more.

Landen shook off his musings and tried to focus on getting through the evening. Ever the conversationalist, Aunt Clara led the small group from one lively discussion to another, while Landen did his utmost to feign interest in anything other than the clock in the corner.

"Alex tells me you're newlyweds." Kit leaned forward on his cane, blue eyes glancing from Landen to Gia. "How did you meet?"

Landen cringed.

Clara glanced from Landen to Gia, frowning at their awkward silence. "A whirlwind romance that took them both by storm," she said with her usual resourcefulness.

"How sweetly romantic," Kit said with a grin.

"So, tell me, Kit. Why isn't a handsome young man like yourself married?"

Clara's directness never ceased to amaze Landen, but Kit's lighthearted laughter said he took no offense.

"I'm still waiting for the perfect woman."

Clara waved him off. "Then you'll be waiting forever," she said. "Besides, perfection is dull. It's the flaws that make people interesting."

Landen choked back the sick taste that rose in his mouth. Flaws, indeed...

"My last sweetheart was a beauty but had one major flaw," Kit said.

Clara's brow arched as she tilted her head. "And what was that?"

"She didn't love me." He punctuated the somber statement with a smile that was as surprising as the disclosure itself. "I found that anything but interesting."

Landen couldn't imagine revealing such personal information to a roomful of strangers. Men didn't bare their souls in public. Hell, most men were loath to bare their souls in private. Obviously, Kit Richardson was unlike most men. Despite Landen's best effort, he couldn't help admiring the man for his honesty.

Aunt Clara admired it too.

"There are plenty of fish in the sea." Clara patted Kit's knee.

"And some sharks," Kit replied.

"Those you must learn to outswim." Clara pointed her finger. "Lest you be eaten alive."

Kit laughed. "I'll not argue with that."

"No one argues with Aunt Clara," Alex chimed in.

"Then I shan't be the first to do so," Kit said with a playful bow of his head. "If only I'd had Clara's wise guidance back then," he said, playfully. "Nothing saps a man's pride like being jilted a week before his wedding."

Kit's statement hit Landen like a fist to the gut. Even Clara fell silent.

Alex lifted his brandy toward Landen. "Expect, perhaps, being jilted the night before."

Landen gaped at his brother's low blow. His clenched jaw trembled as he bridled his fury.

Gia shot to her feet. "Shall we head to the dining room?" she asked through the thunderous silence.

"By all means," Clara said as she rose. "Come along, everyone."

Gia held out her arm to Landen, cuing him to rise. Landen stood, glaring over Gia's shoulder at Alex. The regret on his brother's face was too little too late. The damage was done.

"Landen?" Gia took hold of his arm. With a gentle squeeze, she prodded him to move. Grateful for her assistance, he led her from the room. The weight of her touch on his arm calmed the anger boiling beneath his skin as they filed down the hall to the dining room.

The sound of laughter during the meal made Landen's head ache. Even the roasted pheasant didn't lift his spirit from the bog of his troubles with Gia and now Alex. And as unfair as Landen knew it was, he found Kit's mere presence at the table annoying.

The man had Aunt Clara and Gia giggling like schoolgirls throughout the meal. Even Alice seemed comfortable around him. Observing Kit keenly, Landen understood why.

Kit chatted on as though he'd known them all for years. His manner was easy, and his stories amusing. Under different circumstances, Landen might have found himself enjoying the man's company. Presently, he couldn't wait for him to leave and for this evening to be over.

Alex and Sissy mooning over each other, Alice and Aunt Clara mooning over Kit, even his own mooning over Gia, all conspired to make Landen angrier.

When dinner was finally over, cake was served. Landen's sour mood sweetened a tad as he settled back in his seat. Watching Gia devour dessert had become an evening ritual, and one he truly enjoyed. The wild abandon on her face as she savored every delectable bite, the lazy sweep of her tongue on her lips as she suckled every last taste, was erotic as hell.

Clara gave a sharp clap of her hands, snapping him back to his senses. "It's time for Denny to open his gifts," she announced.

The room quieted and all eyes settled on Landen. His misery intensified tenfold as Clara prepared to give a toast.

"Here's to Landen. And many happy returns of the day," Clara said, raising her glass.

Alice walked to the sideboard.

"Gianna's gift first," Clara advised.

Alice rolled her eyes. "Of course, Aunt Clara," she said as she searched through the collection of gifts. "Where's your gift, Gia?"

Gia blinked. "I..."

"She gave it to me last night," Landen said, hoping against hope his aunt would leave it at that.

"Well?" Clara lifted her hands. "What did she give you?"

"A medal." He downed the remainder of his brandy, craving another.

"A medal?"

"Saint Christopher." He forced himself to look at Gia, regretting it immediately. The memory of her presenting the gift, still naked and flushed from their lovemaking, stirred heat through his veins. Every kiss, every touch, every damn detail of those hours wreaked havoc on him now. She'd given him the medal to protect him from her vision. But who would protect him from her?

"The patron saint of safe travels," Clara said with a nod. "Splendid gift, Gianna."

"That's a fine wife you have, Denny." Alex smiled. "You're a lucky man."

Alex's admiration for Gia didn't surprise Landen. She had that effect on people.

"Hear, hear," Kit chimed in, raising his glass.

Kit smiled at Gia, his gaze lingering longer than a mile, and Landen seethed, wanting to snatch the cane from his hand and crack him over the head with it.

Instead, he opened his gift from Aunt Clara. A wooden shoe kit with his initials engraved in the lid. "Thank you, Aunt Clara."

Alice handed him her gift next.

He admired the thick beveled glass of his new shaving set. "It's very nice, thank you, Alice."

"Florence told me you broke yours." His sister's smile warmed him inside as she leaned in with a peck to his cheek.

Alex stepped toward Landen, then held out a box.

"Arsenic?" Landen's jab earned him a smile.

"Kit helped me procure a fine box of cigars," Alex said. He placed a hand on Landen's shoulder. Landen accepted the silent apology along with the cigars. "Thank you," he said, feeling lighter."

"Open my gift next," Sissy said. Her blue eyes gleamed in anticipation as Landen unwrapped the box. "I hope you like it," she said. "I made it myself."

Hoping he could act sufficiently appreciative, he opened the lid and peered inside. He blinked hard, his heart pounding, as he lifted the item clenched in his hand.

A red scarf.

Chapter 21

Gia stared at the scarf clenched in Landen's hands, feeling faint. Her heart pounded so wildly she could barely catch her breath. She shot to her feet. "Excuse me, please, I'm not feeling well."

She swept past Clara, disregarding the alarmed concern on her face, as she hurried from the room. Tears blurred her vision as she climbed the stairs. Her legs felt heavy as lead, each step a struggle, each moment an eternity. Landen's fate was looming closer. And he didn't believe her.

She stumbled into her room, closed the door behind her, then sagged against it. The door opened against her back, forcing her to move to allow Landen access.

He stomped into the room, slamming the door behind him. "Is this some sort of joke?" he asked, raising the scarf.

She sighed. Even now, with the proof dangling from his hand, he refused to believe what she'd told him.

"It's no joke, Landen," she said. The sight of the scarf sent her mind reeling. Panic erupted inside her, spewing chaotic thoughts she couldn't control. "We must destroy it at once." She glanced to the empty fireplace. "Yes, that's what we'll do. We'll destroy it." She spun toward the scarf, then the fireplace, trying to focus. "We must start a fire and burn it to ashes." She started toward the task, but he pulled her back.

"Calm yourself," he said, with a squeeze to her arm. "We still have company downstairs."

She sighed at the reminder, knowing he was right. She had to calm down. She had to think. "Promise me, Landen, you will burn it as soon as they leave. You will—"

"Yes. Yes, I will burn it," he assured her in a soothing tone.

She nodded, relieved. "It's happening," she uttered. "It's all happening."

Exhaling a long breath, he tossed the scarf aside. "What precisely is happening?"

"I told you," she said, unable to hide her frustration. "And now you own a red scarf."

"It's one hell of a coincidence, I'll admit," he said, sinking into a chair. "But it's just a coincidence, nothing more."

His words lacked true conviction, though, as if he'd spoken them as much for himself as for her. She had to strike now while his defenses were low. She had to convince him that her ability was real, that her visions weren't born of her madness.

"My vision is coming true, Landen. There is no coincidence. You're in danger. I saw it. As clearly as I saw Clara's illness."

His eyes widened.

"As clearly as I saw her recovery and Georgie Toomey in the root cellar. As clearly as I saw Alice dancing at the ball."

He shook his head, running a hand through his hair. He struggled, fighting against the absurdity of what he was hearing, fighting against believing it. He gazed up at her, conveying the same alarm she'd seen on her parents' faces. The same bewildered revulsion.

"What the hell are you talking about?"

She paced the room, unsure where to start. He was listening and she had to tell him everything. "It all began after the accident," she said. "I told you about Mark and Miles, and how I was pulled from the water."

He nodded.

"At first they all thought I was dead too," she said. "I was unconscious and remained in that state for eighteen hours before I woke up."

"Christ," he muttered.

"As I recovered, something strange began happening."

"What do you mean?

"I started seeing things. Pictures in my mind. At first I thought they were dreams. I was still very weak and in and out of it most of the time. I thought the episodes were my mind's way of escaping the grief of losing my brothers and the endless hours of loneliness."

"Loneliness? Where were your parents?"

"Downstairs," she said, her heart aching at the memory. "They were grieving." She brushed a stray tear from her cheek. "They had no wish to see me then—as they've no wish to see me now."

"Why?"

"Because my brothers were dead." She shrugged. "And it should have been me."

He swallowed hard, and she averted her eyes.

Shaking off his pity, she cleared her throat. "Anyway, the visions kept occurring. Small things at first, the maid burning her hand, the prediction of the evening's dessert. Things like that. Then one day I had a vision of my father's friend, Mr. Delemere, winning a large sum of money at the horse track. Two days later he visited the house, informing us of his windfall. My parents called it coincidence at first, but then even they began to realize something odd was happening." She lowered her head. "Everything changed after my vision of Prudence."

"Who's Prudence?"

"Prudence Alber. Our neighbor. I had a vision of Prudence lying dead in a field. I pleaded with my parents to warn the Albers, but they refused to listen to me." She lifted her trembling chin. "A week later, Prudence was dead."

Landen blinked.

"She was thrown from her horse and broke her neck."

He stared, speechless.

"After that, my parents called in the doctor. He prescribed laudanum for my delusions. For months I lived in a stupor. The more laudanum I took, the more I craved. That's when I knew I had to stop. But once I refused the tonics, my parents began concealing it in my food. So I stopped eating and drinking. I got so sick I feared I might die. Instead of accepting my ability, my parents threatened to have me committed to the asylum." She gazed into his eyes. "That's when I left."

"You ran away?"

"It's not truly running if no one is chasing you." She swiped the tears from her eyes. She had to get through this. "The sale of my jewelry was enough to get me to Troy. I found employment at the Female Seminary. I let down my guard and told Mrs. Amery about leaving home. She released me from my position but took pity on me, I suppose, because she gave me your card."

He stared.

"And that's when it happened. That's when I had the vision of you. I had to come here, Landen. I couldn't stand idly by and let someone else die."

He shook his head, looking lost. "I can't believe this, Gia. I won't."

"You must." She knelt beside him, grasping his hand. "Your life is in danger, Landen. Please trust me on this. If not for yourself, for your family."

* * * *

Landen felt sick as he sat there, absorbing her words. She desperately believed what she was saying. He thought of the medal she'd given him. For protection. The scope of her fear for him was overwhelming. He longed to sweep her into his arms and reassure her that all would be well, but he couldn't move. She was asking too much of him, asking him to believe her. Trust her.

"You must stay clear of Mr. Whithers," she said as she stood.

He blinked. "What has Whithers to do with this?"

"I believe he's the man who wants to kill you."

With a shake of his head, his senses returned. Anger chased off his tender emotions. Anger that he was being forced into this nightmare, anger at her accusations against Whithers, a man she barely knew. That she was now involving his business associates—that her illness or whatever the hell it was—might affect the reputation he'd worked so hard to earn, was beyond acceptable. He shot to his feet. "This is ridiculous."

"It's not."

"Gia," he said as calmly as he could manage. "You have been through a lot. Anyone who'd survived what you had would have trouble discerning fiction from reality. But you're safe now. I can help you."

"Help me?" She glared at him. "I came here to help *you*."

He held up his hand. "Please stop. Let me help you."

"You can help by helping me prove I am right about Whithers."

"I will not do that."

"Then I will do it without you. I will go see Mr. Whithers tomorrow and—"

"You will do no such thing!" He pointed his finger. "You will cease this nonsense immediately. You will stay away from Whithers, and you will stay out of my business!"

Anger flashed in her eyes. "Do you honestly still believe I am addled?"

His mother's antics ran like a sequence of dreams through his memory. The humiliation his father had suffered at the hands of her illness. Her suicide.

"I don't know what the hell to believe. But I will not allow you to destroy this family's reputation."

She stared at him, gritting her teeth.

"Do you understand what I'm telling you?"

She opened her mouth to protest, but the furious look on his face must have warned her against challenging him any further.

"Do you?" he repeated.

She glared at him, stiffening her spine. "I understand perfectly. You'd rather believe I am mad than consider the alternative." She shook her head in disgust. "Just like them."

Chapter 22

Gia sat alone on the patio, admiring Alice's beautiful garden. The sweet scent of roses and lilacs filled the fresh morning air, but even the serenity of her surroundings did little to ease her troubled mind.

She was a fool for thinking Landen might believe her. What had she hoped? That he might take her into his arms and reassure her that everything would be fine? That he might help her stop Whithers—help her save his life so they could go on to live happily ever after?

She was so furious at Landen for refusing to even consider she might not be addled, but she was angrier at herself for hoping he'd do so. Angry at having to hide her strange ability from the world. Angry she had to live every moment never knowing when a vision might strike.

But at least I'm alive. Small punishment, she supposed, for what she'd done to her brothers. Her guilt was consuming. Was this curse the tradeoff for surviving?

But then she thought about Georgie Toomey and how she'd saved the missing boy's life. Perhaps her ability was not a curse after all. If she could save Landen as she'd saved Georgie, she would deem it a gift.

To her relief, Landen had burned the scarf last night after Alex and his guests had left. Gia knew Landen had destroyed the scarf merely to placate her, but at least the damn thing was gone. She could only hope the absence of the scarf would change things.

She hadn't had another vision since the one of Mr. Whithers over a week ago. She wondered if the diminished occurrences meant anything. She glanced at the trees in the distance. Tinges of orange and red mingled with the green leaves, an insistent reminder of summer's looming demise.

She had to find out more about Mr. Whithers. Landen would be no help in exposing the man's nefarious intentions, so it was up to Gia to do so. But how could she find out more about the man without actually visiting him?

She could search Landen's office.... He was out on his morning ride, and this was as good a time as any. She hurried into the house and headed for Landen's office.

"Good morning."

Gia started, turning to find Kit in the hallway behind her. His warm smile stilled her heart for a beat.

She tensed at the unwelcome response and tried to sound nonchalant. "Good morning." She gave a nervous pat to her hair. "Are you all settled in?"

"The last trunk has been delivered to Sissy's room." He fanned his face. "Tall staircases are a challenge," he said. "Alex mentioned a patio. Would you mind showing me the way?"

Gia glanced toward Landen's office. "Of course," she said, abandoning her mission in lieu of helping the man get some much-needed fresh air. "It's right this way." She led Kit down the back hall and through the sunroom. They stepped out to the patio, and Kit plopped onto one of the wooden benches.

"Ah," he said, enjoying the breeze. "I haven't the stamina for traveling with Sissy."

Gia laughed.

"By the time my dear cousin is finished unpacking, it will be time to pack up and go." He smiled. "She brought more gowns than she could ever wear during our visit, but you females like to be prepared."

"Yes, we do," she agreed in a playful tone.

He gazed around. "Pretty flowers."

She followed his gaze to the blooming rose bushes surrounding the patio. "Alice is passionate about gardening."

"Her talent for it shows. I must compliment her on her work when she's finished helping Sissy unpack. Of course, that task may detain her until Sunday."

Gia smiled. Kit had a way of putting people at ease.

"So, where is your husband this fine morning? I didn't see him inside."

"He went riding."

"Alone?"

"Yes," she uttered, staring out at the lake.

"You don't ride, then?" he asked.

"I do. I mean, I know how." She sighed, embarrassed by her stammering attempt to evade the fact that her husband never asked her along on his morning rides.

Kit's blue eyes dimmed as they settled on the cane between his knees. "Riding is a fine sport. And one I miss very much."

With a nod, she acknowledged his loss, feeling sorry for him.

"I was quite skilled at riding. Even won a race or two," he said proudly.

"Really?"

"Oh, yes." He leaned forward on the cane. "I thrilled in the competition. The speed. But I was young." He slumped back on the bench. "And too arrogant to consider my horse might ever lose its footing." He tapped the cane to his bad leg. "Crushed my knee to pulp."

"I'm so sorry."

He shrugged. "Such is life. But we do what we must to overcome."

The words struck a chord. Kit had lost a lot too. But unlike Gia, he was not bitter or blue. He was quite the opposite, and she admired his fortitude. She liked him. The realization came with a spike of fear. Was Kit the man in her dream? She tried to deflect the disturbing thought but was soon struck by another. Had she altered her own fate by falling in love with Landen?

* * * *

Later that weekend Gia sat with Sissy, watching Alex and Kit playing croquet. After spending the morning readying the yard for the guests he'd invited, Alex insisted he and Kit take a break from their preparations with a quick competition.

Alice was busy tending to her garden, and Landen had been holed up in his study since he'd returned from his morning ride. Gia bristled at the thought his ride might have led to another visit with Charlotte.

She turned her attention to the game. Alex laughed with Kit in the good-natured humor he engaged with everyone else, except Landen. The cruel comment he'd made about Landen being jilted on the eve of his wedding still rang in her ears.

Gia couldn't shake the feeling that Alex enjoyed humiliating Landen. And she couldn't help wondering why. Alice had told Gia that Alex had a heart of pure gold. After spending only four days in his company, Gia's assessment of the man differed. While he was charming and Gia liked him well enough, something tarnished Alex's goodness when it came to his brother, something ugly and mean.

Sissy clapped, cheering Alex on as he positioned himself with the mallet. Gia smiled at the excitement on Sissy's face. Gia liked this girl. Alice did too. Even Aunt Clara could find no fault with Sissy, and that was saying something. Like Alice, Sissy was charming and sweet. But Sissy was flirtatious and confident as well. Her big blue eyes sparkled with the promise of life, and the lovely sound of her laughter was honest and warm. Alex adored her.

The way he looked at Sissy, with such admiration in his eyes, filled Gia with sorrow for her own situation. Gia couldn't imagine Alex ever looking at Sissy the way Landen looked at Gia now. Of course, Sissy would never do anything to deserve such contempt.

Gia sighed. On the night Landen had received the red scarf and refused to believe her warning, she'd been relieved he'd made no move toward her in bed. Although she was still angry and hurt, two more nights had passed and still he'd made no advances. Now the fear he might never touch her again frightened her to the core.

Kit hit an excellent shot, and Sissy clapped, prompting Gia to join. In mock humility, he bowed his appreciation of their applause, looking quite dapper in his white pants and shirt. He bent to place his cane on the ground before swinging the mallet again.

"Kit told me about his riding accident," Gia said.

"He did?"

Sissy's stunned expression made Gia feel as though she'd said something wrong.

"I'm sorry," Sissy said. "I didn't mean to sound so surprised. It's just that he's never even spoken of the accident to me. He's barely spoken of it to the family since it happened."

Gia sighed at the hurt in Sissy's eyes. "Perhaps he felt more comfortable discussing it with someone who doesn't know and love him as you do. To spare you from worrying."

Sissy shrugged. "Perhaps. But I still worry for him, just the same."

"He seems to be getting on quite well," Gia said.

"Yes, he's always been strong. Even as a boy. After his mother's abandonment, Kit cared for his father as though he were the adult." Sissy shook her head. "But the accident… It happened years ago, but it's not the injury to his leg that worries me."

Gia tilted her head. "What do you mean?"

"Kit was on his way to see his fiancée when the accident happened. By the time he'd recovered, she'd married someone else."

Gia winced. "Oh, poor Kit."

Sissy nodded. "His heart was as badly broken as his leg."

Kit's remark to Clara about his sweetheart not loving him played through Gia's head. The man had lost even more than Gia had thought.

"If something ever happened to Alex, I would wait for him forever to get well," Sissy said.

Gia nodded. "In sickness and in health," she uttered as her marriage vows echoed through her ears.

"That's what love means," Sissy said. "To me, anyway."

Gia could see that Sissy truly loved Alex. A part of her envied the purity of their love. No pretenses, no secrets, no lies.

"I hope Alex agrees," Sissy said.

Sissy usually beamed when she spoke Alex's name, and her sudden coyness made Gia curious. Sissy turned to the lawn, gazing at Alex with something other than adoration in her eyes. Something other than concern for Kit.

"Is something wrong?" Gia asked.

"May I confide in you, Gianna?"

The pleading in Sissy's eyes as she clasped Gia's hand was impossible to resist.

"We will be sisters one day, and I feel I can trust you," Sissy said.

"Yes, of course."

"Sometimes love comes in the strangest of ways. Sometimes it comes in mischievous ways. Less honorable ways."

Gia squared her shoulders against the fear Sissy had discovered the truth behind her marriage to Landen.

"Kit introduced me to Alex to secure my future," Sissy said.

Gia narrowed her eyes. "What do you mean?"

"My father made some very bad business investments. He lost everything we had, except our house. Kit had received a hefty inheritance from his late father, and he's been helping us stay afloat." She lowered her voice as though someone might hear her. "Kit thought Alex would make a good husband."

"I see."

Sissy let go of Gia's hand, her cheeks flushing with shame. "Kit wrote me one day out of the blue, telling me about Alex, and how he thought we'd make a nice match. He arranged to bring Alex along when he finally came to visit. Kit sent me the funds to buy some new gowns. He thought it best we keep my family's financial situation to ourselves. Alex listens to Kit's advice. When Kit suggested we might make a good match, Alex agreed."

"But you love Alex."

She nodded. "More than I'd ever imagined." She shrugged. "But I can't help feeling as though I've done something wrong." She fiddled with her hands. "Do you think I should tell him?"

"Yes, I do."

Sissy blinked at Gia's quick response.

"When it comes to love, trust is everything." Gia swallowed back the pain of her own disheartening failures.

Sissy considered this.

"Alex will appreciate your honesty," Gia said. "You don't want a future that starts on a lie. It will follow and haunt you forever."

Sissy nodded. "You're right of course. I will be honest with Alex and tell him the truth. I love him. And if he loves me, he will forgive me."

Gia smiled at Sissy's optimism and trust in their love.

"Kit only wants what is best for me," she said. "Alex will understand that. Besides, he'd forgive Kit of anything," she added.

Gia didn't doubt this for a moment. It was obvious Alex was impressed by Kit, and Gia suspected this bothered Landen. She also knew Landen would not be pleased by the motivation behind Kit's matchmaking.

Landen loved his siblings and was more like a father than a brother to them. Perhaps that was where Alex's resentment toward Landen came in. Landen could be domineering when it came to his family's welfare, and this couldn't be easy for Alex, a second son, trying to come into his own.

"Kit brought Alex and me together. I only hope I can someday repay the favor. He'd make a good husband, but because of his lameness, I fear he finds himself lacking."

Gia could sympathize. She and Kit had more in common than she'd realized. Perhaps Kit truly was the man she'd dreamed of marrying.

She stiffened against the foolish thought. It no longer mattered. She was married to Landen now. She loved Landen.

And because she loved him, she had to save him. A selfish reason, perhaps, but it was true. She had to save him, not to spare Alice and the rest of his family from the heartache of losing him, not even to spare Landen, but to spare herself.

She was daring to hope for a real future with him—a future without this threat looming over them. She had to live with her visions for the rest of her life—if only she could share that life with Landen, she would happily do so.

Someday he might love her, and all the pain she'd endured would be worth it. And then, perhaps, she would trust him enough to tell him the rest of her secret.

Chapter 23

Landen headed outside, wishing he hadn't agreed to the badminton match he knew he would lose to his brother. Alex had invited several of his friends to the house, no doubt to witness his victory over his older brother, and they all gathered down on the lawn. Many families from the city spent the season in Misty Lake, and Landen recognized several of the people in the distance as those who returned year after year. To his relief, the group was currently engaged in a croquet tournament.

He stood on the patio, procrastinating with his thoughts and his reluctance to face Gia. He'd spent hours reviewing Whithers' investment proposal, and although the man's business reputation seemed solid, Landen had felt compelled to delve deeper into the man's history by making a few discreet inquires in town.

Questioning the man's integrity with no proof of wrongdoing other than his wife's hysteria as the basis was risky, but the risk would be worth it to Landen if he could convince Gia her fears about the man were unfounded. Until he heard back with any news on Whithers, Landen would postpone his plans to invest in the man's venture.

A part of him felt like a fool for acting on Gia's suspicions, but reassuring her of Whithers' innocence might be the only way to put her mind at ease and end this madness once and for all.

He had no idea how to help her, and for the first time, he found himself in his father's shoes. Landen had always resented the man for the way he'd denied his mother's illness. For pretending it didn't exist. Even after her most public tantrums, his father continued to sweep her erratic behavior under the rug. He'd tried in vain to protect her, to fight the truth of her condition and the scandal that came with it. But in the end he could not protect her from herself.

Now that Landen was married, he could better understand his father's reasoning. Landen had been young and ignorant to the matters between a man and a woman. The intimacies shared within the haven of marriage, in the dark of the night, created powerful bonds. The need to protect and defend one's bedmate was just as strong.

Landen pushed thoughts of his past from his head and tried to concentrate on helping Gia. Gia had invested everything in her delusions. Christ, she'd married him because of them. She'd sacrificed her future to save a stranger. If her actions weren't so inconceivable, he might deem them commendable. Courageous.

Running a hand through his hair, he thought about that moment he'd received the scarf. For that one brief moment, he'd been frightened by the shocking coincidence. Paralyzed by the possibility Gia might be right. She'd been so damn convincing. What would happen to Alice and Alex if something were to happen to him? What would happen to Gia?

He had to keep his head and be logical. Life was full of strange coincidences. Gia was bright with a keen sense of intuition, nothing more. The trauma she'd endured had skewed her perception of reality. She'd shaped a few striking coincidences into some fantastical design and created an oracle. There had to be some way to make her realize this.

He thought about her parents. Perhaps contacting them might help. Surely, they had to be worried about their daughter. And yet they'd made no effort to find her. After the way they'd treated her, he couldn't blame her for running away and not wanting to see them again. They'd pushed her into a drug-induced stupor, then held her there to smother her illness. The mere thought of their abuse roused a white-hot anger inside him.

Landen just wanted things to go back to the way they were before his meeting with Charlotte. Before he was faced with the truth about Gia's deception, and before she told him about this delusive ability she claimed to possess. But now he knew, and now he had to deal with his marriage to a woman who believed she saw visions of the future. A woman who had upended his life and changed everything. A woman he still desired more than any before her.

He took a deep breath as he walked toward the assembly situated in the shade beneath the cluster of oaks. Gia sat in one of the several wicker chairs that had been relocated from the sunroom to the lawn for the occasion. During these outside gatherings, Alice usually took shelter inside the gazebo down by the water, but to his surprise, she'd joined Gia on the lawn. Kit lounged on a nearby chaise, entertaining the group of Alex's friends that surrounded him. After a boisterous bout of laughter, Kit rose and headed toward the mallets.

Gia pursed her lips beneath the brim of her bonnet as Landen approached. After everything she'd done, she had the audacity to be angry with him. She'd fed him a steady diet of lies from the moment they'd met, and yet she played the one who'd been wronged. He bristled at how bothered he was by her rebuff. These past nights lying in bed next to her had been torture, and he'd tossed and turned in frustration for more hours than he'd slept. Perhaps he could harness some of his pent-up energy for the game. God knew he'd need it if he were to give Alex a decent match.

He took a seat next to Gia, cursing the intoxicating scent of her.

"Anyone care for a game of croquet?" Kit asked from the lawn. "Alice and I are teaming up for a game."

Landen blinked.

"Alice, you're playing?" Gia asked, clearly as surprised as he was.

"No, I am not." Alice crossed her arms.

"Have it your way, Fair Alice," Kit called. "But be prepared. I intend to hound you all day until you relent." He waved Alice toward him. "You've already watered your flowers, so come play. I need a pretty partner to help distract the competition."

Alice blushed.

Landen frowned. "If she doesn't wish to play—"

"All right," Alice said. She shot to her feet. "I will play."

Landen and Gia gaped at each other.

"But Denny and Gia must play as well," Alice said as she breezed past them.

Landen glanced to Gia, and she shrugged her assent.

"All right," Landen said as he rose. He held his arm for Gia, and they walked across the lawn.

The game progressed, and Landen couldn't help noticing Kit's flirtations with Alice. Whether Alice noticed or not, he couldn't say.

"He's just being friendly," Gia said, as if reading his thoughts. "To help put her at ease."

Kit had his hand on the small of Alice's back as he instructed her on the proper way to hold the mallet. Landen stiffened as Kit worked his charms on his sister. Alice had been playing croquet since she was in pinafores; she scarcely needed lessons.

"Besides, Alice has eyes for someone else," Gia said.

"Yes, I know. The gardener."

"He happens to be a very nice young man," she huffed. "And he seems quite fond of your sister."

Landen scowled.

"Well, he does," Gia affirmed against his cynicism.

"So, why isn't he here? Everyone else is," Landen muttered.

"Alice told me he's working at the Westcott Estate. He'll be here later."

"Wonderful." He jutted his chin toward Alex and Sissy. "At least my brother's choice in companionship has improved," he said. "Until he gets bored."

Gia frowned. "Your brother is in love."

"With Kit?" He smiled.

She frowned at his quip but couldn't hold back a smile. God, how he'd missed that smile. The taste of those lips.

"He is in love with Sissy, and you know it." She took her turn at the mallet and missed by a mile. "And Sissy loves Alex. That's more important than other people's opinions."

"Especially mine." He bent to hit his ball, and it rolled, smacking the others from their positions.

Alice made a fine shot, and she jumped up and down. "We win!"

Gia laughed. Landen laughed too.

"That was a fine shot, Alice," Landen said. Despite his irritation at losing to Kit, Landen conceded defeat with a bow. "But we shall like a rematch."

"Yes, a rematch," Gia chimed in.

"What do you say, Kit?" Alice asked, twirling her mallet victoriously.

Her confident stance took Landen by surprise. This summer had sprouted a budding rose more beautiful than any blooming in the garden she tended, and his heart swelled with warmth.

Kit laughed. "I could not deny you if I wanted to, Fair Alice."

"Good Lord," Landen muttered.

"She's enjoying herself, Landen. She's coming out of her shell. Isn't that what you wanted?"

It seemed like a lifetime ago that he'd hired Gia to be Alice's companion. Something in Gia's eyes said she felt this way too.

He turned to watch his little sister, looking so happy, so beautiful, so much like a woman. "Yes, I suppose it is."

* * * *

"All right, no more stalling," Alex called to Landen. "Let's play badminton." He smiled, twirling the racket in his hand as Landen approached the net. "Are you ready to play?"

"I'm ready." Landen grabbed a racket, then ducked beneath the net. The sun shined in his eyes, but not enough to inhibit his vision. Alex served, and the match commenced. The game was fierce, the sun hot, and as usual, Landen was losing.

Alex taunted Landen with every shot he scored. Alex's friends cheered and applauded, growing rowdier by the competition between the brothers and the bets they'd placed on the outcome.

Alex jumped high, hitting a shot Landen was certain he'd miss. "You're looking weary, old man." Alex laughed, hamming it up for his friends.

Landen raced to the birdie coming over the net and swung hard.

There was no returning the shot that hit Alex square in the face.

"Ugh!" Alex bent forward, clasping his nose.

"Alex!" Sissy rushed toward Alex, and the others followed.

"Are you all right?" Landen asked.

Alex raised his head slowly. "You tell me." He flashed opened his palms. Blood trickled from his nose.

Landen's stomach lurched. Alex covered his nose, but it was too late. Landen froze, staring at the spatters of blood staining Alex's white shirt. Everything swam before Landen's eyes. His weight shifted beneath him. The racket slipped from his hand. He stood alone, wobbling on his feet amid the blurred commotion on the other side of the net.

His thoughts spun through the droning buzz in his ears, the weightlessness in his limbs. Alex was the injured party, but in a few short seconds, Landen would swoon like a woman in front of them all.

"Landen."

The sound of Gia's voice was a beacon through the din.

"Landen, look at me." She tugged at his arm.

He blinked hard against the lure of nothingness pulling him under.

"Landen." She grasped his shoulders, alarmed, but her voice remained calm. "Take a deep breath."

He inhaled a long breath, and she nodded, urging him on. "Good. Now focus on me. On me." Her eyes held his, and he steadied as her face came more clearly into view. "Keep breathing."

He felt himself moving as she slowly led him to a chair. He plopped down in relief.

He glanced up toward Alex, who was being ushered to the patio.

"Alex will be fine," Gia reassured him. "You just focus on breathing."

The buzz in Landen's ears faded with every breath he took, every word Gia spoke. He leaned forward, elbows on his knees. He felt the soft caress of Gia's hand, rubbing his back.

"Are you feeling better?" she asked.

He nodded, but he couldn't yet speak.

"Good." She kept rubbing his back, up and down, soft and steady.

The lightheadedness dissipated, as did his blurred vision, but he didn't move.

Gia's touch felt so good. So soothing. Conflicting emotions battled inside him. He couldn't trust her, and yet in this moment there was no one he trusted more. No one who knew him as well as she did. No one else who saw him for who he truly was.

Sitting back in the chair, he turned to face her. Her small smile of relief washed over him, drowning him in a flood of emotion. She blinked against the sunlight, gazing intently at him. It took every ounce of strength he possessed not to pull her into his arms and kiss the hell out of her.

In her sparkling eyes, he saw no traces of madness. But what he saw frightened him almost as much. All the facets of the woman she was flashed before him. He saw her compassion as she'd consoled him through the night of his aunt's illness. Her loyalty as she'd defended his sister at the garden party. Her determination as she'd led the search party to the missing Toomey boy.

He saw it all—and more—with a startling clarity that scared the hell out him. "We should go see how Alex is faring," he finally said, breaking the trance he was under.

She held his arm as he rose, concern stamped on her lovely face.

"I'm all right," he said as he eased from her grip.

She nodded, releasing him.

They headed across the lawn to the patio. Thankfully, Sissy and the others had taken Alex inside the house.

"Florence will see to Alex," Gia said with a smile. "He'll be fine."

Landen nodded as he took a seat on the patio.

"I'll get you some lemonade." She walked to the table of refreshments Florence had arranged.

His gratitude for Gia's assistance overwhelmed him. Landen would have been mortified to have fainted in front of Alex and his friends. He never would have lived it down.

He doubted anyone had noticed his earlier distress. Except Gia. Landen took care of others. No one took care of him. But when everyone else had run to help Alex, Gia had run to help Landen.

He still couldn't believe she was the same woman who claimed to see visions of the future. The same woman who'd pleaded with him to believe her delusions.

Despite every warning screaming in his head, she was the same woman he loved.

Chapter 24

Gia lay in bed, wide awake and craving something sweet. She glanced at Landen's sleeping form beside her. Truth be told, she craved something else. The warmth radiating from his bare shoulders begged her to touch him, to kiss the soft skin, trail her mouth along the muscles beneath. The pull of her yearning for him was so strong her body ached with the force of it. She missed him so much. His presence outside this room had been scarce all week, as though he were avoiding her, but now it was clear, he intended to avoid her in bed as well.

She blew out a long breath, disappointed another night would pass without making love. She'd have to settle for satisfying her sweet tooth instead.

She slipped from the bed and into her robe. Creeping through the moonlit room, she made her way to the door, then turned the knob slowly.

Once in the hall, she hurried for the stairway. The wood stairs beneath her bare feet were cold, and she wrapped her arms around her chest, surprised by how cool the house was on the lower floor. She hurried through the dim hallway, past Landen's study. She slowed. Perhaps this might be a good time to search for proof against Whithers.

Gazing inside the dark room to Landen's desk, she decided to wait for an opportunity to conduct her search in the daylight. She continued toward the kitchen. The aroma of the evening's chicken dinner lingered in the air, whetting her appetite. She opened the cupboard and grabbed the canister of cookies. Opening the jar, she smiled, relishing the smell of gingerbread.

"Good evening."

She jumped, spinning around.

Kit laughed. "I'm sorry. I didn't mean to startle you."

She exhaled, her heart still pounding. Mortified by her careless attire, she secured her robe around her. She'd forgotten there were male guests in the house, and she shuddered at the thought of what this man might think of her now. All at once she thought of Landen and what he might think if he happened upon the scene. Her pulse quickened in the sudden urge to bolt from the room.

Pushing through the awkwardness of the meeting, she said, "I was just getting a snack." She returned the canister to the cupboard, providing him with ample time to excuse himself so she could retreat back to her room.

"I was just enjoying a brandy."

He remained where he stood. Surprised by his lack of propriety, she narrowed her eyes.

He held up his glass in response. "Would you like some?"

The smell of alcohol assaulted her senses as he stepped toward her. He was drunk.

"No, thank you," she said with a shake of her head.

He seemed like a different man suddenly, not at all like the charming gentleman whose company she'd enjoyed this past week. She didn't like the inebriated Kit. She knew all too well how one could lose oneself while in the midst of a stupor, and Kit seemed clearly lost.

"Good night." She moved to pass him, but he blocked her path with his cane.

Her heart pounded as she stared down at the thing.

"Aren't you forgetting something?" he asked.

She glanced up into his bleary eyes.

He tipped his head toward the forgotten cookie on the table.

"Suddenly I'm not very hungry," she said coolly.

"You look hungry to me."

Something in the way he said it sparked her ire. "Pardon me?"

With a smile, he reached for the cookie, then held it before her.

She snatched the thing from his hand, felt it snapping to pieces as she shoved it into her pocket.

"Beautiful women like you are always hungry for something." Lowering the cane, he moved closer. "And men like me are always happy to oblige."

She gaped at him, too stunned to move.

In one swift motion, he grasped the back of her neck, pulling him toward her.

"What are—"

His lips covered her mouth, stifling her words. A cry of alarm caught in her throat, fear shot through her veins. She wrestled against him, the sickening taste of brandy, his tight grip digging painfully into the nape of her neck. He was stronger than he seemed, surprisingly steady on his feet.

She pushed him with all her might. He stumbled back against the table, his cane crashing to the floor. The sound of her slap to his cheek filled the room as she stood there, gasping for air. He rubbed his face, looking stunned before bending slowly to retrieve his cane.

Tears stung her eyes as she moved for the door.

"Pleasant dreams," he called after her as she ran from the room.

* * * *

Landen opened his eyes at the sound of the door closing. He rolled over to face Gia as she climbed into bed. "Are you all right?" he asked.

Through the shadowy light, he could see her face, her eyes shimmering in the moonlight. She breathed hard, as though she'd just run a mile.

"Yes, I am fine."

She didn't seem fine at all.

"Where were you?"

"I went downstairs for a cookie."

While her craving for a late-night treat came as no surprise, she seemed strangely out of sorts. He eyed her warily.

"Good night," she said, turning away and nestling into her pillow.

Her breathing still stounded labored, and he could feel her body trembling beneath the thin sheet. Had she had another of her nightmares? That he may have slept through her terror and left her to face her demons alone made him feel like a heel. He moved toward her. Without a word, he pressed his body against the warmth of her back.

The sound of her small sigh of pleasure filled him with joy. He kissed her neck, burying his face in the citrus smell of her hair. God, he'd missed her so much. She rolled over to face him and kissed him fiercely, almost desperately.

The taste of gingerbread invaded his senses. She plunged her tongue into his mouth, surprising him with the force of her fingers raking through his hair. She'd missed him as much as he'd missed her, and her eager response drove him wild.

He kissed her face and her throat, yanking open her robe. He kneaded her breasts. The feel of her soft flesh in his palms sent a surge of heat through his veins. He lowered his head, sucking a taut nipple into his mouth. Moaning against the luscious mound at his lips, he savored the taste of her skin on his tongue as her quick breaths of pleasure spurred him on.

Parting her legs, she cued she was ready, arching her wetness to the press of his thigh. His heart raced as she ground against his leg, writhing for more. Shifting between her legs, he drove his rock-hardness into the heat of her.

Pleasure engulfed him, seeped through his flesh to his bones. She cried out, clutching his back. Glancing into her face, he saw her eyes flutter in desire, her lips parted and uttering those beautiful sounds he'd come to live for. Sounds only he, and he alone, could inspire.

He moved faster, pumping into her body with the force of his need. He was so close to the edge of perfection, so close to falling. But he wanted her to plunge with him, needed her to cling to his body as she soared through that space where nothing else mattered and all was right with the world.

The sound of her release freed it all, sent him reeling. Through his shattering orgasm he heard her sweet moans, felt her breath on his cheek. She stared up at him, disheveled and spent and so damn beautiful he could barely breathe.

She had consumed him completely, but he no longer cared. He was hers—mind, body, and soul. Kissing her softly, he succumbed to this truth. If Gia truly was insane, so was he.

* * * *

"We get on so splendidly here, in this bed." Had she said that out loud? A flush of shame heated her face.

Landen laughed. "That is true."

He kissed her temple, and her eyes fluttered closed. The tender gesture affected her more than she could have imagined. She nestled into the crook of his arm, wanting so desperately to tell him about what Kit had done to her downstairs. The man was despicable, and Landen deserved to know the truth about the man he'd allowed under his roof.

A shiver of fear crawled up her spine at the memory of Kit's kiss. Even the gingerbread she'd forced down hadn't erased the sickening taste of brandy—of him—from her mouth. The sound of his laughter still echoed in her head. As did Landen's words.

I can't believe a word that comes from your mouth. No. She couldn't risk telling Landen about Kit. He might not believe her. Why should he after all the lies she'd told?

She'd feared he'd never touch her again, but she was back in his arms—back in the bliss of these nights she'd come to need so much. No. She'd not ruin this moment with him. She'd keep quiet about Kit. There was really no reason for Landen to know. Kit certainly wasn't about to tell anyone, and she wouldn't, either. Kit would only be here for another few days. Gia could tolerate his presence until then.

After that, she'd never have to lay eyes on the reprehensible cad again.

Chapter 25

Gia was arranging Alice's hair for the picnic at Sandy Cove when Aunt Clara swished into the room to check on their progress.

"Sissy is almost ready," Clara announced, plopping into a chair. "And the picnic hampers are packed."

"Are you certain you don't want to come with us, Gia?" Alice asked.

The hopeful look in Alice's eyes made Gia feel guilty for abandoning her. She knew Alice would be more comfortable at the picnic with Gia at her side, but Gia had other plans for her morning. She had to search Landen's study for something that might inspire a vision of Mr. Whithers. Landen had gone into the city this morning, and once the others departed, she would have the perfect opportunity. "I prefer to wait for Landen and go with him."

Alice sighed. "But what if he's detained in the city?"

"Denny left for Troy at the crack of dawn this morning," Clara reminded her. "He'll be back in plenty of time to meet us for lunch."

Clara's reasoning seemed to suffice, and Alice conceded with a nod.

"We shall see you there," Gia said with a reassuring pat to Alice's shoulder.

Alice gave a small smile, looking so pretty. She was still the shyest creature Gia had ever known, but she was also the sweetest. The possibility Kit might turn his unscrupulous attentions to Alice snaked through Gia's mind. Alice's intelligence outweighed her naivety, but she felt comfortable around Kit and thought him a friend. Gia shook off her trepidation. Aunt Clara would be there, and Gia couldn't imagine Kit would be so foolish as to try anything inappropriate with the perceptive woman nearby.

"Will Ben be joining you for the picnic?" Gia asked.

"Not today," Aunt Clara interjected. "We have only a short time left in Misty Lake, and we can't have the young man monopolizing all of her time."

"He is not monopolizing my time," Alice said.

"He most certainly is," Clara shot back. "I imagine by now even your roses are feeling neglected."

Alice huffed. "I would never neglect my flowers. I've been rising with the birds every morning to care for the garden to free up my afternoons for…visitors."

"Visitors?" Clara humphed, turning to Gia. "The girl finally peeks out from beneath her shell but sees only the gardener."

"They have a lot in common," Gia said.

"Precisely. And one Green Fingers in the family is quite enough." She tilted her head. "I am counting on you, Gianna, to act as chaperone while I'm in Saratoga tomorrow."

Alice rolled her eyes.

"Of course," Gia said.

"I wouldn't usually leave guests to their own devices, but this is the last chance Bea and I have to indulge in a soak at the Springs before the close of the season." Clara waved her arm. "Hurry along there, Gianna, the others are waiting. We must be on our way."

Gia put the finishing touches on Alice's hair, then followed them downstairs. A few excruciatingly long minutes later, Gia had the house to herself.

She hurried down the hall toward Landen's study. She had to locate something that Whithers had touched. Perhaps he'd given Landen one of his cards. Since Gia had had a vision upon touching one of Landen's cards, this seemed the most likely object on which to focus her search.

Suddenly she was stricken by the fear her ability might have deserted her. She swallowed back a surge of panic. The failure to summon a vision at the creek, despite her best efforts, came as no true surprise. Her visions appeared through objects, and yet she hadn't had a single vision in weeks.

Pushing her doubts aside, she regained her confidence as she strode to the desk. She pored through the clutter of ledgers and documents. Finding no cards or correspondence bearing Whithers' name, she directed her search to the pile of portfolios next to the inkwell on the opposite side of the desk.

Opening the portfolio on top, she scanned the contents inside. Landen would be furious at the invasion to his privacy, and she hastened her search. Like a thief, she ransacked past the risks to the pay dirt beneath. And there it was—Whithers' name listed on a document regarding a business investment or some such matter. A jolt of excitement shot through her.

Grasping the page in both hands, she took a deep breath, clearing her mind. She closed her eyes.

The feeling hit quickly, and she swelled with relief. Welcoming the familiar hum in her ears, she released herself to the consuming sensations, the dark embrace of the future and its unmerciful truth. Her heart pounded. The buzz in her ears grew louder. Clouds of darkness parted to the picture forming behind her closed eyes.

Whithers stood here, in this room, arguing with Landen. Their mouths moved with angry words she could not hear, but she felt every one. Their rage bit like teeth through her skin. With a violent swipe of his hand, Whithers cleared the desk's surface. A blizzard of papers flew through the air, and then the vision was gone.

Gia clutched at the desk for support. Her knuckles were white against the paper still trapped in her grasp. Her legs trembled. She took several deep breaths to combat the crushing wave of exhaustion.

"What are you doing in here?"

Gia spun around, leaning back on the desk for support. Landen stood in the doorway, arms crossed, feet planted, impatiently awaiting an answer.

She fought to collect herself, fought for her voice. "I didn't expect you would be back so soon."

"Obviously." His arms fell to his sides as he walked into the room. "I passed the others on their way to the cove," he said. "Is this why you didn't go with them? So you could spend the morning snooping through my study?"

"A good part of the reason, yes."

He blinked at her honest response. "And here I thought nothing you could say could surprise me." He pointed to the paper she held. "What do you have there?"

She lifted the page. "You must be careful, Landen. Mr. Whithers—"

"Is not your concern." To her surprise, Landen didn't seem angry. He merely shook his head, then eased the paper from her grip. "I will take care of Mr. Whithers." He tossed the page to the desk. "I made some inquiries in Troy," he said. "To find out more about him."

"You did?" Her voice rose with the joyous lift to her spirit.

"Yes. I wish to put an end to this matter, and I will do my best to make that happen." He tilted his head, his words soft yet stern. "If there is any chance to set things right between us, you must do the same. You've lost much in your life. I understand that. But you are safe—I am safe," he added before she could object. "You must try and get past this fear." He placed his hands on her shoulders, his touch as gentle as the look in his eyes. "Can you do that for me?"

She stared into his handsome face, knowing she would promise him anything if it meant he would look at her like this. She nodded, too moved by his tender regard to speak.

"Good." He smiled, touching his forehead to hers. "Very good." He released her. "What do you say we go for a ride?"

She blinked. "Really?"

"You can borrow Alice's horse," he said. "We can take the long way to the cove before meeting up with the others at the picnic. Since you've agreed to leave the spying to me, you have the spare time."

She smiled, so pleased by his invitation to join him on his morning ritual she was tempted to kiss him, right there where he stood. "All right."

After changing for the ride, Gia found Landen in the stable, saddling Alice's horse. Gia watched as he moved, bending to tie the cinch. His broad back and firm shoulders strained beneath his shirt as he worked. Suddenly she wanted nothing more than to touch him. Kiss him.

The pull of her attraction affected her like the onset of a vision, but in a good way. Her body felt feeble against the potent impact of her desire. Her pulse quickened. Her blood stirred with the restless need that consumed her whenever she looked at him, thought of him, dreamt of him.

"Are you ready?"

The question drew her from her reverie, and she nodded as she came down to earth.

"It's been years since I've been on a horse," she said.

"Velvet will take good care of you." He patted the horse. "Won't you, girl?"

Gia smiled at his affection for the horse. For whatever reason, Landen smiled too. All at once he looked so young and carefree. She basked in this lighthearted side of him as he led Velvet from the stable.

After helping her mount, they were on their way. The ride was lovely. The sun shone overhead as they rode side by side through the nearby field. Gia hadn't realized how much she missed riding, and she picked up the pace, smiling against the wind as they trotted along.

"Let's stop over there." Landen pointed to a tall tree atop a hill in the distance.

He hopped from his horse, then helped her dismount. She slid from the horse and into his arms and the heady scent of him. Soap and wind, and the heated flesh of a virile man. The feel of his hands on her waist rippled through her. A drift of tingles branched from her core. He led her to a large boulder beneath the tree. They sat on the flat rock in the peaceful seclusion overlooking the glistening lake in the distance.

"This is my favorite spot in Misty Lake," Landen said.

"It's lovely." She gazed at the mountains in the distance. The beautiful view seemed hauntingly familiar, but she was too consumed by the happiness of the current moment to reflect on the strange feeling.

"I will miss the country and the long summer days," he said. "Some people have already headed back to the city."

Clara had mentioned yesterday that Charlotte and Maude had left Misty Lake early. The relief Gia had felt at their departure now turned to despair. Was Landen missing Charlotte already? Had that been the purpose of his early morning trip to Troy?

"Like us, several people you've met here this summer reside in the city, so we'll reunite there," he said.

"Several people?" she asked. "Like who, for instance?"

He shrugged. "The Martins live across from us on Pawling Avenue. And the Downeys live just next door."

She couldn't help herself. "And Charlotte?" she asked. "Is her home in close proximity as well?"

He frowned. "She lives a few blocks away."

How convenient. She bristled, straightening her spine against her aching dismay.

As if reading her thoughts, he said, "I have not been unfaithful to you, Gia."

Her heart stilled. She took in the words, the firm look in his eyes, and hope spread through her veins.

"Truly?"

He nodded. "Since our very first kiss, there's been no one but you."

Her spirit soared on a gust of delight. The endearments he offered in bed were inspired by his lust. But these words… She'd never heard anything sweeter.

He was hers… She smiled, blinking back tears.

"I never thanked you for coming to my rescue yesterday," he said, changing the subject.

"You still haven't." She bumped her shoulder to his, and he smiled at her teasing.

"There's no need to thank me," she said.

"You saved me from making a fool of myself in front of my brother. Thanks are well justified." He shook his head. "Alex would have enjoyed seeing me swoon, though."

She smiled at the truth in his words. "I know." She tilted her head. "What happened between the two of you?"

He shrugged. "If only I knew. When we were younger, we got on so well. He used to look up to me, if you can believe it. All that changed after my father and step-mother died."

"But you took care of him and Alice."

"Yes. And he despises me for it." He shook his head. "He fights me on everything."

"Such as?"

"Such as everything. We fought for months before he finally agreed to go to school in Syracuse."

"Which school did he wish to attend?"

He narrowed his eyes, considering this.

"You didn't ask him?"

"There was no need. I knew Syracuse would be best for him."

She pinned him with a recriminating look she could not contain.

"I know what you're thinking, but my father entrusted me to take care of his children."

"An enormous responsibility for someone who was as young as you were."

He looked at her as though no one had ever acknowledged the fact before now. A part of her ached for him and the thankless task set upon him. The other part of her felt pride for his efforts. Alex and Alice were a handful. Gia had never been responsible for anyone but herself, and she now understood more clearly why Landen tended to be so controlling with his siblings.

"Aunt Clara offered guidance as well," he said.

"Oh, I've no doubt about that." She smiled. "But you've done a fine job with them, Landen. I'm sure your father would be proud."

"You didn't know my father," he said, turning to face her. "Expressing pride in his children was not his strongest suit." He shrugged. "But I appreciate your sentiment." He averted his eyes, staring out at the view.

"The point is you are doing your best. Alex is a grown man and will do what he's going to do."

"Yes, and all to spite me." He shook his head. "Good God, I sound like Aunt Clara," he said with a grin.

Gia laughed.

"But it's true. I can't even talk to him anymore," Landen said. "I merely asked him about Sissy's family, and he all but took my head off."

He sighed. "Alex is planning to marry this woman. I have every right to know about her family's financial standing."

"That may be a sore subject," she uttered.

"What do you mean?"

For a moment, she gauged answering. While she didn't want to break Sissy's confidence, the deep concern on Landen's face convinced her that she was doing the right thing. Besides, Sissy had probably told Alex by now. "Sissy's family has no money. Her father lost everything."

Landen's eyes widened.

"How do you know this?" he asked.

"Sissy told me. Kit has been helping them stay afloat with his inheritance."

"And I suppose Kit also arranged the meeting between Alex and Sissy?"

"Yes."

Landen nodded, looking more reflective than angry. "Does Alex know?"

She shook her head. "He didn't. But I advised Sissy to tell him at once."

He stared at her for a long moment before he gave her a nod. "Sound advice."

"Trust is everything." She fiddled with her hands on her lap. "I have learned just how important trust is between people. And how difficult it is to earn back once it's lost."

She glanced up, fearing his reaction. But instead of the skeptical frown she'd expected, his expression remained thoughtful and serene. He was, no doubt, too concerned for his brother to focus on Gia's admission, but she needed no acknowledgement. She'd needed only to say it, to let him know she was sorry for her hurtful deceptions. Despite the necessity of her actions.

"Sissy promised to tell Alex," she reassured him. "She's a good girl. I believe she truly loves him."

"And what if she doesn't? Am I to sit back and let him make a mistake?"

"What is the alternative? Demanding he break off their relationship will only push him further away."

He ran his hand through his hair, considering this. His shoulders slumped with the weight of his dilemma.

"Alex is happy. And Alice is too. Be there for them if they need you, but trust them enough to let them live their own lives."

He turned to face her. "And if I can't do that?"

"Trust should run both ways, Landen. If you refuse to accept this, you will lose them."

* * * *

After seeing Aunt Clara off to Saratoga the next morning, Landen looked forward to enjoying some more private time with Gia. He'd considered asking her along on the ride, but he hadn't the heart to wake her. The memory of her sleeping so soundly, her glimmering hair surrounding her lovely face, made him hard with arousal. Even the heated discussion he'd had with Aunt Clara on the way to the stage depot hadn't tempered his present lust for his wife. He quickened his pace up the stairs.

He stepped into their room to find Gia reading in the window seat. Her hair hung in loose waves down her shoulders. She still wore her nightclothes. His pulse jolted.

"Did Aunt Clara depart as scheduled?" Gia asked.

"Thankfully, yes."

Gia smiled.

"I saw Kit fishing down at the lake," Landen said. "Is Alex fishing as well?"

"No." Gia glanced down at the book on her lap. "He and Sissy took Alice into town."

"To see the gardener?" He tossed his coat to a chair. "Let's hope she continues her newfound enthusiasm for socializing once we return to the city," he muttered.

Gia pursed her lips at his sarcasm. "Alice will miss Ben."

"Alice will get over it."

"Despite your obvious reservations, you must admit her fondness for Ben has helped her come out of her shell."

"Yes," he said. "But seeing her these past weeks mooning over that boy makes me want to push her back into it."

Gia smiled. "You're her big brother, that's natural. But if you spent some time with the young man, you might feel differently about him. He's really very sweet."

"Sweet or not, she could have a variety of suitors in the city. She needn't settle on the first one that comes along." He shook his head. "Nor the first one Aunt Clara finds charming."

"Aunt Clara?"

He sank to the bed. The conversation with Clara in the carriage had sapped his patience, but he'd held his ground. He wanted to do right by Alice, and his aunt's plans for his sister did not feel right. "She enlightened me with her latest brilliant idea."

"What brilliant idea?"

"She wants to match Alice with Kit."

"No!"

He flinched at her reaction and the stricken look on her face. His heart sank like a rock. The last thing he wanted was to have Kit as a brother-in-law. The man was too old, too worldly for Alice, and he'd told Clara as much. Landen had had every intention of telling Gia the same—until now.

"I mean, he's not right for her," Gia said to cover her outburst. "Besides, Alice cares for Ben far too much to consider Kit."

Landen eyed her warily, doubting that was Gia's reason for her opposition. Yesterday at the picnic, he'd noticed Kit stealing glances at Gia. Landen sensed Gia had noticed it too. Throughout the day, she'd gone out of her way to avoid Kit, as though it pained her to be near him. There'd been an awkward tension between the pair that made Landen furious. And jealous as hell.

That damn dream Gia had had about the man with a cane still dogged him. Ridiculous, he knew, but true just the same.

"Is that your only objection?"

She tilted her head. "What do you mean?"

He shrugged, feigning nonchalance. "I got the impression you liked him."

"I don't like him for Alice."

Landen believed her. The question was why didn't she like him for Alice? Would having Kit in the family be a painful reminder to Gia of what she'd lost by marrying Landen? Would having the man around be too tempting for her to resist?

"Well, Aunt Clara does."

"You must talk her out of it, Landen."

"And why is that?" He feared the answer, but he pressed for it, anyway.

"Because he's not good enough for Alice."

"And the gardener is?"

"Yes. Wealth isn't everything. And I told you. Alice cares for Ben. He'd make a far better match, money or not."

"Well, Clara thinks Kit is good enough, and once she sets her mind to something—"

"You must dissuade her against him. He's not the right man for Alice, and I couldn't bear her unhappiness."

"Her unhappiness?" He couldn't help himself. "Or yours?"

"What is that supposed to mean?"

"Come now, Gia. Surely you haven't forgotten about your dream. The man who walked on a cane and all that?"

She gaped at him. "How dare you insinuate such a thing."

Fueled by his uncontrollable jealousy, the flames of his anger spiked higher. "It truly isn't so difficult."

She winced at the insult. The hurt in her eyes turned to anger. "If you care for your sister, as I do, you will not allow it."

"And why is that?"

She gritted her teeth as though biting back whatever sharp-witted response she wanted to voice. He stared at her, egging her on, daring her to tell him what he dreaded to hear.

"Give me one reason why my sister shouldn't be matched with Kit Richardson."

She took a deep breath, lifting her chin. The defiance in her stance chased the air from his lungs.

"Because the despicable man kissed me."

Chapter 26

The words stabbed through Landen like a knife. He shot to his feet, inhaling a sharp breath through the clench in his chest, his clenched teeth. "He kissed you?"

She nodded, staring into his eyes. "Yes."

His first reaction was to storm from the room, find Kit, then beat the living hell out of him. His second reaction was to grab Gia and shake the truth from her. The chance she might be lying was the only thing stopping him from heading to the door. The knife twisted in his gut. She'd told him her parents were dead—he couldn't put anything past her.

Her eyes narrowed, as though sensing his thoughts. "I've told you about my visions, Landen. And you know all about my past. I have no reason to lie."

He searched her face for the truth, his jaw trembling with anger.

"He kissed me," she said. "In your house."

"When?"

"The other night in the kitchen. He was drunk."

"And you said nothing?" He stared, incredulous, as she averted her eyes. They'd spent all day yesterday together, and all of last night. She'd had ample opportunity to mention she'd kissed another man, and yet she'd kept Landen in the dark. "Why didn't you tell me?"

She lifted her chin. "You know why."

He couldn't deny her answer. He didn't trust her, and she knew it. He'd told her enough times.

"But I am telling you the truth. The man kissed me."

The image of Gia kissing another man—especially Kit—ignited something infernal inside him. He stood helpless against the burning pain and the rage he could not tamp out. "And you let him?"

She gaped.

"Did you?"

She flinched at the accusation, shaking her head. "I did not." Indignation flamed in her eyes. "I slapped him."

He clung to the words, wanting so badly to believe them.

"I have learned to take care of myself," she said. "But I am thinking of Alice." Her voice cracked with emotion. "You mustn't let him near her. He's not who he seems."

The plea for his sister's welfare wrenched in his chest. Despite everything, he could not deny Gia's affection for Alice. And despite all Gia's previous lies, he felt himself believing her now. He was either the most gullible man on earth or the most pathetically besotted.

He was definitely the most furious. He shoved on his boots.

"What are you doing?"

Ignoring her, he charged across the room.

"Landen, wait. You need to calm down."

"The hell I do," he called over his shoulder as he stormed out the door.

* * * *

Landen charged across the lawn toward the lake, his pulse thundering at his temples so loudly he could hear little else. From a bench on the shore, Kit cast his fishing line into the water. Landen bridled the urge to toss Kit in after it.

"Richardson!"

Kit turned toward Landen. His eyes flashed wide at Landen's furious demeanor. He reached for his cane, then shoved to his feet. "Good morn—"

"Did you accost my wife?" Landen asked.

The air stilled around them, tense and thick.

Kit's expression turned deathly sullen. "Is that what she told you?"

"Answer the question."

Kit shook his head sadly. "It pains me to have to tell you this, friend, but you've got it all wrong."

"Are you denying it?" Landen took a step closer.

Kit held up a hand in surrender. "I'd had too much to drink and failed to foresee her intention. But her kiss stunned me sober. I stopped it at once."

The confirmation that this man's lips had touched Gia's churned in Landen's gut. Fury roiled like hot lava inside him, about to erupt. His body trembled. The only thing stopping him from beating Kit bloody was his lameness, and Landen sensed the bastard knew it.

"I did not reciprocate. You're my best friend's brother."

That Kit might have divulged this story to Alex—that he would disgrace Gia this way—was too infuriating to fathom.

Kit shook his head, as though reading Landen's thoughts. "Of course, I did not speak a word of it to anyone," he said. "You and your wife are newly wed. I did not wish to stir trouble." He tilted his head. "Perhaps she feared I might tell, and the clever thing turned the table on me. Or perhaps in her shame, she has distorted what occurred, even to herself, by denying her actions."

The rough edge of Landen's anger was smoothed by Kit's articulate tone. He spoke calmly, each placid word enunciating his innocence. Gia's guilt.

Landen's head spun amid his confusion. His doubts. Gia had been upset that night when she'd returned from the kitchen. She'd been trembling, and he'd attributed her distress to another of her nightmares. Had her attentions toward Landen been nothing but merely a consolation to her disappointment of Kit's rejection? Had she made love so eagerly to Landen because she couldn't have Kit?

The thought hurt too much to consider, and he balled his fists to contain his emotions.

"You're understandably angry," Kit said. "As a man who's suffered the heartache of an unfaithful woman, I know how you feel. There are unscrupulous men in this world who don't care if they compromise another man's woman. But I assure you that I am not such a man."

"And I do not know you well enough to make that determination."

"I suppose not," Kit said.

The pity in his eyes made Landen angrier.

"She is your wife, and you are duty-bound to defend her. No matter what."

The statement hit home. A man should be able to defend his wife's honor without doubting her honor. Only Kit and Gia knew what really happened between them that night. That the pair shared this secret made Landen feel sick.

Whether Kit was guilty or not simply didn't matter. The man's presence—his mere existence—roused doubts Landen could not bear. Doubts about Kit. About Gia. About Landen, himself.

Did Gia feel this same torment when she looked at Charlotte? Or was he fooling himself on that score as well?

"I suppose this unfortunate business puts an end to my welcome," Kit said.

"You suppose correctly," Landen ground out. "Now go pack your bags and get the hell out of my sight."

* * * *

Landen holed up in his study, trying to calm down. He felt so angry, so damn betrayed, he didn't know which way to turn. Love and doubt waged a battle inside him, pulling him apart.

His control over his emotions was slipping away. Or perhaps he'd ceded the reins to his stability the moment he'd laid eyes on Gia.

With every tattered fiber of his being, he wanted to believe in her. She'd wedged open a part of him, invaded a place he'd forced tightly shut with the pain of his past. A place so deep and dark and remote, he'd forgotten it was there.

And she'd filled it completely.

He'd married a woman he didn't trust, but if there was any hope for their future, he had to trust her now. He needed to. He loved her. The fact made him angrier.

The door to Landen's study flew open, and Alex stormed inside. His eyes looked wild. "What the hell did you do?"

Landen sighed in dread of this conversation.

"Kit and Sissy are packing," Alex said. "Kit told me they're leaving, and I want to know why."

"What reason did he give?" Landen asked warily.

"Some twaddle about being summoned home, but I do not believe it."

Whether Kit's discretion was out of honor or guilt, Landen hadn't a clue. The bastard was protecting himself, plain and simple. While Landen would have preferred to keep the whole sordid incident under wraps, Alex deserved to know the truth.

"Have a seat," Landen said.

Alex lifted his chin and remained where he stood. "Why are they leaving?"

"It's for the best. Trust me."

Alex narrowed his eyes. "Trust you?" He slammed his palms to the desk, leaned forward, and glared. "I am not a child."

"Then stop acting like one and sit down." Landen ground back his own anger and tried to stay calm. Their sibling discord had been brewing stronger for months, but this situation had the potential for disaster.

"What happened?" Alex demanded.

"Kit and I had a disagreement," Landen said. "Sit down," he repeated, "and I'll explain."

"There's no need to explain. I already know. You don't think Sissy is good enough for me because her family has no money."

Landen stared at him. Just once, Landen wished Alex didn't have to think the worst of his every move.

"I know Gianna told you about Sissy's financial situation," Alex said. "Just as I know you told Kit to take Sissy home."

"That's not true. This has nothing to do with Sissy."

"Why can't you let me be happy?"

The stricken look on Alex's face wrenched Landen's heart. Did Alex truly believe Landen would purposely hurt him? Memories of the boy Alex once was and the brotherly bond they had shared poured over Landen, a dose of the past that reminded him of all he had lost.

"Alex—"

"I'm sick and tired of you controlling my life. You're my brother, not my father."

With each verbal blow Alex struck, Landen's temper spiked higher. He inhaled through his nostrils to restrain his anger. "Let's discuss this—"

"No! No more discussions. I'm finished listening to you!" Alex started away.

Landen shot to his feet. "But you listen to Kit!"

"Kit is my friend," Alex said, turning to face him. "A good friend. Unlike you, he treats me like a man."

Landen stood speechless, his heart hammering. His brother, whom he loved so much, was singing the praises of Kit, the son-of-a-bitch who'd accosted Gia under his roof.

"You're a damn fool, Alex."

"And you're so damn envious you're green," Alex shot back. "You've always been envious of me for being father's favorite. Now that he's gone, you're making me pay for it."

Landen winced, shocked by what he was hearing. He'd had no idea how much his brother resented him. How little he trusted him. The disdain in Alex's eyes was so blatant, so foreign, Landen could have been looking at a stranger. Or his worst enemy.

"Well no more," Alex said. "I am finished. I'll not live my life under your thumb any longer."

"And how do you propose to live, little brother?"

Alex narrowed his eyes at the veiled threat Landen posed. "I will make do with the paltry allowance father left me, or I'll borrow from Kit. You've no control over that." He pointed his finger. "Either way, I am going to marry Sissy Richardson as soon as I finish school. And nothing you say or do is going to stop me." He lowered his hand. "Until I head back to school next week, I will stay at the hotel."

"Alex, wait!"

But Alex turned his back and stormed out the door.

Chapter 27

Dinner that evening was a dismal affair. Gia glanced at the solemn faces around the table. Only three of them remained at the house, and while Clara's absence always resulted in less chatter, other than the sound of clinking utensils as they ate, the room was unusually silent.

Alice had been surprised by Kit and Sissy's sudden departure, but when Alex had stormed from the house shortly after, there'd been no denying something was wrong.

Landen refused to speak of the argument he'd had with Alex, and his foul mood had only grown fouler at any mention of it. He had barely spoken a word since Alex left. Gia feared he blamed her for his falling out with Alex, but she couldn't truly blame him. Damn Kit Richardson for causing all this trouble.

"So, why didn't you go to Saratoga with Aunt Clara?" Landen asked Alice.

Alice started at his unexpected attempt at conversation. "I have other plans."

"Such as?"

"Ben is taking me out for a sunset boat ride, remember?"

Landen frowned. "Those plans were made with Alex and the others," he said.

"Well it's too late to cancel now." Alice poked her fork at the peas on her plate.

"You're not going alone. It's out of the question."

Alice's shattered expression was too much to bear. Gia dreaded the water, but she had to face her fear some time. "I am going with them," she said to defuse the situation.

Landen pinned Gia with a frown that made her want to shrink in her seat. "Of course you are."

She shook off the sting of his sarcasm as he turned to Alice.

"Very well. But from now on, you will inform me of any future plans with this man. He's been here every day for a week, and I'll not have you giving him the wrong idea."

Alice set down her fork. "The wrong idea?"

"We'll be going back to the city soon. There's no sense attaching yourself to a man you may never see again."

Alice gaped at him. Her wounded look turned to anger as she shot to her feet. "Excuse me, please. I must get ready."

She swished from the room in a huff, leaving Landen staring after her.

Gia shook her head at his unnecessary censure. "You're angry with Alex, and you're taking it out on Alice."

"Is it too much to ask that my wife might support me on this?"

"You're being—"

"She's spending too much time with him," he said. "And your encouragement will not make it any easier for her when she has to leave him behind."

While it was true Alice wouldn't be able to see Ben as often once she went back to the city, there was no reason they couldn't continue their courtship. "She cares very much for him, Landen."

"She deserves better."

"Because he's not wealthy?"

"Because she's my sister," he said. "She's just beginning to gain some confidence in herself. I want her to explore her options and not settle for the first man she feels comfortable with. I want her to take her time, to get to know other young men, other young men who might be better suited for her."

"You're sounding more like Aunt Clara every day," Gia muttered.

"I am nothing like Aunt Clara. I would never push her to marry the way she pushed me."

Was he referring to Gia or Isobel? At the moment it didn't matter. He seemed angry at the world, so she did her utmost to ignore his hostility.

"It's a boat ride, Landen."

"It's more than that, and you know it," he said.

After what had happened with Kit, Gia assumed Landen didn't hold much trust for any man at the moment, especially when it came to his sister. While she understood his fears for Alice, he was being unreasonable. "But I will be with them, so you needn't worry." She tilted her head. "Why not join us?"

With a frown, he considered the invitation for barely a moment, during which she knew he'd decline. "I am in no mood for boating."

"Alex will come around," she said. "Just give him some time."

Her attempt to broach the crux of his anger earned her another frown. She didn't care. The tension between her and Landen had grown tauter in the wake of this rift between the brothers. She had to find some way to fix things.

"What did you tell him about Kit?" she asked.

"I didn't get the chance to tell him anything. He believes I oppose his plan to marry Sissy because of her financial situation."

"Well, you must tell him the truth about what Kit did."

"I will not grovel at his feet and beg him to listen to me."

She saw in his eyes his anger at Alex. She saw his anger at her as well. Perhaps Gia shouldn't have told Landen about what Kit had done. But she loved Landen, and she had to be honest with him. No more secrets or lies. She also loved Alice and could not allow the sweet girl to be matched with the likes of Kit Richardson.

Besides, Alex deserved to know the truth about Kit. Sissy did too.

"Don't let your pride become another obstacle between the two of you," Gia said.

"I doubt he'd believe me, anyway. He worships Kit. He despises me."

The hurt behind his frustration was as clear as a bell. She sighed, wanting so much to console him. "I'm sure that's not true. Just go talk with him."

"No."

The man's stubbornness was infuriating. "Then I will."

"No, you will not." His face turned to steel, and she knew she had pushed him too far.

"Damn it, Gia. This is between me and my brother. You will not speak a word of it to anyone, including Alice," he said. "Understood?"

With a reluctant nod, she conceded defeat. For now, anyway.

"Go get ready for the boat ride," he said.

She stood, frowning at his dismissal as she made her way to the door.

"Gia."

She turned to face him.

"Keep a sharp eye on them."

* * * *

The surprising visit from Whithers had not gone well. Landen slumped into the chair behind his desk, his heart still pounding from the heated exchange long after Whithers' carriage had torn down the drive.

Fortunately, Gia was still out with Alice on the boat ride. She'd be more frightened than ever had she heard the argument, and he could do without having to deal with her now, while he was still processing what had occurred.

Whithers' reaction to Landen's inquiries made Landen suspicious. Instead of defending his reputation as any honest man would, Whithers had sputtered and spouted in circles before he'd resorted to warning Landen to cease his probing into his affairs at once. He'd offered nothing that might encourage a reluctant investor, nothing that might aid in his case to secure Landen's trust.

Or, perhaps, Landen had read the man wrong. God knew he was losing faith in his own judgment lately. Landen had never had so much strife with so many people—and all in the course of one day. He'd never felt such a loss of control over things.

His mind reeled to Gia. What if Whithers was innocent? What if Kit was innocent as well? Landen had sacrificed a lot in service of this woman, and he couldn't help feeling angry at her. And angry at himself if it turned out he'd been a fool to believe her.

He rose to clean up the mess Whithers had made when he'd cleared Landen's desk before Gia returned to see it.

The sound of footsteps in the hall told him he was too late. He uttered a curse as the door to the study opened. Gia froze on the threshold, mouth agape.

"Whithers was here," she uttered.

Landen narrowed his eyes, wondering how she had known. He walked through the mess of papers strewn on the floor. "He's unhappy I backed out of my deal with him. And he got wind of my inquiries. He's understandably upset."

"He threatened you."

"Yes," he answered as he stared at her.

"You must never go anywhere with him, Landen," she said. "And you must stay out of the woods and away from the creek along the estate."

"Gia, please." He held up a hand. "I haven't the stamina for any more right now. I've put my reputation in peril. I've alienated a business associate based on no proof of wrongdoing other than you have a *bad feeling* about him. Let that be enough."

She pursed her lips, looking more hurt than angered by his trivializing her concerns about Whithers.

"He's going to try to hurt you," she said.

The stark fear in her eyes stopped him cold. She was so damn worried for his safety, so damn insistent that he was in danger, he could almost believe it himself.

"I don't think so," he said honestly. "But if that is the case, I will be ready."

* * * *

The next morning Gia sat at the breakfast table alone. The visit from Whithers had left her tossing all night, as did her worries for Landen. He had assured her he would be prepared for any threats from Whithers, but the man could be more dangerous now that he knew Landen was on to him.

The knot in her stomach tightened. Gia also couldn't help worrying about her relationship with Landen. There was no denying his falling out with Alex had damaged something between her and Landen. Despite her efforts to stay positive, her heart ached with the possibility their marriage might fall apart too. He hadn't joined her in bed last night until after she'd finally fallen asleep.

Landen stepped into the room, looking tired. He took a seat, and Gia poured him some coffee.

"Where's Alice?" he asked.

Gia shrugged. "She's been getting up with the birds to tend to her garden. Perhaps she went for a walk afterward."

He nodded as Florence stepped into the room.

"Only two messages this morning, Mr. Elmsworth." She placed the tray on the table.

"Thank you, Florence."

Apprehensive about any news about Whithers, Gia watched with keen interest as Landen read the first message.

He glanced up at her, brows raised in surprise. "It seems your suspicions about Whithers were right," he said.

Her heart stilled.

"It's come to light that he's bilked several former investors. According to my solicitor, a full investigation into his dealings is currently underway." He set down the note. "I have to admit, I'm surprised." He studied her face, tilting his head. "You're a good judge of character," he said as though he could hardly believe it. "Your intuition saved a lot of people a lot of money."

She slumped back in her seat.

He eyed her warily. "I thought you'd be happy."

"I'm afraid."

"The man is finished, Gia. It's right there in black and white," he said with a tap to the page. "It's over."

Gia considered his words, wanting so much to believe them. Could it be true? The red scarf was long gone, and Whithers had been found out. Had she done it? Had she saved Landen from the fate depicted in her visions?

The possibility that the nightmare might truly be over made her heart soar. She floated on the newfound lease on life, reveling in the prospect immensely. Could they finally build a life together? A family? Or would the means to this end—all her deceit—be too much for him to overcome?

"You can rest easy now," he said, "and put your fears to rest once and for all."

Encouraged by his reassurance that all would be well, she broke into a tremulous smile.

He smiled back at her, and her heart refilled with hope for their future.

With a nod to end the matter, he proceeded to open the second message.

His face turned stark white.

"What's the matter?" she asked.

His eyes bulged as he read, and her short-lived happiness turned swiftly to fear.

"What has happened? Is it Clara?"

He shot to his feet. "It's Alice." Anger flushed his face red. "She and the gardener have eloped."

Chapter 28

Gia blinked, not believing her ears. "What?"

"Eloped." He spun from the table, stumbling into the chair behind him. With a curse, he heaved the heavy thing from his path, and it slammed to the floor.

Cringing at his violent reaction, Gia fought to stay calm. She'd sensed all along that Alice loved Ben, but she still couldn't believe she'd eloped. "Are you sure?"

"It's right here," he said, raising the page in his fist. "I knew something like this would happen." He strode toward the door, a succession of curses trailing behind him. "I'll kill that son of a—"

"Where are you going?" She shot to her feet.

"Where do you think I'm going?" he tossed over his shoulder.

"Landen, please. Let's calm down and think—"

"I don't need to think. I need to stop them."

Gia chased after him as he stormed out the door and proceeded across the lawn. He flung open the stable door. "Her horse is gone. She wrote that they were going to the city to get married."

"To Troy?"

"I don't know." He shook his head, glancing down at the page still clutched in his hand. "Maybe Troy, maybe Albany." He rambled more to himself than to her. "I have to find them."

He ran his hand through his hair, and his angry expression waned beneath the sudden shift in his features. His eyes filled with the same frantic worry he'd displayed the night Aunt Clara was ill, and they'd feared she might die.

Gia's vexation at Alice bristled under her skin. Her thoughts spun. They had no idea where Alice was heading nor when she'd left, for that matter. Alice could be married already. The dull ache of dread inside her intensified as she considered the repercussions of the elopement. Landen would never forgive the girl.

Gia had to do something. “May I see the note?” she asked, determined to summon a vision that might help locate Alice before it was too late.

“It says nothing more than what I’ve told you.” He stuffed the crumpled note into his pocket, then started toward the stalls. “Now, get out of my way.”

She scrambled from his path, watching as he set to saddling his horse.

“I’m coming with you.”

“No.” He dropped the saddle on the horse, then spun to face her. His jaw was like steel, and she flinched at the anger in his eyes. “You’ve done enough.”

His meaning was clear. He blamed her. “Landen—”

“This is your fault. All of it.” He pointed his finger, stabbing it like a knife through the air. “*You* encouraged this courtship. *You* encouraged me to trust her.” He glared at her, shaking his head as he lowered his hand. “But my biggest mistake was trusting *you*.”

Gia stared at him, stunned. In his savage expression, she saw that all they had shared, all the progress she’d thought they’d made, was for naught. Her despair turned to anger in the course of one breath. “Trusting me?” The preposterous assertion dredged up months of frustration—a lode of worthless effort and disappointment and ire. “You’ve never trusted me.”

“And rightly so,” he fired back.

His smug shot pushed her over the edge. “Yes, Landen. I have made some mistakes. We both know that. But I have been a good wife to you. I’ve tried my best to earn your trust, but I see now that’s an impossible feat.”

“Right again,” he said as he turned back to his horse.

She grit her teeth, but her fury was too much to contain. “You will never trust me, because you trust no one! Your mother and Isobel saw to that!”

She froze, startled by her own words.

His shoulders tensed as he straightened.

The air stilled. She stood in the wake of her strike, in that ominous space between lightning and thunder, and braced herself for the boom.

He turned to face her. His expression conveyed more than anger. More than accusation and blame. Bitter regret surfaced in his eyes. “Be that as it may, it was you who ruined my life. You used every trick in the book to seduce me—in and out of bed.” His nostrils flared. “You made me marry you. You made me care for you only to destroy me in return.”

“That’s not true!”

"I've lost everything because of you! My freedom, my brother, and now my sister! You're like a toxin, poisoning everything you touch!" He gnarled his lips in disgust. "No wonder your parents wanted you gone."

The piercing words cut through her, and she winced against the depth of her pain.

He averted his eyes, but it was too late. She'd seen his true feelings. Felt his utter disdain. Her heart splintered to pieces. She stood amid the ringing silence, unable to speak, unable to move.

He turned away from her, finished saddling his horse, and then tore away.

* * * *

Gia slumped to a hay bale, trembling. It was over. The finality of it all echoed through her empty soul like the memory of that first shovel-full of dirt dropping over her brothers' caskets—that unforgettable sound that scraped through the shock and denial to the dreadful realization that things would never be the same.

Another man, perhaps, might succeed in forgiving her lies, but not Landen. He'd been hurt and betrayed by the women he'd loved; he'd not allow himself to risk trusting another again. Or, then again, maybe he might have—on a woman who was worth it.

A woman like Charlotte…

But Gia had forced an end to that affair and that prospect for his happiness. The ponderous thought sunk her lower. The desire for a dose of laudanum had never felt so strong. The desperate urge to escape her inadequacies, to vanish into the sweet numbness slithered like a snake through the maze of her troubled mind.

Hating herself for her weakness, she cried into her hands, bleeding her misery, her guilt, her failures. She'd saved Landen from Whithers but at what cost? Landen lived for his family, and without them, he would shrivel away. As she would shrivel away without him….

The ache in her chest spread outward. She could barely breathe through the press of sorrow crushing her lungs. She'd given him her heart and her soul, and now she had nothing.

With an angry breath, she staved off her self-pity. She'd survived the icy water and the opiates—even her parents' rejection. If she had to, she could survive Landen's hatred as well. She straightened, wiping her eyes. Despite her stark grief, she could never regret all she'd done to save him. Because as long as she lived, she would love him. And she could not let him go.

A vision of a stranger had brought her to Misty Lake. Her promise to Pru had kept her here. She'd fulfilled her objective, and in the process, she'd fallen in love. She'd forged a new life—a home and a family. She lifted her chin. And she would fight like hell for all of it.

She had to find Alice. If only she had the note. Jumping to her feet, she collected her wits. She raced back to the garden.

Alice's watering can sat on the stone bench on the patio. Gia grabbed the thing, clutching it between her trembling hands. Her ability was at her control, and she commanded it forth with more confidence than ever before. The vision struck quickly. Alice huddled on the ground. Below her terror-filled eyes, her mouth was gagged. Her hands were tied to the wide base of a tree. The gnarled tree.

Alice hadn't eloped. She'd been kidnapped.

And Landen was riding into a trap.

Gia bit back a sob. Exposing Whithers had changed nothing. More likely, her actions had prompted it all. The instinct to open her eyes and escape the scene in her mind was strong, but she had to be stronger. For Alice and Landen. Trembling with the fear the pair would be killed as she watched, she plowed through her terror, regaining her focus.

The steady hum in her ears droned through her head. Alice whimpered and squirmed near the pair of booted feet next to her. Gia forged deeper into the morbid scene. The buzz in her head grew louder as the picture expanded toward Alice's captor. And then Gia saw him. Her shocked gasp caught in her throat. She flashed open her eyes, heart pounding. The man standing over Alice's cowering form at his feet was not Whithers.

It was Alex.

* * * *

Gia sank to the bench, panting for air. A shiver took hold of her and wouldn't let go. She hugged her arms to her body as the vision registered. Alex had kidnapped his own sister. And he was going to kill his brother.

Disbelief muddled her thoughts. How could Alex do this to the people who loved him? Why? Her thoughts whirled in a dozen directions. She fought to stay calm, to figure out what to do.

She had to get to the creek. She had no weapon, no horse, no plan. She knew only that she had to stop Alex from this madness. She dropped the watering can, then hurried into the house to the kitchen.

"Florence!"

Florence froze, dishrag in hand.

"Run to town and get help. And bring back the doctor." Gia paused to catch her breath. "If I'm not back when you return, have them search the woods along the creek."

The woman's startled eyes narrowed in question. "What's wrong?"

"Florence, please, just do as I ask. There's no time to explain. You must hurry."

With a nod of alarm, Florence moved into action.

Relieved, Gia rushed from the kitchen. She tore up the stairs to their room. Landen kept a pistol in his bureau. She pulled open the drawer and snatched up the gun. The very sight of it, the weight of it in her hand, added to the sick churning in her stomach. She swallowed hard, shoved the thing into her skirt pocket, and then raced from the room.

She hurried down the stairs, breathless as she ran out the back door.

"Gianna!"

Gia froze. A chill of fear shot through her veins. She turned to face Alex, ready to run for her life.

"I just saw Florence," he said. "What's happening? What's wrong?"

Clutching the gun in her pocket, she took a step back. "Where is Landen?" she croaked through the lump in her throat.

He narrowed his eyes. "I was about to ask you the same question."

She shook her head, gazing into the handsome face of the man Landen and Alice loved so dearly. "Why are you doing this to them?" Her voice broke on thoughts of the painful betrayal.

"What are you talking about? What's the matter with you?"

She eyed him warily, backing farther away. He looked so genuinely baffled by her questions she couldn't think straight.

"What the hell is going on?" he said. "Where's Kit?"

She blinked. "Kit?"

"He was heading this way."

"Kit?" she repeated.

"He never left town. Henry Whalen saw him this morning. On horseback."

Gia stiffened against her surprise. "I do not believe you."

"I didn't believe Henry either when he told me. I was sure he must be mistaken. I can't believe Kit let Sissy travel alone." His face tightened with anger. "But it was Kit."

"How do you know?" she asked skeptically.

"Kit was wearing the scarf Sissy made him."

Gia's stomach dropped to her feet. Blood rushed from her head. "Sissy made Kit a scarf?"

Alex nodded. "A red one," he said. "Like the one she made Landen."

Chapter 29

Landen pulled back on the reins, slowing his pace. Up ahead, a riderless horse meandered in the weeds at the side of the road. Landen squinted, honing in on the sight. Alice's horse.

He jumped from his horse and rushed toward Velvet, scanning the area for Alice.

"Good morning."

Landen spun around. He saw the red scarf first, and his every instinct screamed danger. "Kit." His pulse lurched. "What are you doing here? Where is Alice?"

"Come with me, and I'll show you," Kit said.

"What the hell is going on?" Landen charged toward him, balling his fists.

"I wouldn't." Kit flashed open his coat.

Landen halted at the sight of the gun tucked into Kit's waistband.

"You'll come peacefully," Kit said.

The bastard had Alice. Landen's heart thundered. "The hell I will." He started toward Kit again.

Kit drew the gun and aimed it. "Perhaps I should clarify." He spoke in that melodious tone Landen had come to despise. "If you hope to ever see your sister again, you will come peacefully." He tilted his head. "Of course, you can try to overpower me. Perhaps even kill me." He shrugged. "But as you're considering those options, consider this as well. Fair Alice will be dead before you ever find her."

Landen inhaled through clenched teeth. "Why are you doing this? What the hell do you want?"

"Revenge."

"Revenge?" Landen scoffed. "For tossing you out for kissing my wife?"

Kit frowned, shaking his head. "For defiling my fiancée."

Landen winced in disbelief. "Gia was your fiancée?"

"Not her, you fool. Isobel."

Landen blinked. "Isobel?" He shook his head in confusion. "You knew Isobel?"

"I was going to marry her. And you knew it."

Landen shifted his weight against the force of this news. The faceless man of his past, the man he had wronged so long ago was Kit Richardson. The inconceivable twist of fate that had forced them together stifled his breath.

"I knew no such thing," Landen said. "I knew there was another man, but I never—"

"You never cared!" Kit's outburst echoed through the trees. "You never gave a thought to the man she was promised to. The man you made look like a fool. You just took what you wanted."

Landen stared, lost for words. He had no defense. It was true. "That was a lifetime ago," he said. "And in case you've forgotten, Isobel left me as well."

"That changes nothing," Kit shot back. His sneering mouth curved into a smile. "Though I must admit your being jilted did bring me some pleasure." His smile faded. "But not nearly enough to make me forget. I can never forget." A shadow of pain crossed his face. "I live with the reminder every day of my life." He tapped the gun to his leg. "Because of you, I'm a cripple."

Landen shook his head, trying hard to comprehend.

"After I received the news that Isobel was marrying you, I took off after her." Kit steadied the audible quake in his tone. "I never made it."

And suddenly Landen understood. Gia had told him that Kit's accident occurred while on the way to see his fiancée. The gravity of this revelation struck hard.

Landen swallowed. "We were young. Isobel—"

"Was replaceable. My leg was not!" He took a long breath, reclaiming his calm. "I've waited years, but you'll soon pay for what you cost me." He smiled, awaiting Landen's reaction. "Thanks to your brother."

Landen swallowed, feeling sick. "Alex knows who you are?" he choked out.

"Your brother knows nothing. That self-absorbed brat hasn't a clue. Fortune smiled upon me when I happened to sit next to him at a card game. My plan took root that night, but I bided my time. Ten months confined to a bed taught me patience." Despite the contempt in Kit's words, his expression remained unnervingly civil. "I introduced Alex to Sissy." He shrugged. "Her family needs money—two birds with one stone." He puffed his chest proudly. "I even managed to get her chaperone ill so I could come here myself."

"This is lunacy. You're insane."

"And it will be my insane pleasure to rid the world of one more man like you. Men who lure foolish women away from the men they belong to. Selfish bastards who leave broken husbands and motherless children in their wake."

Landen's blood turned to ice. Each word made it clear that Kit's deep-seeded hatred was born of much more than what Landen had done. But there was no doubt the unstable man intended to make Landen pay for it all.

"Get on your horse."

Landen watched in surprise as Kit moved to mount Velvet. Hefting himself into the stirrup, he fumbled with his cane as he attempted to lift his lame leg over the horse. After two failed attempts, he finally managed the feat.

Despite everything, Landen couldn't help pitying the man.

As though sensing this, Kit straightened his frame in the saddle, lifting his chin to reclaim his pride. He pointed the gun, looking angrier than before.

"Get on your horse," Kit ground out.

Having no other choice, Landen complied.

"Now move," Kit ordered. "That way," he said, with a nudge of his head.

Landen turned the horse off the road. They rode into the woods, along a trail Landen hadn't known existed. His mind searched for a way to unarm the man. Did he really have Alice? Landen knew that he did. Just as he knew Kit meant to kill him today.

Just as Gia had foreseen.

Landen's heart clenched with regret. She'd been right all along. Somehow, some way, she'd known this would happen. Her visions weren't a symptom of illness or lies; they were real. Gia was not insane. She was gifted.

As unbelievable as it was, he believed it. Despite the hell of his current circumstances, a sense of relief filled his lungs. Everything Gia had done—all the lies—were to save him.

And he'd broken her heart.

He cringed against the memory of his final words to her. Why couldn't he have believed her? Trusted her? Gia had tried so desperately to help him—to gain his forgiveness. But now it was too late.

They reached the creek, and the path grew steeper. Kit remained silent behind him as they trudged the treacherous terrain. With each footfall of the horse, Landen feared he'd be shot in the back. The urge to dismount and make a run for it grew more tempting. But then he thought about Alice....

The narrow ledge above the creek widened into a small plateau surrounded by tall pines and a half-dead gnarled tree. And then Landen saw her.

"Alice!"

Landen jumped from his horse.

"Hold it right there," Kit ordered. He slid down from Velvet, stumbling to his feet.

Landen froze, heart pounding at the sight of his sister huddled on the ground. Tied to the tree, she look terrified. Tears poured from her eyes.

"Fair Alice is a brave one," Kit said. "Only agreeing to write that letter after I threatened her family. I never wanted to hurt her. She wasn't part of the plan. Seducing Gianna was." His face twisted in disgust. "But then you had to have a faithful wife. You don't deserve a faithful wife." He shook his head. "I had to adjust my plans accordingly after she told you about the kiss." He smiled. "But I must admit, it was worth it. She tasted so sweet."

Landen's fury overpowered his reason. He charged toward Kit, felt the burn in his shoulder as the shot rang out. Alice's muffled screams filled his ears. He grasped his shoulder. Blood seeped through his trembling fingers. His ears buzzed. His body swayed. Spots formed before his blurry eyes.

He struggled against the force of the darkness luring him under. He had to stay conscious. For Alice. He blinked hard. Gia's soothing words echoed through his mind. *Keep breathing and focus.*

In the midst of repeating the mantra, Landen felt the first blow. Kit struck Landen with his cane again, knocking him to the ground. The man somehow managed to maintain his footing as he kicked Landen's ribs.

Landen grappled blindly against the assault. The cane whipped through the air, striking his head. Landen yanked at Kit's leg, and Kit fell to the ground. The gun flew from his hand. Landen clung to the man, fighting to keep the gun from Kit's reach. They struggled and rolled in the dirt. Kit straddled Landen's back, driving his head into the ground, again and again. Something cinched his throat, stopping his breath. Kit was strangling him with the scarf. The red scarf.

Landen yanked at the thing, gasping for air. He couldn't go like this—in the dirt, at the hands of a madman, with Alice watching him die. He wouldn't. He fought with all his might. He fought for Alice and Alex. For Gia—the woman he loved more than he'd ever realized until now.

They wrestled, rolling over each other. Landen could no longer breathe. They were getting closer to the ledge, and he was getting closer to death. Kit would kill Alice next….

The light dimmed. He thought of Gia. Of how much he loved her. She'd known this was his fate all along. The stunning truth roused his faith in her—his trust that she would save them. He trusted her with his life, and he'd prove it now.

With the last ounce of his strength, he made one final move. He rolled hard, taking Kit with him. The image of Gia's beautiful face filled his mind. That was the last thing he saw before they hurtled over the ledge.

Chapter 30

Gia's chest heaved with exertion as she and Alex raced through the woods. Branches slapped at her face, her feet throbbed. She'd done her best to explain the situation to Alex, without mentioning her visions. Baffled by her ramblings, he'd refused to believe Kit would do anything to harm anyone, but Gia's frantic pleas for his help had convinced him to go with her. Despite her relief that he'd agreed to help find his siblings, Gia couldn't help fearing he might be a part of Kit's scheme.

She still had the gun in her pocket, and she'd use it if necessary—even on Alex—to protect Alice and Landen. The path grew steeper as they neared the plateau high above the creek.

The sound of a gunshot stopped them in their tracks. Her rioting panic escalated, dizzying her senses. As did the fear in Alex's eyes. Without a word, she drew the pistol from her pocket.

His face paled as he stared down at the gun in her hand.

"This way," she said, reorienting herself. "It's up here."

They raced up the trail to the plateau above the water. Only the sound of the birds filled the eerie silence around them. Gia shivered against the prickle of dread that ran down her spine. The sound of a snapped twig made her jump. Alice's horse peeked its head through the tall brush. Gia glanced to the gnarled tree, and the sudden sound of whimpers behind it.

"Alice!"

The girl's muffled cry tore at Gia's heart.

"Oh my God." Alex raced toward his sister, and Gia saw in his horrified reaction he had no involvement in Kit's plan.

Her relief was confirmed as he stood over Alice, as he had in Gia's vision, before he sprang into action. Alice's muffled cries became more frantic as he fumbled to unknot the long rope binding her wrists and ankles. He cursed aloud, his hands trembling as Gia moved to loosen the gag over Alice's mouth.

"They fell!" Alice pointed, chest heaving. "He shot Denny, and they fell over the ledge!"

Gia's heart thumped madly. She ran toward the ledge. Her heart stopped. She took in the sight—her vision come true. Landen lay deathly still in the shallow water below, a red scarf floating around him.

"Landen!"

It took only one glance at Kit's broken body sprawled atop a large boulder on the rocky shore to know he was dead. She bit back the sick taste in her mouth.

"Why? Why would Kit do this?" Alex called out.

Staring at Landen's still body, she feared they might never know. She swallowed hard, focusing on getting to Landen. She scrambled to climb down the steep embankment, clinging to rocks and bushes as she moved. Her skirts snagged and tangled as she struggled to lower herself. Alex appeared suddenly at her side, skidding past her in his haste to get to his brother. He directed her descent from below her, forging their path over the jutting rocks. He jumped to safety at the shore, then helped Gia down.

They waded into the shallow water, then turned Landen to his back. A deep gash on his forehead bloodied his pale face, and his lips were an alarming shade of blue. They dragged Landen from the water and up to the shore.

Gia knelt next to him, tears pouring down her face as Alex uncoiled the scarf from Landen's neck, then tore open his shirt. The medal Gia had given Landen winked in the sunlight as Alex pressed his ear to Landen's chest.

"He's alive," he said.

Gia's heart lifted. The blood seeping from Landen's shoulder quickly squelched her relief.

Alex gazed up the embankment. "We'll never get him up there." He glanced down the shoreline and then back up the embankment. "Alice! Toss down the rope!"

Alice did as directed.

Alex worked to uncoil the long rope, shouting to Alice again. "Get the horse and meet us down stream!" He hesitated, rope in hand, staring up at his sister. "Can you do that?"

With a frantic nod, Alice disappeared from sight.

"Let's get him back in the water," Alex said.

"In the water? But why?"

"We'll be able to move him easier that way. We'll use the current to float him along."

With a nod, Gia drew a deep breath for the challenge ahead as Alex worked and knotted the rope. Together they struggled to drag Landen back into the water. Fashioning the rope like a sling beneath Landen's torso, they each took a side as they guided him carefully on the current. The distance from the steep creek bank to level terrain seemed endless as they floated Landen along. Bedrock underfoot hindered their pace. Gia's sopped skirts grew heavier with each step as they waded with the force of the current.

Sweat beaded on her brow, trickling into her eyes, and her throat was so parched she could barely force air into her lungs. Landen was alive. She had to keep him that way, and the urge to save him gave her the strength to push onward.

"I'm here!" Alice waved on the shore up ahead.

The girl had made surprisingly good time, and Gia couldn't help being impressed. And grateful.

They grunted against Landen's weight as they dragged him to shore. Alex took a deep breath, clearly exhausted. "I'll need you both to help me get him up on the horse," he said. "But first we have to stop the bleeding."

Gia tore a piece of dry fabric from the tattered hem of Alice's skirts. Alex took the long strip, then tore it in half. He packed a wadded piece against the wound, then tied it in place with the other.

Landen moaned, and his eyes fluttered open.

"Gia." A quivering smile touched his lips. "You found us."

"Shh. It's all right, my darling." She smoothed back his wet hair.

"Alice?"

"She is fine," Gia said. "Alex is here too."

"We're all fine, Brother," Alex said, securing the dressing. "Just hold on, and let us take care of you for a change." Alex's voice clogged with emotion, and Gia realized suddenly how much Alex truly loved his brother. Alex squeezed Landen's hand. "We're taking you home."

* * * *

The trek back to the house took forever. Gia led the horse through the woods as quickly as she could with Landen slumped against Alex's chest to keep him mounted as they moved. When they finally reached the edge of the woods, Florence and a group of people hurried toward them.

"He's bleeding badly! He's been shot," Gia cried. Tears streamed down her face as all the pent-up emotion and fear spewed forth.

The men carefully pulled Landen from the horse, then carried him across the lawn toward the house.

Alice flew into Florence's arms, hugging her tight. The girl had been through quite an ordeal. She was stronger than Gia had ever realized, and she loved her all the more for her surprising inner strength.

"Where's Doctor Reed?" Gia cried, searching the faces around her.

"He is away. I am Doctor Merrick, Mrs. Elmsworth. I'm filling in for Doctor Reed this week."

Gia nodded as the doctor hurried after the men. A young woman appeared at Gia's side and took her by the arm. "I am Madeline," she said. "Doctor Merrick's wife." She inspected the scratches and cuts on Gia's face. "Are you hurt?"

Gia shook her head. "No, I am fine."

"Come on, let's see to your husband."

Gia let Madeline lead her into the house while Florence attended to Alice.

"He fell over the cliff," Gia murmured. "He's been shot."

"Don't worry," Madeline said. "We'll take good care of him. I promise."

Gia followed as the men carried Landen upstairs to their room. She sidled her way to the bed. Brushing back the wet hair clinging to his face, she leaned to whisper in his ear. "Please don't leave me."

She clutched his cold hand. Closing her eyes, she hoped for a vision of his recovery, like the one she'd had of Clara that night, but nothing appeared. The frightening possibility he might die, here in their bed, chased the breath from her lungs.

Doctor Merrick ordered the men from the room, then placed his hands on Gia's shoulders. "Let me tend to him now," he said softly.

"I can help," Gia uttered, though she wasn't sure how.

"My wife will help me." He turned to Madeline and gave a firm nod. "She knows what to do."

Madeline peeled off her gloves, then tossed them aside. She took Gia's hands firmly in hers and gave them a squeeze. "Wait downstairs," she said gently. "Let us care for him."

The vision struck quickly. Madeline leaned over Landen's still form, her eyes closed in a trance, her palms pressed to the bleeding wound on his shoulder. The flow of blood oozing between her fingers slowed beneath her small hands and then stopped completely.

Gia gasped in surprise, opening her eyes. Blinking back her amazement, she eased from the woman's tight grip on her hands, blinking again.

"Are you all right?" Madeline's eyes filled with concern.

Gia stared into her pretty face, too stunned to speak.

"Please bring her downstairs," Madeline instructed Alex. "And get her something to drink."

Gia moved in a daze, in a maelstrom of bewilderment at what she had seen. She glanced back at Madeline as Alex led her from the room. The sound of the door closing firmly behind them echoed through the din in the hall. Alex took Gia's arm, and they joined the others as they filed downstairs.

Gia sat in the parlor with Alex and Alice, the low chatter of the crowd outside wafting in from the open windows. Despite what she'd seen Madeline do in the vision, her mind reeled with fears for Landen, and everything else that had transpired today—these past months.

She wiped at her misty eyes, remembering everything. The first time she'd set eyes on Landen, their first kiss. The first time he'd made love to her. How she longed to be in his strong arms again, hear the sound of his laughter.

A long hour later, Madeline stepped into the parlor. "Your husband wishes to see you, Mrs. Elmsworth."

Gia sprang to her feet.

"He's lost a lot of blood, and his ankle is badly sprained, but he will be fine."

Gia smiled. She hugged Madeline with all the relief flooding inside her. "Thank you," she uttered against her hair. "Thank you for saving him."

Madeline drew away. "You can thank my husband—"

"No," Gia said, shaking her head. "It was you." She clasped Madeline's hands and gave a firm nod. "It was you."

The woman's dark eyes flashed wide. Her defensive look softened into a look of perplexity. "But how… How could you know—"

"It doesn't matter right now," Gia said with a smile.

Madeline tilted her head, studying Gia. After several long moments, a tremulous smile touched her lips. "Perhaps the two of us should have tea sometime," she said. "I've a feeling we may have a few things in common."

Gia nodded. "As do I." Gia hugged her again before hurrying up the stairs to see Landen.

She raced into the room. Landen lay in bed, his ankle set in a splint and raised on a pile of pillows. His bandaged shoulder hung in a sling.

"Kit is dead," he said bluntly.

Gia nodded. "Yes."

Landen averted his eyes. "He was Isobel's fiancé," he said. "Before I stole her away."

Gia gaped, stunned by the news.

"All these years he's been waiting to take his revenge…." He turned back to Gia. "I'm so sorry for the things I said to you, Gia."

She shook her head and tears rolled down her cheeks.

"I'm so sorry," he repeated.

"It's all right." She grasped his hand, and his warm flesh spurred a sigh of relief. "You're all right."

"Because of you," he uttered. His eyes filled with sorrow. "Alice and I would have died out there. But you knew where we were. The red scarf. You knew all along."

She nodded.

"I should have believed you," he said. "I should have trusted you." He straightened in the bed, grimacing at the effort. "You were telling me the truth. You really came to Misty Lake to save me. A complete stranger," he said as though he still couldn't believe it.

She nodded again.

"Why?"

"Prudence," she uttered. "I didn't fight to save her." She gazed into his face. "I had to fight to save you."

"And you did." He smiled. "As I knew you would."

She tamped back her elation. Suppressed the joy bubbling inside. She'd told him about her visions, and he believed her now. But if there was to be a future with him, she had to tell him everything. "There is something else you should know."

His brows rose above humor-filled eyes. "There is more?"

He tilted his head at her solemn nod as she summoned her courage. "My brothers…" She'd never spoken of it aloud; she'd barely let herself think of it. The pain and guilt hurt too much. The fear of confessing the horrible truth right now—to the man she loved—of risking any hope for their future, threatened to swallow her whole. She stared into his handsome face through her teary eyes. "The accident was my fault."

He winced, narrowing his eyes.

"We were in town and heading home. I'd arranged to meet someone that night. A beau," she said. "And I was late. It was my idea to cross the frozen pond to make better time. I insisted. It was my birthday, you see, and they had to oblige." She lowered her head. "My brothers died because of me. Because of my selfishness."

"Oh, Gia." He shook his head, looking stricken. "It was an accident. A terrible accident. And you are anything but selfish. You proved that to me a dozen times over. In a dozen different ways."

She wiped at her eyes.

"We've all done things we regret. Things we'd give anything to undo. But we have to forgive ourselves and move onward." He shrugged. "Because that's all we can do."

Landen's sorrow for his part in Kit's plight shined in his eyes. Gia swallowed hard, absorbing his comforting words.

"No one knows why things happen as they do," he said. "But we must trust that there's a reason." He lifted her chin. "Trust is everything."

He smiled at the use of her own words to him, and in that moment, she loved him more.

"You survived that accident for a reason," he said. "And whatever that reason, it brought you to me."

"A vision brought me to you," she reminded him. "You are married to a woman who has visions. Unexplainable, inconvenient visions that can strike any time."

"Life with you will never be dull." He smiled again. "And I'd have it no other way. Your visions—this gift—is a part of you. A part of the compassionate, beautiful, enticingly sensual woman that makes you who you are." His voice quaked with emotion as he squeezed her hand between his. "And I love all of you."

She smiled through her blinding tears. She couldn't remember the last time she'd felt loved. But she felt his love now as clearly as she felt the firm hold on her hand. Her heart swelled to overflowing. "I love you too."

He smiled, looking relieved. "I did not make it easy."

She laughed. "No, you didn't, my darling." She pressed a kiss to his lips. "But then again, neither did I."

Epilogue

Two weeks later

Gia nestled closer to Landen in the wagon as they rode through the field. The sun hung low in the cloudless sky, but the brisk nip in the air reminded her that summer was over. Shades of yellow and orange tinged the leaves of the trees along their route. The summer residents had returned to their homes in the city, leaving a peaceful quietness in their wake.

With Landen's blessing, Ben had escorted Alice and Clara back to Troy. The young couple would continue their courtship, and Gia couldn't be happier for them. Even Landen had defended the young man to Aunt Clara, who wasn't quite so in favor of the idea.

Alex had left immediately after that horrible day at the creek to inform Sissy of Kit's death. Hearing the details had been difficult, but according to the letter they'd received from Alex yesterday, Sissy was doing her best to manage her grief, and Alex was doing his best to console her. As expected, Sissy had been stunned by Kit's crimes. But he'd brought Alex and Sissy together, and for that, the couple would always be grateful.

Gia had much to be grateful for as well. She loved Landen and her new family to pieces. And they loved her in return. Her mind drifted to her parents. Perhaps, someday, she might reunite with them. She'd forgiven them, as she'd forgiven herself, for what happened in Boston. But their lack of effort to find her made clear they'd found peace in letting her go.

Pushing the sad thought from her mind, she nestled closer to Landen. They'd decided to spend a few extra weeks in Misty Lake and were using the privacy of the house to celebrate their belated honeymoon. Although Gia missed the rest of the family, she welcomed the serenity of being alone with Landen and had enjoyed the past week immensely.

She'd had only one single vision since the ordeal. She smiled, touching her stomach. She looked forward to telling Landen about that wonderful vision tonight.

Landen stopped the wagon at his favorite spot on the hill overlooking Misty Lake, and Gia helped him down from the wagon. His ankle was healing nicely, but it would take some time before he could walk unassisted.

They stood, gazing out over the sparkling lake and the sun setting behind the mountains in the distance. Once again, the lovely view felt hauntingly familiar. Landen had taken her here before, on the day he told her there'd been no one but her since the first time he'd kissed her.

Landen took her hand in his. She stared down at their interlaced fingers and something sparked in her memory. She'd lived this moment before.

"It wasn't a dream," she uttered, warmth spreading inside her. She glanced up into Landen's question-filled eyes. "This place. You." She glanced down at their hands. "It wasn't a dream."

A slow smile curled his lips as her words registered. "It was a vision."

She nodded. "A wonderful vision that foretold I would stand here one day, overlooking a lake and feeling so happy."

He clasped her hand tightly, blue eyes shimmering as he spoke. "With a man who truly loves you—and leans on a cane."

THE END

Meet the Author

A three-time RWA Golden Heart® nominee, **Thomasine Rappold** writes historical romance and historical romance with paranormal elements. She lives with her husband in the small town in upstate New York that inspired her current series. When she's not spinning tales of passion and angst, she enjoys spending time with her family, fishing on one of the nearby lakes, and basking on the beach in Cape Cod. Thomasine is a member of Romance Writers of America and the Capital Region Romance Writers. Readers can find her on Facebook and follow her on Twitter: @ThomRappold.

Keep reading for an excerpt from the first book in the Sole Survivor series

The Lady Who Lived Again

Madeline Sutter was once the belle of the ball at the popular resort town of Misty Lake, New York. But as the sole survivor of the community's worst tragedy, she's come under suspicion. Longing for the life she once enjoyed, she accepts a rare social invitation to the event of the season. Now she will be able to show everyone she's the same woman they'd always admired—with just one hidden exception: she awoke from the accident with the ability to heal.

Doctor Jace Merrick has fled the failures and futility of city life to start anew in rural Misty Lake. A man of science, he rejects the superstitious chatter surrounding Maddie and finds himself drawn to her confidence and beauty. And when she seduces him into a sham engagement, he agrees to be her ticket back into society, if she supports his new practice—and reveals the details of her remarkable recovery. But when his patients begin to heal miraculously, Jace may have to abandon logic, accept the inexplicable—and surrender to a love beyond reason…

Chapter 1

Misty Lake, New York, 1882

Everyone wished she had died with the others. Maddie Sutter had accepted this truth long ago. But much to the small town's dismay, she insisted on living and breathing despite it.

Straightening her shoulders, she lifted her chin against the barrage of eyes watching her every move as she forged down Main Street. After three years of suffering this unwelcome attention each time she ventured to town, one would think she'd have grown used to the assault.

Maddie had resigned herself to many things since the accident, but she'd never adapt to the dread her presence induced in those she had known all her life—those who had once loved and cared for her.

With a fortifying breath, she approached a cluster of young boys on the corner. The same wretched imps had greeted her earlier when they'd spied her arrival in downtown Misty Lake. She braced herself for a repeat performance of the cruel rhyme they'd composed in her honor.

"Four dead girls on the slab, on the twelfth day of May. On Friday the thirteenth, one girl walked away."

Refusing to alter her course, Maddie strode straight toward them. Her lungs swelled with triumph as the alarmed little brats scattered like mice. With another fractional lift of her chin, she swept onward and rounded the corner.

She entered the general mercantile, the jingling bell on the door her only greeting as she stepped inside. Along with a handful of patrons, the store housed a hodgepodge of scents. Aromas of charcoal and beeswax mingled with the sweet smell of cinnamon and apples. Renewed by the boon to her senses, she enjoyed the whiff of fond memories that came with it. She shopped quickly, spurred on by the hushed whispers echoing through the aisles as she browsed the shelves.

Gathering a bag of sugar, a tin of baking powder, and the other items on her list, she headed to the front of the store, then placed them on the polished counter.

"Good morning, Mr. Piedmont," she said with a smile.

He wiped his hands on his bibbed apron and took a step forward.

"Madeline."

With a curt nod, he lowered his somber eyes to the items on the counter and began to tally her purchases.

Maddie's smile faded, her mind drifting back to the days when Mr. Piedmont's face would light up to see her and her friends bounding into the mercantile. The Fair Five, as they were known back then, had charmed everyone. The girls had hardly put away their pinafores when they first learned to use their collective wit and beauty to full advantage. The Five always left Mr. Piedmont's store lapping at complimentary peppermint sticks, pressed upon them by the kindly merchant with a playful wink.

Maddie took a deep breath, forcing away thoughts of the past and the accident that had snatched her friends from this world. At twenty-four-years old, Maddie was a living reminder and the sole survivor of the worst tragedy in Misty Lake's history. People could barely stand to look at her. And Maddie couldn't blame them. She could barely stand to look at herself.

Mr. Piedmont worked swiftly, the sound of crumpling paper filling the awkward silence as he wrapped her purchases and bound the tidy parcel with string. By rote, his freckled hand reached to the nearby jar of candy. Placing a single peppermint stick on top of the bundle, he slid it toward her, then turned to face the shelves lining the wall behind him.

Tears blurred Maddie's vision as she stared down at the red-striped treat, the simple reminder of who she once was—who she still was, if only one of her neighbors could manage to look her in the eye long enough to see it. She swallowed hard.

"Thank you," she murmured to the shopkeeper's back before he walked away.

Maddie left the store and proceeded to her final errand. As she'd anticipated, a letter from Amelia awaited her at the post office. Maddie would wait until later to open it. Their recent correspondence had rattled her to the bone, and she knew any public display of emotion would be ripe fruit for hungry local gossips.

Not that maintaining decorum could help her cause now. People already believed the worst about her. These rare trips to town only served to remind her that nothing had changed.

Shoving the letter into her skirt pocket, she headed south on Main Street. To her relief, the band of young hooligans that had taunted her earlier was nowhere to be seen. She hurried out of town nonetheless. Each dreaded trip was a tax on her nerves, and when added to the anxiety of what awaited in Amelia's letter, Maddie yearned for the comfort of home.

When she reached the outskirts of town, she took the path through the woods that opened to a large field. She welcomed the sound of chirping crickets and birds. As always after she exerted herself with a lengthy walk, her leg was beginning to ache. She slowed her pace, then stopped to rest at her favorite spot on her grandfather's sprawling property. Sitting on a felled birch log in the broad clearing, she stretched out her leg. The cramped muscles unfurled as she enjoyed the serenity of the surrounding forest, the gentle spring breeze through the swaying trees. The sun felt heavenly, and she lifted her face to bask in its glow.

She'd avoided town all winter, hibernating like a bear in a cave. She'd emerged from seclusion renewed by foolish hopes, but the first outing of the new season had been just like the last. A bear would be better received.

Maddie sighed in defeat, dug out the letter that was fairly vibrating in her pocket, and unfolded its pages. The bold strokes on the delicate cream sheets conveyed Amelia's confident tone and dramatic style.

My dearest Mads,

I received your response denying my request, but I refuse to take no for an answer. I simply cannot get married without you!

You swore an oath to one day serve as my bridesmaid, and it is time for you to honor it. My deep love and concern for you force me to hold you to your promise.

The past is the past, my dear friend, and you must lay it to rest. Eventually, the town will follow suit. Consider attending my wedding as your first step toward getting on with your life.

We arrive in Misty Lake in three weeks. I look forward to seeing you then.

Forever yours,

Amelia

Maddie's breakfast turned in her stomach. How on earth could she attend? No one, save Amelia, wanted her there. Certainly not Daniel. The mere thought of facing her former fiancé and all the others who'd blamed and abandoned her…no. Maddie hadn't the courage. Amelia didn't understand. How could she? She was not present when it happened. Nor was she here for the aftermath.

Something rustled in the woods across the field. Squinting against the sun, Maddie scanned the trees. A deer hobbled into the clearing, took one final step, then collapsed to the ground. Maddie gasped at the arrow protruding from its shoulder.

Without a thought, she ran to the deer and dropped to her knees at its side. Blood flowed, a crimson stream from the gaping hole around the arrow. The trembling doe stared up at her, eyes wide with pain and terror.

Maddie glanced around to ensure she was alone. The arrow was a direct hit to the vitals, and the poor creature couldn't have traveled far. Someone might be tracking it. Glancing into the deer's desperate eyes again, Maddie tossed caution to the wind.

She grasped the arrow, clenching it as hard as she could. The blasted thing was in deep. Mustering her strength, she pulled, grunting as the arrow ripped through the torn muscle and flesh in which it was lodged. She fell backward, arrow in hand. Blood gushed everywhere. Tossing aside the arrow, she leaned over the deer and pressed her hands to the wound. Blood oozed between her fingers. Life drained from the deer, the warm flow filling her nose with the acrid scent of looming death.

She squeezed her eyes shut, swallowing against the bile rising in her throat. Behind her closed lids, pictures flashed in the darkness. The wagon careening out of control. The approaching tree. The bodies hurling through the air. Sounds of terrified screams filled her ears. Tears poured down her face as she opened her soul. All the pain, all the guilt, manifested inside her, raging through her veins. Heat radiated to her hands, transferring everything onto the dying deer.

Her hands grew hotter and hotter. Her heart pounded and she could barely breathe. She opened her eyes, watching through her scalding fingers as the stream of blood slowed and the torn hide around the wound began to close. The deer stirred, and Maddie sat back on her haunches, panting for air.

The deer sprang to its hooves. Its wide eyes met hers before it darted across the field, white tail raised like a flag as it hurdled the birch log, then disappeared into the forest. Maddie exhaled a shaky breath. The thrum of her pulse waned in relief. Once again, she felt worthy, if only for a moment, of surviving when no one else had.

She'd awakened after the accident with the ability to heal, and the absolution implied by this power helped her cling to her sanity. The mysterious gift was her only justification for living now, a token she'd smuggled back from some place between heaven and earth. One she had to keep hidden if she hoped ever to regain any semblance of a normal life.

"Hey, there!"

Maddie spun toward the voice in the trees. A man charged into the clearing, a large bow in his hands. With a curse, she pushed to her feet and turned her back to him as she gathered her wits. Wringing her bloody hands furiously between the folds of her beige skirt, she fought for composure, concocting her lies.

She inhaled a sharp breath and turned to face him. He stopped, startled by the sight of her. "Are you all right?" He rushed toward her. "Did it hurt you?"

"I'm fine," she said, backing away from the tall stranger.

He glanced down at the pool of bright blood at his boots, then looked around for the deer. "What the devil happened? Where is it?"

Maddie pointed toward the trees. "It ran into the woods."

"It's still running?" His blue eyes narrowed. "Impossible. I struck a kill shot."

"Unfortunately for the deer, your aim was not so precise." She gauged his wary reaction. "Nor is your eyesight if you thought you struck the vitals," she added, pinning her lies firmly in place with an angry nod. "Your clumsy shot to the gut will prolong the poor animal's misery. I dislodged the arrow to lessen its suffering."

His brows shot up. "You dislodged… Are you addled?" He stared in disbelief. "What possessed you—?"

"Senseless torment possessed me," she shot back. "And I assure you, my mind is quite sound."

The man was not convinced. Lowering his chin, he yanked off his hat and scratched his dark head. "I could have sworn I hit the…" Tousled black hair gleamed in the sunlight as he bent for the arrow. "You dislodged it, you say?"

He analyzed the bloody hair on the arrow, clearly distracted. She could see the questions forming in his bewildered eyes. She had to get rid of him.

"Your deer bolted, but it won't get far." She gave a nod toward the trees. "You should hurry."

Ignoring her suggestion, he took a step forward. "What's your name?" He dropped the arrow, his gaze fixing on her bloody hands. Reaching into his coat, he pulled out a handkerchief. He grabbed her wrist and attempted to wipe at the blood.

Maddie yanked back her hand. "My name is Madeline Sutter, and I can do that myself."

With a frown, he relinquished the cloth and let her proceed with the task.

"I'm Jace Merrick, Miss Sutter. I've taken over Doctor Filmore's practice in town now that he's retired."

The news surprised her. Doctor Filmore was eighty years old, if he was a day, and she'd always assumed he would die wearing his stethoscope. She was equally surprised by the youthful mien of Filmore's replacement. And by this new physician's obvious appetite for hunting. Weren't doctors supposed to be devoted to preserving life? Not that Doctor Filmore had gone out of his way to preserve hers. He'd pronounced her dead for God's sake. She slapped the cloth between her palms.

"It's about time that old fool retired," she muttered.

Pushing her disdain for the elderly doctor aside, she focused on the man before her. Jace Merrick possessed a palpable confidence, but dressed as he was, he didn't look like a doctor. His brown trousers were tucked into large boots, and a green flannel shirt peeked out from his open tweed coat.

And yet, even in his casual hunter's uniform, the man was impressive. The words ruggedly appealing sprang to mind. He stood taller than most, surely taller than Daniel. Doctor Merrick's build was broader than Daniel's as well. A twinge of longing fluttered in the pit of her belly.

The queer sensation took Maddie aback. She straightened her spine, steeling herself against her attraction to the handsome stranger. As she knew only too well, a man in the medical profession could destroy her. The doctor's stern voice snapped Maddie out of her reverie.

"Wild animals can be dangerous, Miss Sutter. Especially when they're wounded. You were fortunate in this instance, but I'd advise you against taking such risks in the future."

"I appreciate your advice, Doctor Merrick, and I have some for you." She took a step toward him. "There is no hunting allowed on Sutter land, so please do your murdering elsewhere." She finished wiping her hands, then handed him back the bloodstained handkerchief. "Now take your belongings and get off my property."

* * * *

Jace blinked, staring at the woman. Whatever he'd done to earn her hostility, he'd obviously done it well.

"This is your property?"

"My family owns twelve acres. Hunting is restricted on all of it." Her spine stiffened like a broomstick. Beneath her simple straw bonnet, wisps of dark hair fringed her pretty face. Specks of hazel and gold sparked in her brown eyes, along with an annoying tinge of righteous indignation. "My grandfather makes exceptions in cases of necessity only." She eyed him from head to toe. "Since there are several eating establishments in town, and you're clearly not starving, you can pursue your sport elsewhere."

"In my defense, Miss Sutter, this hunt *was* necessary."

"Is that so?"

His business was none of her concern, but the challenge in her skeptical tone got the best of him. "Your elderly neighbor, Mrs. Tremont, is a patient of mine. Her weight has dropped drastically, and her appetite continues to wane."

Her smug tone faded. "I'm sorry to hear that," she muttered, looking genuinely distressed.

"The woman has a craving for fresh venison. I apologize for trespassing, but I intend to provide it."

She lowered her eyes, and Jace couldn't help enjoying her contrite response.

"Had you not intervened with my deer, I'd have no reason to dally here. On *your* property," he added, just for the hell of it.

"Well, don't let me keep you," she snapped. "Good luck with Mrs. Tremont." Her hard look softened again, as did the harshness in her voice. "Please send her my regards."

With a lift of her chin, she collected her market basket from where it sat beside a log, then hurried away. Jace stared after her, absorbing the view. She held her head high, her stance rigid and aloof. Her frame was small but curvaceous, possessing the perfect measure of female proportions. Ample breasts, narrow waist, pleasing backside.

Of course, one had to get past the bloodstained dress to appreciate what lay beneath, but as a doctor who'd seduced dozens of nurses whose aprons were soaked with far worse, this posed no problem for Jace. Her slender form moved swiftly as she made her way down the path through the field, but her pace was slowing. He detected a slight limp in her gait, though from this distance, he couldn't be sure.

"Madeline Sutter," he mumbled, shaking his head. What kind of woman went about pulling arrows from dying deer?

Jace had met some odd people during the month since he'd arrived in town, but he'd yet to meet anyone like Miss Sutter. Dragging his gaze from the fading view of her, he squatted before the patch of blood in the grass where his deer had fallen.

From the amount of blood and crimson color, Jace agreed with Miss Sutter's assessment of the situation. The animal was certain to bleed to death before getting far. It had to be dead on its feet to have allowed her anywhere near it, let alone remove the arrow. How it summoned the stamina to move on, Jace hadn't a clue, but he knew it would bed down in dense cover as soon as it could. Like any diligent hunter, Jace was obligated to recover it.

He reexamined the arrow. The hair attached was coarse, dark gray with dark tips, and two or so inches long. This evidence indicated a perfect kill shot behind the shoulder, not in the gut, as the girl had claimed.

With a shake of his head, Jace stood, preparing to track the deer. He would find out the truth soon enough, though with a wounded deer, one could never be certain as to how soon that might be. Mrs. Tremont was in dire need of protein. Since the old woman had no husband or sons, Jace would do what he must to provide it.

It had taken only one house call to discover that the duties of the country doctor entailed catering to each patient on a more personal level than was possible with the human wreckage he'd treated at Pittsburgh Hospital. Although his office had yet to open officially, he already knew the hell of the emergency ward—and the endless misery that flowed through its wide double doors—was a stark contrast to a small-town practice. He could make a real difference in Misty Lake, and not just to the wealthy summer visitors. Here he'd have the time to focus on each patient case without the patch-them-up-and-ship-them-out approach of the hospital. The change would be just what he needed to replenish his spirit from the toll of the daily tragedy that had sucked him dry.

Inhaling deeply, he forged past the memory of his internship in the city and the suffocating despair that came along with it. The pine-scented breeze coursed through his senses, anchoring him back to the present. The beauty of his current surroundings lifted his mood. There was nothing like a walk in the woods and reconnecting with nature to remind him that he was alive.

Perhaps if he'd found some comparable diversion from his rote existence in the city, he might have fared better there. Not that it mattered now. He'd made a decision to build a practice in the country, and he intended to succeed come hell or high water. Even so, he knew that, as a stranger, he should expect some initial hostility and skepticism from Misty Lake's residents. Miss Sutter had merely acted upon the resentment that a lot of her neighbors were nursing privately.

Swatting at a horsefly, he took a few steps in the direction in which the deer had bolted, searching the ground for the blood trail that would lead to his prey. Bloody hoof prints led from the scene. Hunching down for a closer look, he followed the tracks to a birch log, scanning the ground as he moved. "What the…?"

Not a single droplet of blood lay anywhere in the vicinity of the tracks. Had the deer's wound simply stopped bleeding? He scratched his head, glancing around. The blood flow might have ebbed somewhat, but to cut off entirely without leaving a trace? Preposterous. There had to be a logical explanation. There always was. As a man of science, Jace was curious to know what the devil that explanation was.

He inspected the peeling bark on the decaying log, then saw something flutter on the ground behind it. He reached for the discarded leaf of paper trapped in the weeds. Miss Sutter's? He collected the thing, then read with interest the letter that was, indeed, addressed to Madeline Sutter.

The past is the past, my dear friend, and you must lay it to rest. Eventually, the town will follow suit.

Who was this strange woman he'd encountered in the middle of nowhere? The woman who refused to attend her friend's wedding, but had no qualms about dislodging an arrow from a wild animal or ordering a man twice her size off her property?

Madeline Sutter intrigued him, and few women accomplished that feat. Jace looked forward to meeting her again. He glanced toward the path through the field. Locating her residence wouldn't be difficult. And her dropped letter gave him the perfect excuse to pay her a visit. For the moment, though, he had a deer to track in the opposite direction.

He gathered his things, then headed into the woods. When he returned to town, he would ask around about his latest acquaintance. Whoever she was, he couldn't wait to find out more.

CPSIA information can be obtained at www.ICGtesting.com
Printed in the USA
LVOW08s2318060616

491432LV00001B/59/P